James DeMonaco and B. K. Evenson

# FERAL

James DeMonaco is the writer and director of the feature films *The Purge, The Purge: Anarchy, The Purge: Election Year,* and *Staten Island, New York.* He also wrote the films *The Negotiator* and *Assault on Precinct 13,* as well as created and executive-produced the cable television miniseries *The Kill Point.* He lives in both Staten Island and Manhattan with his wife and daughter. He is an avid New York Yankees fan.

B. K. Evenson is the pen name for Brian Evenson, who has been a finalist for the Edgar Award, the Shirley Jackson Award, and the World Fantasy Award and a winner of the International Horror Guild Award and the American Library Association's award for Best Horror Novel, as well as having one of his novels selected as a *Time Out New York* top book. The recipient of a National Endowment for the Arts fellowship and three O. Henry Prizes, Evenson lives in Southern California.

# FERAL

# FERAL

## James DeMonaco
## B. K. Evenson

Blumhouse Books | Anchor Books
A Division of Penguin Random House LLC
New York

A BLUMHOUSE BOOKS/ANCHOR BOOKS ORIGINAL, APRIL 2017

Library of Congress Cataloging-in-Publication Data
Names: Demonaco, James. | Evenson, B. K.
Title: Feral / James DeMonaco, B. K. Evenson.
Description: New York : Blumhouse Books/Anchor, 2017. |
"A Blumhouse original novel."
Identifiers: LCCN 2016033239 (print) | LCCN 2016058703 (ebook) |
ISBN 9781101972700 (paperback) | ISBN 9781101972717 (ebook)
Subjects: LCSH: Young women—Fiction. | BISAC: FICTION / Horror. |
FICTION / Thrillers. | GSAFD: Horror fiction.
Classification: LCC PS3604.E466 F47 2017 (print) | LCC PS3604.E466 (ebook) |
DDC 813/.6—dc23
LC record available at https://lccn.loc.gov/2016033239

Anchor Books Trade Paperback ISBN: 978-1-101-97270-0
eBook ISBN: 978-1-101-97271-7

Book design by Steven Walker

www.anchorbooks.com

Printed in the United States of America
10  9  8  7  6  5  4  3  2  1

*For our girls . . .*

# Epilogue

# THE WORLD BEFORE

*I was nine, just a little girl, at the time, though trying my best to be older than that. Concerned about all sorts of things that just one day later wouldn't matter. Worried about boys. Worried about clothes. Worried that my name, Kim, wasn't a cool enough name, didn't make me stand out enough. I was at the start of trying to figure out how I fit into the world, but before I could, the world went away.*

*That last morning, I was sitting in the kitchen, in my usual chair, eating breakfast. Or eating what I could of it, since Dad was still cooking the eggs—or overcooking the eggs, I should say. He had already put on his uniform and couldn't find the apron, which was probably in the wash, which made him extra cautious not to get splattered with grease. It also meant that he was trying to keep an eye on the eggs from the other side of the kitchen.*

*"Dad," I said. "Eggs."*

*"Coming right up, honey," he said, and continued to ignore them.*

*"Mom," I said, "make him stop cooking them. They're done."*

*"Mmmm? What do you need, Kim?" Mom asked. She was putting together lunches, a row of four brown paper bags, one for me, one for herself, one for Allie, one for Dad. We all got the same things, which meant that usually none of us was completely happy—half the time Dad probably just threw the bag away and went out for a burger. But it was quicker that way.*

*In the end, I got up and walked over to the stove and took the pan off. I carried it over to the table and dumped some eggs onto my plate, then left the rest in the pan on the trivet. A few minutes later, when Dad looked down and found the pan gone, he got the most amazing look on his face, like the world had just pulled a fast one on him. If he'd conducted police business like he scrambled eggs, our little town would have been in a whole heap of trouble.*

*The TV was on, like it always was in the morning. Not the big one in the living room: the small one hanging from the underside of the cabinet. It's probably still there like that, unless someone has trashed the place, but there are no working TVs now, of course; no power, either. I haven't been back and never will be. A lot has changed since then.*

*A news reporter on screen. I was only half listening until I saw Dad swivel toward it. The reporter was just reading from a script, but I remember a few words. They changed everything. "Fire" . . . "Arcon Pharmaceutical" . . . "Human gene engineering."*

*"That's less than an hour away," Dad was saying, kind of to Mom, kind of to himself, kind of to nobody. "I wonder . . ." And then he was looking past the TV, his brow furrowing. It didn't take much for me to guess what he was looking at. Or, rather, who.*

*"Hold on," he said. "Way too tight."*

*I turned and there was Allie. She was wearing jeans that Dad would describe as "painted on."*

*"Very provocative," I said. It was a word she'd taught me just a few days before. When Mom and Dad heard me say it, they both stared.*

*"What?" said Mom. "How old are you?"*

*Now they listened. Allie usually ignored Mom and Dad, so I figured that I would, too. And, lo and behold, it worked—Mom turned to Allie instead.*

*"You need to grow up a little, Allie," said Mom, arms crossed. "Start setting the example for your little sister. Start looking out for her." But when Allie didn't say anything, either, just grabbed a plate and a fork and shoveled most of the rest of the eggs onto it, Mom sighed.*

*Dad, though, had another way of getting Allie to pay attention. Before she could get comfortable, I saw his eyes flash and he spun and whirled a tennis ball at her. I'm not even sure where he got it from—it was just suddenly there. Not even a "think fast" or a "heads up" or any kind of warning—and the look on his face made me think that he'd be just as happy if it hit her in the head: it'd teach her a lesson. If you had a warning, Dad always thought, what was the point of even throwing the ball?*

*But Allie caught it one-handed with a whump just like she always did, and this time the eggs didn't even fall off the fork that was raised halfway to her mouth. She threw it back just as hard and then fist-bumped Dad when he came over, grinning.*

*"Quickest hands in the conference," said Dad.*

*"Toughest girl on the field," Allie said coolly.*

*Dad loved that mantra, always had. He gave Allie a big hug.*

*"You're going to be MVP this year," he said. "Just like your old man." He kissed his Lacrosse Championship ring, which he still proudly wore, every day without fail. My mom used to joke that he'd forget to put on his wedding ring before he'd forget to wear his championship ring, and then, one day, he left his wedding ring off to tease her and she stopped telling that particular joke.*

*I was never going to be like Allie: by the time she was nine she'd already been playing Little League for four years, and had the coach eating out of her hand. Dad tried that with me, too, but when I tried to throw a ball, half the time it ended up behind me. Usually, Allie would do something to make me feel included, to bring Dad's attention back to me, but today she already had her bag slung over her shoulder and was heading for the door.*

*"Change into some pants that aren't painted on!" Dad yelled after her, but she was already gone.*

*So—an ordinary day, totally normal, more or less. Except that this would be the last time our family ate together, ever. We'd be together one more time, but I can't talk about that. I won't. I'd rather remember us in that kitchen, eating burnt eggs. That last happy moment before the end of the world.*

## Chapter One

# Allie

It all starts with a sex video. Real hot and heavy, shot on a cell phone propped up against a wall. You wouldn't even notice it unless you were looking for it.

*Which you weren't*, you're probably thinking. And, yes—no, I wasn't. But you're already on the wrong track, because I'm not even in the video. I'm at home alone, in my own bed, my bra flung over one bedpost, the net of my lacrosse stick cupped over the other. I'm fast asleep, with not a care in the world.

No, I'm not in that room, the one with the camera—I'm blocks away, four and a half to be precise. But I know who is.

Or was. By the time I see the video it's the next day. I wake up, sleep still clogging my eyes. I sit up in bed, and, like I do first thing every morning, grab my iPhone. There's a text there, blocked number, that says, "Check it out!!!" Below is a link, and so I do what any other half-asleep sixteen-year-old would do and open it.

It's grainy and hard to see what exactly is going on. The angle is skewed and the lighting is bad, shining right into the camera. There are flashes of motion, maybe a limb here and there, but it's hard to make out what limb is where. The sound is clear enough, ragged breathing and the smack of lips. It's animalistic, and I feel I should look away, but I don't. I'm curious, too, and maybe a little scared.

Then they move a little and block the light and I see it clearly. A boy and girl kissing, rolling around, panting, light going from okay to bad and back again, but there's something familiar about . . . And then I hear one of them, the girl, she giggles and says, "Come here," and, yeah, I know that voice. Fuck. This is going to be a bad day.

It's Brit, and her boyfriend, Damon. My best friend, Brit, is half of a sex tape. And by now probably half the school has seen it. Holy shit. Shit. Shit. Shit.

And then, before I know it, they're really going at it. Brit's on top and Damon's inching across the floor beneath her, and I feel guilty for watching but I can't stop, either. *What is he doing? Why is he moving?* I think for just a second and then, suddenly, realize: he's positioning her for the camera. You can hardly see him at all now, just the side of his neck where he went too close to the camera, and his torso. You can hear him, though, grunting like some kind of animal. But her, you can see all of her, grinding back and forth with no idea the whole world is watching. It's so clear: he's set this up. He's set *her* up. What kind of shithead *does* that to his girlfriend? She doesn't even know it. Not yet.

But she will.

I shut off the video, wishing I could unsee what I just saw. I mean, seeing your best friend having sex is weird enough, but knowing she doesn't know the camera was on, knowing for sure that all sorts of people are going to know before she does, that's so much worse. I thumb Brit's number from the top of my favorites and dial.

The phone rings and rings and then:

"Why the hell would you call me?" Brit says. "Just text."

I open my mouth to speak and then hear the beep—she almost got me with her stupid message.

"It's Allie. I can't text you because I have to talk to you! Stay away from Damon, he's a total asshole. You can't trust him, just stay away until I find you. Fucking call me! Now!"

I hang up, and then I sit for a while, staring at the phone in my hands, willing it to ring. When it doesn't, I glance at the bedside clock. Already late. With a groan, I run for the shower.

## Chapter Two

# Allie

It figures: when I track Brit down in the hall, right before first period, and ask her if she got my message, she says, "Well, I saw you left one . . . but I figured if it was important you'd text."

"And what if it was something I couldn't text?" I ask.

"Like what?" she says, and I can see her getting interested. She thinks I'm about to tell her something crazy about myself, reveal some big dark secret, some secret lover, or maybe some weird addiction or that I've joined a snake-handling cult. She doesn't know what's about to hit her.

I don't know how to break it to her. How do you tell your best friend that dozens, maybe hundreds of people have seen her having sex? "You and Damon are having sex," I say, and she says, "So? You knew we were heading that way."

"He wanted everybody to know," I say. "I mean, really know."

She narrows her eyes. "Is he going around telling people?"

"He made a video," I say.

"What do you mean? Like, he taped himself saying that we had sex and posted it to YouTube or something? That's kind of sweet."

Fucking clueless. By this time, people are staring and whispering as they walk by. They've seen the video, I know it, and I can also tell that at least some of them have figured out that I must be telling her the film is live. They're the ones that are slowing, loitering around, waiting to see what will happen, how she'll take it. They've got their phones out, ready to record how she reacts. I won't give them the satisfaction.

So I get her into the bathroom and block the door and only then explain it to her.

"No," she says with a look on her face that I've never seen before. "No fucking way."

"Way," I said. "He definitely did." And when she still won't believe me, I get my phone out and play the video for her.

Which ends with her running out and taking my phone with her. I go out after her, but by the time I catch up she's already found Damon and has him pinned against a locker and then is dragging him outside, people staring and pointing and filming, and I can't help thinking, *Third wheel.* I'll let them solve this one for themselves—I'd only be in the way. And then, when she needs it, I'll be her shoulder to cry on. And when she's done crying on my shoulder, I'll try to get my phone back from her.

It's like Mom always says: "Us girls have to stick together when the 'you know what' hits the fan." That's a direct quote, especially the "you know what" part. Me, I'd just say "shit." I don't mince words.


Only it doesn't work out exactly like that. Next time I see her, Brit doesn't need a shoulder. She's not crying. She seems serene, not even bothered by the stares she's still getting from people around her. She strides languorously down the hall, sixteen going on twenty-two, like it's just a normal day.

I'm a little shocked at first, don't know what to say. Every scenario I've worked up in first and second period for what Brit must be feeling is just wrong, *off*. Is this some kind of intense, deep denial? If I say anything about the video will she simply say, "What video? There is no video," and keep walking?

She hands me my phone. "Thanks," I say, and wait for her to say something back. But she doesn't say a thing.

Finally, I can't stand it anymore. "They've all seen you having sex," I say as we walk. "Holy goddamn shit. How are you not having a breakdown?"

"Because I look good naked," she says. She gives that fake exasperated sigh that I've seen her practice in the mirror. "I really don't care, Al."

My jaw drops. "You don't care?"

She continues on, hurrying her words. It's like she's trying to convince a part of herself as well as me. "I spoke to Damon—he knows it was stupid, he wasn't thinking, he's really sorry, and I accepted his apology." She stops, swallows. "They're all just jealous anyway," she says.

Wow. I mean, just wow. How can she forgive him for what he did? He's a monster. It's insane. And now she's in my space, a grin I don't fully recognize on her face as she points her finger at me and kind of jabs it under my collarbone.

"And what about you?" Jab. "When are you going to *do it*?" Jab. "Jared's not going to wait much longer."

What the hell is happening? If she jabs me one more time, I can already see myself grabbing her finger and snapping it in two. What, she wants to drag me down with her? Maybe Damon will offer to give Jared some filming tips. After all, he's a veteran now.

But I make a supreme effort and rise above it. I ignore her, don't even bother to answer, lips pressed tightly together, and she realizes maybe she's gone too far.

"Allie," she says, her voice more like it usually is. "Allie?"

I still don't answer. Before she can say my name again, we hear sirens. They are quiet at first, then growing louder, and louder still, until the noise is almost deafening. People in the hall are stopping, looking around anxiously, and a few are even going to the windows, looking out. Then the roar starts to ebb away again.

"What's going on out there?" asks Brit. "Wow."

I need to clear my head. I think, *I'm going to just keep walking and not say anything, just let all this slide*, but my mouth's already talking, saying whatever it wants to say. Sometimes my brain can't control it.

"What the hell's wrong with you, Brit?" is what I say.

"He's just a boy," she says, beginning to get defensive. "What do you expect?"

And there, ahead, down the hallway, is the boy in question. Tall, good-looking, and a total asshole. He's wearing a beanie pulled so low it's a little hard to recognize him at first. He waves, and the boy beside him waves, too—my own boyfriend, Jared. *Why are you hanging out with that asshole?* I want to shout down to Jared, but instead I wave back and walk forward, keeping pace with Brit.

When we get there, Damon scoops Brit up in his arms, a totally melodramatic embrace, and I can't help thinking, *He's acting.* Maybe he has another camera hidden around here and is filming it all to watch later: the romantic reconciliation scene. Jared's a lot more subdued, which is to say normal. He comes close and hugs me and kisses me, and then whispers:

"I would never do that to you."

The video, I know he's talking about the video. It should go without saying. I never even remotely thought he would. But, then again, I never thought Damon would to Brit, either.

I'm still thinking it through when I realize that something's wrong with Jared. He feels like he's on fire. I reach out and touch his forehead.

"Wow," I say. "You feel like you're overheating, Jared. You okay? Sick or something?"

"I'm fine. Just a little hot. Come on, let's go."

All four of us walk to homeroom. The three of them seem fine, almost oblivious to the other people in the hall. I'm still hyperaware of all the students who are staring at Brit. And now staring at me, too: if I'm friends with a slut like her, probably that means I make sex videos, too. Guilt by association.

We walk by three emo girls—cardigans over band T-shirts, Converse shoes, geek glasses: you know, the usual emo uniform—and even though their faces are partly hidden by their swept hair, I can still see them clearly enough to know they're eyeing the four of us with pure venom. The tallest of them sees me watching and silently mouths "Sluts" as we pass. I'm the only one of us who notices. What can I do but glare and walk on?

Maybe it's that everyone seems to have seen the video by now, maybe it's spring, but there's a charge in the air. Every boy I see is so amped up that he practically can't stay seated. The boy next to me, Peter

Reed—straight A's and on the fast track to Harvard—doesn't have his mind on his schoolwork today, which isn't like him. Today he can't keep his eyes off my legs, and I can't help thinking about Mom and Dad's comments on my tight jeans. Christ, it's the twenty-first century. When are things going to get better? I'm tired of the looks, the glares. I'm tired of playing nice. I'm tired, even, of being there for Brit, particularly since she doesn't seem to need me, is just shrugging off something that would floor anybody normal. She's buying Damon's bullshit. "Boys will be boys."

I'm looking forward to this morning's lacrosse scrimmage even more than usual. I've got to take my aggression out on something, and a few good stick checks will go a long way. I really want to hit someone.

And that's exactly what I do. At first I'm wound as tight as a spring, but then, like always, I relax into it, get to the point where I'm no longer thinking about where I'm moving on the field, the shots I'm taking—I'm just doing it, my body is thinking for itself. It's not like I feel like I'm out of control, but I've let go of the reins because I know exactly where the horse is going to run. Everything is moving quicker than normal, but everything feels serene, colors are brighter, and I feel like I'm noticing everything, missing nothing, like my senses are suddenly tuned in on the slightest detail. It feels . . . great, and the whole time my body's moving, rushing here and there, but without wasting a gesture, a stride. Maybe that's what sex is like, when it's real. If so, why am I still waiting?

And then, late in practice, things get even more precise, everything fluid, and there's that amazing moment when I can't do anything wrong. There I am, running fast, spinning, pivoting, sprinting toward the goal. Nothing can stop me—I know it somehow, really know it—and even when the way looks blocked by three other players I serpentine my way through. I take a hard hit, but it doesn't slow me, then another, and today I don't even feel it. I'll welcome the bruises tomorrow. The ball's passed, and even though it's off, a little high and wide, I catch it cleanly in my crosse. The goalie's moving and ready, and the catch has thrown me off balance, is sending me down. But I dive headfirst, shooting on my way down.

Perfect shot. If I do say so myself. Only then, lying on the ground, do I realize that my lungs are gasping for breath. I begin to feel the aches and pains. I wince pulling myself up, but the wince quickly changes to a smile. Teammates and coaches are clapping and cheering me on—"Great run!" "Way to go, Allie!" They know the game and know what a hard shot it was, and they also know that it wasn't luck—or not *just* luck: luck never hurt anybody, but a good player makes her own luck.

I'm psyched, pumped, ready to get back in formation and get back into that killing zone. But then I hear the usually sedate Hannah Shaw say, "Fuck me, is that Mikey Stewart?!" There's a strange excitement and urgency in her voice, so I turn her way, and so does everybody else.

She's gesturing, pointing toward the nearby track, where a group of students are holding up their cell phones. They're filming a scrawny freshman, Michael Stewart, who is getting ready to throw the javelin. He's clutching it oddly, almost too tight. He lifts it high, and then takes his approach run. His form's ragged—even I can see that, and I've only thrown javelin maybe twice, because I had to for PE. Why is everybody watching him? Do they think it'll be an epic fail?

And then he performs his delivery and I get it. Jesus, did he really throw it as far as I think he did? Michael Stewart? It sails across the field in a high arc, glinting in the sun, and comes down hundreds of feet away, impaling the running track that circles the field. Holy shit, that's *really* far, almost impossibly far. Like verging on Olympic-record far.

Everyone around me is going nuts. They're cheering, but there's an edge to it, a bit of scary panic behind it.

"He just broke the school record by, like, thirty yards," says Hannah. "This is unreal." She cups her hands around her mouth and shouts, "Go, Mikey!"

Michael doesn't acknowledge the cheers. He's already back at the start with a new javelin, getting ready to throw again. His walk is off, unsteady and lurching, like he doesn't quite know what he's doing. You'd expect at least a smile, but it's like nobody else is even there for him. And even from here, I can see the sweat dripping from his face.

There's something odd. He's scrawny, yet all his muscles are tensed, and they don't untense.

"He's going to pull a muscle if he doesn't rest," I say to nobody in particular. "At the very least."

But nobody's paying attention. A moment later, he's back at it, making his approach. It's a little more controlled than last time, though not much. But the throw, when the release comes, goes just as far. How is he doing it? Running on pure adrenaline? Tearing his own muscles to get such incredible results? It's weird. Is he on something? Steroids? Bath salts? Something even worse?

A police helicopter suddenly whizzes directly over the school, the roar and chatter of its blades deafening. Where the hell did that come from? My dad never said they had a helicopter. It must be from another town—but if that's the case, why is it here? Isn't there a rule against flying that close to a public school? Half the people are looking at it, half at Michael Stewart, but Michael isn't paying attention to any of it—he didn't even look up, didn't even slow down. He's back at it, choosing his next javelin.

*Something's wrong here*, I think. *Something's really wrong.* Should I call my dad? He'd know, he could tell me.

That's when someone grabs my arm hard, spins me around. My reflexes take over, and I'm just bringing up the heel of my hand to break whoever's nose it is when I realize it's Jared. He's sweating more than he was before. He has a glazed, angry look in his eyes, like he's on something, like he's only partly there.

"Jared," I say, "you're hurting my arm." I try to pull free, but he doesn't loosen his grip. He just stands there, then blinks and shakes his head. For a moment, his eyes are like they usually are, and then, just as quickly, they glaze over again, and he becomes even more angry.

"Are we ever gonna fuck or what?" he whines.

You have got to be kidding me. He's in some kind of fugue state. Part of me is worried about him—I've never seen Jared like this before—but the rest of me is as mad as shit.

"Go to hell," I say as coldly as I can. "You're worse than Damon. Get your hands off me."

I reach out to pry his fingers off my sleeve, but as soon as I touch them I pull back. They're hot, seriously hot—like, way hotter than they should be even if he has a fever. There's something seriously wrong—as in, if he doesn't get into an ice bath in the next ten minutes his brain's going to start to bubble. Maybe it's already bubbling. Maybe that's what the problem is.

"Christ, you're burning up," I say, more gently now, concerned. "Even more than before." I reach out slowly, like you would to a dog with its foot caught in a trap, and place my hand on his forehead. He lets me do it. The relative coolness of my touch seems to calm him a little. "Something's wrong," I say. "Come with me."

I manage to pull my arm free and then take his arm, leading him toward the school building. Michael Stewart is on the ground now, lying facedown, a bunch of people gathered over him, shaking him. He's not responding. There, over and behind the building, not far away, is a cloud of black smoke, growing larger. *Well, maybe that explains the police helicopter*, I think, *though it looks like a fire-department helicopter would be more appropriate*. I want to call my dad, but I can't let go of Jared's burning-hot hand. I can tell, too, from the wind blowing in my face, that the cloud is likely heading our way.

By the time we're inside, Jared seems a little less angry, less dazed, too. He's almost, but not quite, back to his normal self. We're walking down the hall and he's contrite, and confused about what just happened.

"I'm sorry, Al," he says, and there seems to be real agony on his face. "I don't know why I said that stuff to you. You know how much I care for you. I would never want to do anything you didn't want to. . . ."

But I've stopped listening. Outside the nurse's office is a line of fifteen or so boys, mostly kids I know. They're all sweating, and they all have the same glazed look that Jared had. They are staring toward us as we come, but without really seeing us. Oozing from the noses of several of them is a mucus so viscous and white that it looks like pus. It is speckled with blood and coming out thick, totally disgusting, and the boys keep touching it absently and then looking at their fingers as if confused by what they see there. Others are dabbing at a similar blood-streaked white fluid as it trickles from their ears or wiping it away from the corners of their eyes, a look of confusion spread across their faces. Confused, but not panicked—shit, if I had stuff like that coming out of my head holes, I'd be screaming for a doctor! But it's as if they are only partly there. One boy almost looks like he's crying, lines of this strange ruddy mucus spreading down his face, and he doesn't even seem aware it's there.

Weirder still is the way some of the boys have thick purple veins bulging out on their faces and pulsing—like small worms squirming beneath the skin. That's not only disgusting, it's downright scary.

"What the hell is going on?" I can't stop myself from asking. Strange, I think, that only boys seem to have whatever it is. There are only boys in the line, anyway.

"Huh?" says Jared. And then he sees the line. No comment on the pus oozing from all those faces—it's like he doesn't even notice it. "Looks like we'll have to come back later," he says.

"No way," I say. "Get in line."

By the time we get up to the front, pus has started dripping from his eyes, too, and his glazed look is back, his lip starting to curl as well. I can't hold his hand because the heat of it makes my skin crawl, and he keeps on squeezing my hand too tight. He'll say something off, vulgar, like he's drunk and has no filter, and then, a moment later, he's apologizing, seemingly amazed by what he just said, unsure how those words could possibly have come out of his mouth. When we get in, the nurse takes one look at him and points to the floor. He's told to lie down alongside all the guys that arrived before him. The nurse looks anxious, harried.

"What is it?" I ask her.

"How should I know?" she says, pushing her hair out of her eyes. "I'm a high school nurse, I spend most of my time just taking people's temperatures and deciding if they need to go to see a real doctor. Are you sick, too?"

I shake my head. "I just came with Jared," I say.

"Then go to class now," she says. "Or, better yet, go home."

"But—"

"Look at them," she urgently whispers, as if afraid of being over-heard. She gestures to the restless bodies all around her feet. Her movements are jerky, frantic. "Something really wrong is going on here. I called the paramedics over an hour ago and they still haven't shown up. Do you want to catch whatever they have? Honey, get out while you can."

# Chapter Three

## Allie

I'm back in the locker, changing out of my sweaty gear, stressed about whatever the hell's going on. I've tried calling my dad, but nobody answers. I've tried my mom, too; no answer there, either. I'm worried about Jared, but the other boys at the nurse's office have me freaked out, and there's Michael Stewart, who Brit just told me apparently suddenly up and died, his heart giving out or something. Nobody knows for sure because the paramedics still haven't shown up. Why don't they just cancel school?

It's taken long enough with Jared that the period has come to an end, so Brit's cheerleading class is over, too. Shit, I should have asked the nurse for an excuse note.

"It must have been awful for you," Brit's saying. "Just awful."

I nod. I want to start crying, but I won't, I just won't. "And all those other boys, too. It came out of Jared's eyes. It was . . . disgusting. But worse than that, like . . . unnatural. I didn't know what to do. I'm really worried. . . ."

Brit gives me that big, wide-eyed look that says, *I'm paying total attention to you and I feel for you.* But there's something there underneath that look, too, something I'm not familiar with from Brit. And then it clicks: fear. She's afraid.

"We have to get out of here," she says. "It's like everyone has fucking Ebola or something. Someone needs to tell us something. They can't just keep us here."

"If it's bad, wouldn't they cancel school?" I ask.

"Maybe it's so bad that they don't want us leaving. Maybe we're, like, at ground zero, and they want to keep us contained." I know from the way her eyes dart to the side when she says it that she's *really* afraid and that she thinks Jared is going to be lucky if he ends up in the hospital rather than dead.

"Hey, slut."

That came out of nowhere, I think. Who said that? And then I turn and see that tall emo girl from earlier, and she's talking to Brit. All three emo girls are there suddenly, just a few lockers down. An absurd thought flits through my mind. They say "a murder of crows" or "a wake of buzzards." I'm wondering what you call a group of emo kids. "An emote of emos"?

Brit turns. "Forget those idiots," she says.

I ignore her. It's been an awful day, and the last thing I need to cap things off is to have to turn the other cheek to someone wearing a thrift-store sweater. "What did you call her?" I say.

"Slut," says the tall one, a smirk on her face. "And you're a slut, too, because sluts hang out with sluts."

I take a deep breath. I balance on the balls of my feet and look the bitch straight in the eye. "Say one more syllable and I'll beat the piss out of you, stretch."

To her credit, she thinks about this a moment. She opens her mouth and stops, and then I see her lips curl into a sneer and she starts to say, "Really," all sarcastic like. But she doesn't manage to finish even the first drawn-out syllable, because as soon as I hear sound coming from her mouth I tackle her.

She goes down hard, just missing hitting her head on the bench, and before she's even sure what's happened, I've hit her hard enough to make her nose bleed. Then she's scratching at me, trying to gouge my eyes out or whatever, and her two friends, her *minions*, are there before I can get the third blow to connect. At first they are trying to drag me off of her, and then, when they realize that I'm not going to go easy, they start clawing and scratching, too. One of them is a hair puller, so I elbow her in the gut hard enough to knock the wind out of her before she rips my scalp off. The other mainly just seems to want to bear-hug. Still, there are three of them and only one of me, so it's basically a fair fight. As my coaches know, when I set my mind on something I usually get it in the end. And I would have in this case, too, if Ms. Belknap, the PE instructor, hadn't elbowed her way in and thrown us apart and then ordered me down to the principal's office.

Principal Sabian just sits on the other side of the desk, staring right past me, waiting. She is about the same age as my parents, maybe a little older, her hair running to iron gray, her cheekbones sharp and pronounced, sparkling eyes, a steady gaze. I've had a run-in or two with her before—those weren't my fault, either—but she's never acted like this. Usually, she starts right in with "Well, what do you have to say for yourself?" or "Can't you stay out of trouble, Allie?" or "Do you want to tell me your side, Ms. Hilts?" Normally, she looks austere and in charge, like she's got her finger on the school's pulse, but today she looks frazzled and preoccupied. Her movements are sharp and brittle, and this makes me as worried as anything else. Before, she was a rock of consistency, but today I can't predict what she's going to do or say.

She stays silent for a minute longer, her fingers tented in front of her—it's like she's forgotten I'm even there—and then she blinks and sighs. I take that as my cue.

"Look," I say, "I can explain."

But Mrs. Sabian's not listening. Instead, she stands up and goes over to the television and turns the volume up. I'm so surprised, I allow myself to trail off midsentence. It's a small set, placed in the bookshelf. It's on a news station that's showing footage of what the thing on the bottom, the running tape or whatever, says is the "Arcon chemical fire." "Breaking news," it says. "Inhalation might have unexpected effects." Like what? I wonder, and then see Michael Stewart again throwing the javelin over and over, his muscles tensed. The principal just stands there, watching, listening.

"Mrs. Sabian?" I say. "What's wrong?"

She turns toward me, though she still looks distracted. Then her mouth sets in a no-nonsense way that reminds me a little of the old Mrs. Sabian. I'm both glad to see that and nervous, too.

"Don't you think I have more to worry about today than some spat between teenage girls?" she says.

"Excuse me?"

"What's wrong with you kids? Everyone's acting crazy. Exactly why—"

The ringing of the phone cuts her off. The way she rushes to it, I can tell it's a call she's been waiting for.

"Hello?" she says. "Yes, this is she. Yes, I'm listening."

And then she does just that, listens. I watch her from the other side of the desk, watch her face tightening into a mask. I don't know what it is exactly that she is being told, but I know that, whatever it is, it's heavy. It's got to be about the shit that's going on around here—people sick and going crazy. Maybe Brit was right, maybe we are ground zero for Ebola 2.

A scream rings out, a woman's full-throated cry of mindless fear. It's not far away, just out in the hall somewhere. I'm halfway up from my seat and leaning toward the door when Mrs. Sabian reaches across the desk and grabs me.

"Allie, stay here," she says. I can see from her eyes she's serious. "We're evacuating. Something's going on."

"But, Mrs. Sabian," I say, "out there, something's—"

She cuts me off and speaks briefly into the phone—"You'll have to excuse me, we have a situation"—then drops the receiver on the desk and makes her way briskly to the door.

She stops on her way out and says, "Allie," but I'm already staring at the TV, trying to figure out what's going on. "Allie!" she says again. And when I look, "Lock this door behind me and find a way out. Do you hear me?" When I nod she goes out, closing the door firmly behind her.

My heart's beating fast. What could possibly be going on out there? Terrorists, maybe? Some sort of chemical or biological attack?

I stand up and pace a little, back and forth, after a while gravitating toward the TV. The banner at the screen's bottom still reads "Arcon chemical fire." The closed captioning is a mess, just garbled letters that don't form words at all.

Says the reporter, "Critics say genetic manipulation is man's attempt to play God. Further complicating this issue is that Arcon is using a technique called 'viral vector gene therapy'—using live viruses as a means to carry new genes into the primate's cells. This—"

But I don't hear any more, because there's another scream, a blood-curdling one, this time right outside the door. I'm trembling now, and totally freaking the fuck out. Something very bad is going on out there, and my mind's running wild trying to imagine what it is.

I search around for a weapon, but there's nothing beyond a paperweight about the size of a lacrosse ball. I cross to the desk and pick it up. Much heavier than a ball. It'll leave a bruise at least. The phone's there just beside it, a voice coming out of the receiver, a woman's voice, calling "Hello? Hello?" over and over again. I'm reaching for it when there's a crash from behind me as something slams into the door.

I turn and there's another crash and the door shudders in its frame, and the small window of wire-mesh glass high on the door is suddenly smeared with a shroud of blood. *Shit*, I'm thinking. *Shit, shit, shit.*

But, despite how terrified I am, I absolutely have to see what's going on. I can't stop myself from moving toward that door. Curiosity killed the cat and all that, but it is better, I'm telling myself, if I know what I'm up against, know what's happening, and have a way of putting a face to my fear.

So, even though I'm shaking, even though my heart feels like it's pounding up in my throat instead of down in my chest, I take quiet, careful steps toward the door, stooping so I won't be seen. A thud from the hall, another scream, the sound of metal being mangled. There's an unearthly piercing howl that makes the hair stand up on the back of my neck. I can't tell if it's animal or human. Then I reach the door and slowly raise my head until I can see through the blood-streaked window.

A bank of lockers that look like they've been hit by a sledgehammer. They're all crushed in, and some of the doors are torn off. On the floor is Mrs. Sabian, crawling backward as best she can. Some of the hair has been torn from her scalp, and blood runs down the side of her face. One eye is swollen shut, and something's wrong with one of her legs—it flops as she drags herself, the foot pointed the wrong way. Her clothing is torn, and there are deep scratches all along one arm, and a deep gash along her belly that leaves a swath of blood as she pulls herself.

I open my mouth and almost cry out, but then I see what she is crawling away from. Mr. Roundy, who teaches wood shop, and Mr. Barks, who teaches Spanish. I can hardly recognize them. They're just a few yards away from her, and coming deliberately closer. Like the boys outside the nurse's office earlier, they have blood-streaked pus oozing from their ears and eyes and noses, and I can't help thinking of rabid dogs. Their skin is glazed with a thick, viscous sweat, and the muscles undulate grotesquely under it, like something is alive and in pain beneath their skin. As they come, they're howling, emitting shrill, animalistic wails that make me want to get the hell out of there. They're approaching slowly, waiting for their moment. Their pupils are pinpricks, like nobody's home. There's nothing in those faces but hatred, aggression.

They pass by me, just a few feet away on the other side of the door's window, and I'm so stunned by their transformation that I don't think to duck. By the time I can move again, I'm worried that any sudden movement on my part would draw more attention to me than staying still would. So I hold my breath and clutch the paperweight and pray.

They stalk past the door without a glance. They have eyes only for Mrs. Sabian, who has given up crawling now, and lies there, blood puddling around her, watching them come. She turns her head a little, searching, and locks eyes with me through the glass. *Go*, she mouths, and, when I don't move, *Now*.

But even then I don't move. It's like my muscles won't obey me, a feeling that's the complete opposite of what I was experiencing in lacrosse practice today, like I'm trapped in my body. I watch the two deranged men come closer to her, still howling. They dart in and strike her and dart back, toying with her. It's like watching cats toy with a mouse. She resists weakly, her head lolling, her wounds bleeding more and more freely.

And then, suddenly, they leap forward, lashing out at her, roaring. The blood from her broken face spatters the wall. She's not even resisting now. Either she is dead or close enough to it to be as good as.

Which is what I'll be, too, if I don't get out of here.

## Chapter Four

## Allie

There are many ways that people come to realize they're no longer children. I mean, really realize it, not just pretend, not just go back and forth between thinking of themselves as adults and thinking of themselves as children without being quite one or the other. Back in that past world, most people only realized they were adults after the fact, without being able to put a finger on when exactly it had happened, understanding they had become adults only days or weeks later. Some, like Brit, thought that sex would do it for them, that losing their virginity was enough. But most of them, after the act, realized how little had changed. In any case, for most people it's not that one day you suddenly realize you're an adult, but that one day you suddenly realize you've been an adult for a while without quite knowing it.

But I know exactly when I become an adult. It's when I regain control of my body after seeing Mrs. Sabian die and realize that the only person I can count on from there on out is me.

I spin away from the door. By the time I've crossed the room and am facing the outer windows on the opposite wall, I am, for better or worse, no longer a child. I'm scared shitless, but what Mrs. Sabian just said, just mouthed at me, has released me. It has given me permission to be a grown-up, to think for myself, to take my life into my own hands. I recognize that permission and take it as my own. And I will never look back.


I run to the windows and unlatch them and fling them wide. I clamber out. The air outside is smoky and acrid, reeking of something chemical and artificial. I'm coughing and choking from my first breath. The dark cloud I caught sight of earlier is hanging over the school now, slowly sifting down, spreading out into a haze or mist.

I drop to the ground and lope across the grass, sprinting as soon as I hit the pavement. I'm almost out of the parking lot when I hear the crashing sound of windows shattering. There, down a nearby street, are three guys, all students I grew up with. In normal circumstances they are nice guys, nice enough anyway, but these are anything but normal circumstances. Now they're all three spewing blood and mucus from their eyes and noses and ears, their muscles bunching and rippling, and howling that inhuman, dire scream. They've stopped a car. I can't be sure, but it looks like one is actually lifting up the front end of the car as he bellows at the driver. The other two break the windows of the car with their fists, not caring about the way the glass is lacerating their flesh as they try to get inside. Viciously, they drag the two women out of the vehicle. The mucus boys grab and lift them like they're rag dolls, as if each weighed a fraction of what they must actually weigh. One gives a little twist and snaps the neck of the woman he's holding, and she immediately goes limp. He's just fucking killed her.

I don't know how long I've been gawping at them. What snaps me out of it is more women screaming, this time behind me, dozens of screams from dozens of women, from the school, all offset by those terrifying shrill male moans and howls.

The three boys hear it, too, and turn toward the sound. Which is what causes them to notice me.


Coach Ambler always used to say, when he was trying to get me to put on a burst of speed in a game or in practice, "Allie, run like your life depended on it." When he said that, I'd run as fast as I thought I could. But you don't really know what that means, to run like your life depended on it, until your life really does.

As mine does now.

The first of the three, the one holding the car, is the first to start toward me, probably because he doesn't have a lifelike human doll to play with and tear apart, and he wants one. Me. Almost immediately he's running impossibly fast, faster than I've ever seen another human run, a literal blur of speed, sweat and blood and mucus flicking off him. I quickly pivot and sprint back across the parking lot, pulling my keys from my pocket as I go, frantically pressing the unlock button. I can't see him, but I imagine him gaining on me, even catching up. I imagine myself knocked off my feet and hurled, and then, like Mrs. Sabian, crawling backward, broken and bleeding, trying still to get away. But above all I imagine running as fast as I can and with all my heart.

My car is not where I left it—but, no, it's closer than I remembered, and I almost run right past it. I skid to a stop and pull the door open and dive in. My hands are shaking so badly I fumble the keys trying to get them into the ignition. The boy slams hard into the side of the car, but it doesn't seem to bother him. There—the key is in. I turn it and there's no response and I think, *Oh God, I'm dead.* The boy is moving around to the front of the car just as I realize that it's not starting because I don't have my foot on the brake. I jam my foot down and turn the key and this time the engine catches, and then the front end of the car creaks as the boy lifts it up off the ground.

Joke's on him, though, since my car is rear-wheel drive.

I slam it into gear and drive up and over him, smashing into the car behind him. He's nearly cut in two, but he's still scrabbling, still trying to come at me.

I'm just throwing it into reverse when the car shakes again and the other two are there, climbing up on the hood and roof. With a crash they punch their fists through each of the side windows. I know how this goes—break windows, reach in, take woman out, break her neck—so I floor it and burn rubber into the row of cars behind, tossing one of them off. I throw the car into drive and peel out, careening through the parking lot, scraping the remaining one off against a parked car, skidding out and away from them.

I've made it. Or at least I think so, but they're following, running after me. I push the needle up to thirty miles an hour but they're keeping up, even gaining a little. I'm kicking forty and they're still keeping up, though I know that's not possible—no human can run that fast. And yet there they are, both of them, in my rearview mirror, and hardly getting any farther away—all tensed muscles and fury. And then, all at once, one falls abruptly and doesn't get up again, like maybe, as with Michael Stewart, his heart has just given out. The other, still howling, recedes, and a moment later I screech around a corner and he's gone.

Away from the black cloud, away from a school full of those things that used to be human, that used to be boys I knew. All the way back to my house, the streets are deserted: no damaged vehicles, none of those unearthly male shrieks, no people, just an eerie, empty silence. I keep it at forty anyway, just for safety's sake, and keep watching the rearview mirror. Nothing. The suburbs feel deserted. Maybe everything is fine back home. But I have to be sure.

My heart rate is returning to normal, and I almost have my hopes up until, a mile from the house, I see someone. They're walking like a drunk, stumbling, and I only have a moment going past to see clearly, but I'm pretty sure it's an older woman. Pretty sure, too, that her face is shrouded in blood, and that she's stumbling not because she's had too much to drink but because she's dying.

*Please*, I pray, *please, let my family still be alive.*

I fumble out my cell and try to call Dad, but just get an emergency message. Cell service is down. I try again with Mom; same result.

I try to remember breakfast—Mom had a house to sell, Dad was going to work. Kim. Kim was going to school, but her school is close enough that maybe, if things were as weird there as they were at mine, she just ran home. For a moment my foot hesitates over the brake and I think about flipping the car around and going back to look for her, but then I see our driveway. Mom's car is there, so Mom's home. Dad's patrol car is there, too, but parked crooked and half off the slab, the grass all torn up. The side panel is all dented, where he scraped it along something, just like my car. Maybe he had to fight off mucus boys, too.

I skid to a stop, one wheel up on the sidewalk. Dad's going to be pissed about that, one part of my mind thinks; I should straighten the wheels up, but then I think about how Dad parked his own car. When you're trying to make sure your family is safe, the rules of normal life no longer apply. I'm already out of the car and rushing toward the door. The moment I push it open, I hear it: that same primal male howl of frustration and rage, coming from somewhere inside.

"Dad!" I yell. "Mom!" I can't stop myself. I don't know if they're still in the house, but maybe I can distract whatever I hear howling, and buy them a few minutes.

I'm hauling ass down the hall, all the way to the end, to the door to the kitchen, hearing those same ungodly shrieks the whole time. But as I get closer I realize there's something else mixed with them, the broken, weakened cries of a woman.

I push at the door, but it only opens a little bit. Something's blocking it. Those shrieks are making it impossible for me to think. I push it again, a little harder this time, and see a sliver of my dad's uniform, a bit of the back of his head. He's in the way. I can't see his face, but I can see that he's flailing his arms desperately, striking something in front of him. *Fighting for his life*, I think at first, *trying to keep the monster at bay*, and then I push harder and get the door open a little farther, expecting to see him fighting a creature with an oozing, pus-ridden face, with muscles pulsating out of control, with veins writhing like worms under his skin.

But, no, that's not what I see. Not what I see at all.

It's my mother. My dad is beating my mom. He's hitting her again and again. I can't see her face, but I know it's her—I recognize the shoes she put on this morning. He's straddling her body, sitting hard on her hips, pinning her down with his weight. His fists when he hits her sound like he's hitting wet sand, awful deadened moist thumps that just keep coming and coming. She's whimpering, voice more and more diminished, moaning softly. I can hardly hear her over my father's unearthly shrieks.

And there, past them, up against the stove, the unwashed frying pan lying on the floor beside her, prostrate and motionless in a slick of her own blood, is Kim. My little sister. Her head is bleeding, seriously gashed. I can't tell if she's unconscious or dead.

"Dad!" I'm yelling, pounding on the door. "Dad! Stop!"

I push the door into him, and push it again, yelling and shrieking, hammering into his back with the sharp edge of it. He doesn't stop beating my mother, but he slows a little and turns, and that's when I see the pulsing purple veins beneath his skin, the contorted muscles, the pus that's oozed from one ear and down his neck. Holy fuck, he's one of them. I'm still shouting at him, pounding the door into him, trying to squeeze through, when he swats behind him with one hand without even turning around, like he's swatting a fly.

The door splinters from the impact of the blow and slams into me so hard that I'm thrown backward into the hallway, the breath knocked out of my lungs. He's strong, even stronger than the boys who lifted the car.

I scramble up and run the other way, back down the hall. I stop shy of the front door and jerk open the door that's just a half-dozen steps before it, then clatter down the basement stairs as quick as I can, pushing open the door at the bottom. Behind it is a large unfinished room, stinking and musty. I sprint across it to a closet framed on the far wall. It's got a latch on it, and a lock on that, but I grab a spade from where it's leaning against the wall and work it under the latch, using it like a lever.

It's just a matter of a few seconds until, with a groan, the lock pops off and the door creaks open, but they're seconds I don't have to spare. Inside is the rack of Dad's hunting rifles, boxes of bullets. I grab the nearest one, a Winchester model 94 30-30, load it as quickly as I can with my trembling fingers; then it's back up the stairs two at a time, and back down the hall, trying to hold the rifle like my dad taught me, so I can be ready to kill him.

I kick the kitchen door, and this time it opens easily. I'm just through when a shape flashes across my vision and crashes into the glass-fronted cabinets, then falls to the floor. It's my mother, or, rather, my mother's body—from the condition she's in, there's no chance she's alive. Her legs are twisted the wrong way, and her face is a bloody pulp. I step farther in, and there's my father. He's standing across the room, panting and feverish. His face drips with blood and mucus and sweat, and his temples are throbbing as if ready to burst. He watches my mother's body for a moment, and when she doesn't get back up, he turns toward Kim.

He stands over her a moment, just staring down, and then gives that same inhuman howl. He seems to be struggling with himself, as if a part of him wants to do to her what he just did to my mom but another part is resisting, trying to remind him of who he really is. It's terrible to watch, especially because of how quickly the human part of him loses out. He flexes his fingers and begins to reach down to grab her.

"Dad!" I yell.

He turns swiftly and sees me at the threshold of the room, rifle raised. I can't tell if he recognizes me or not. He gives another unearthly howl and starts toward me.

"Daddy! No! Please!"

I'm crying and trembling so hard I can hardly hold the gun. I can still see him underneath that mask of mucus and sweat and rage, I still know it's him. My dad. I can't just think of him as a monster. If I kill him, I'll be killing my father, the man who raised me, the man who loved me, the man who taught me almost everything I know.

His face twists into a snarl and he rushes forward, barreling toward me. I have to force myself to do it, but I pull the trigger.

The shot catches him in the shoulder, slows him down a little. I'm not a bad shot; it's a warning. A way of saying, *I don't want to kill you, so go ahead, leave, and you'll stay alive.* But he doesn't take the hint. He looks down at the blood-soaked fabric on the right side of his uniform and gives a loud howl rife with anger and then comes after me in earnest.

I lever the next round in and fire again. When he keeps coming, I pull the trigger again, but he's still not down. I try to get another shot in, but he's too close now and it goes off into the ceiling, and then he's knocked it away and his hands are on me, rough and hot, unbearably so. He picks me up and lifts me and I'm holding on, scrabbling, trying to get at his belt, at the service revolver still hanging there. He knocks me against the wall and I almost pass out, but I've unsnapped the holster. By the time he throws me across the room, his Glock is in my hand.

I hit the cabinets so hard that for a moment I can't hear anything and I'm afraid I'm going to pass out. My mother is there on the floor beside me, gazing blankly at nothing, and I'm trying to get up, and there he is, starting across the room toward me, preparing to tear me apart. This isn't my dad, this isn't him, it isn't. I keep telling myself that as he comes closer, and it's enough to give me the strength to roll over onto my back and lift the Glock and fire.

And again, and again, and again. Four shots in all, all but the first shot straight into the skull of the monster that used to be my father. He drops, his head a pulpy mass, and dies. I let the Glock clatter to the floor. In a daze, I walk to my mother, check for a pulse; no, there's nothing, she's dead. I turn and cross to the other side of the room, trying to forget the way my mother's dead body looks, making a wide circle around the bodies, going over to my little sister.

I check for a pulse. It's weak but there. She's still alive. Thank God.

I lift her into my lap and cradle her, and try to staunch her wounds. I rock with her back and forth, my eyes staring through the broken bodies of both my parents, unable to look away but trying not to see them. *This is so wrong,* I tell her, *but I've got you. I'm going to keep you safe. I've got you.*

# THE WORLD NOW

*The world, as it turned out, didn't end in either a bang or a whimper, but in pus and sweat and infected men emitting unearthly cries as they destroyed woman after woman. A pharmaceutical company taking advantage of lax federal controls to work with living viruses and genetic splicing. "We have safeguards, we have procedures, we know exactly what we're doing, we're responsible, and if we're not, if we do something irresponsible, you can fine us." Yeah, right. That's how companies worked in those days: maximize profits and weigh loss of life or health against that, a cold-blooded translation of human life into dollars and cents. Whatever their protocols, their gene vector virus mutated and made the leap from animal to human, traveling quickly, airborne. For some reason, the virus only affected males, making those men that survived the initial infection that dramatically sped up their metabolism, and made their bodies go crazy, nearly rabid, aggressive with one another, but incredibly hostile to women. Fines? Nobody was left to enforce any fines against Arcon. Society had collapsed by then. Three years later, it was still collapsed—a little hard to rebuild a society when half the people in it are rabid and trying to kill the other half. And since men are infected and all men seem susceptible, even if we could rebuild, humanity wouldn't last more than a generation.*

*What do you do when you discover your species has a limited shelf life? Do you try to make the most of the time you have left? Do you try to leave evidence behind, in case something else comes along, in case some other animal is foolish enough to evolve and become the next humans? Or do you simply live one day at a time, trying to ignore the ticking clock, hoping without truly believing it possible that some sort of solution will be found? One day, and then the next, and then the next, just trying to stay alive . . .*

Most of the survivors hunkered down, staying alert but never looking for trouble. They locked themselves in ones or twos in basements or survival shelters, eating canned food and drinking bottled water until they had to go outside to forage. Once outside, they usually didn't last more than a day or two. All it took was a single feral catching your scent and then you were hunted down and slaughtered. Allie, though, had grown up hunting with Dad, and she was always one step ahead of the ferals, though every time she went out the door to try to find us something to eat I wondered if this would be the time she didn't manage to make it back.

I remember the first time she came home soaked in feral blood and was confused at first by my concern—I thought she'd been injured. She looked at me with incomprehension for a moment and then laughed. "I'm fine," she said, "but you should see the other guy." It was a way to mask her scent, she explained, so that they wouldn't know she was there.

We never did talk about what had happened with Dad. I didn't want to, and I don't think she did, either. I only knew the first part of it, before he'd knocked me out, but I could at least guess at the rest when I woke up in Allie's arms with her rocking me. Dad dead, Mom dead. That's the past. No use thinking about it. Better to remember the kitchen as it was that long ago morning, before the world went crazy.

After a year like this, Allie found something and everything changed for us. We're now in a much different place. Better, I'd say, but I don't know that Allie would agree.

## Chapter Five

Through the scope, she could see glimpses of the herd of deer, running and leaping through the dense forest undergrowth. They'd been flushed. They were trying to get away from something, something that was hunting them, and Allie suspected she knew what. She kept the rifle's scope steady, let the deer run through, waited. And a moment later, there they were: a group of ferals giving chase. Three in all, running and panting hard as they pursued the deer. She kept them in the circle of the lens, watched them.

They were even more changed now than they'd been three years earlier, back when the virus had first struck. Their bodies now were lean and statuesque, hardened with muscle. The purple wormlike veins no longer writhed or jutted out and were only visible up close or when they'd been exerting themselves; they extended and spread down their faces and through their chests and limbs, like a faded tattoo just below the skin. The bloody pus that had oozed from their eyes, ears, and noses had mostly disappeared, with occasional minor flare-ups, as if the infection had reached a point of equilibrium for those that had survived it. They still ran hot, still sweated a little, but the sweat has become caked and layered with dust, drying and building up on their bodies in a grotesque patina.

They were as fast as the deer, traversing the terrain like agile wild beasts. They were hunting the deer, but Allie was hunting them.

She tracked them with the scope, following them as they gained on the deer and came down closer to the deserted town. Strange, she thought. From a distance, they looked like ideal specimens, attractive, lithe, and with rippling muscles, washboard abs, in perfect physical condition. The kind of testosterone-soaked men that all those boys training at the gym back before the world ended had been striving to be like. It was only when you got close that you began to see what they really were—the strange veins that up close marred their skin, the pus still present in the corners of their eyes marking the infection always waiting to run rampant again, the emptiness in their gaze, the way they moved their heads and sniffed the air more like wild beasts than humans. And, if you got too close and they caught your scent in the air, the way that emptiness turned into a rage, and they tried to kill you.

She took a deep breath, then let it out evenly, slowly, and took her shot.

Or, rather, three shots, one at each of the ferals, in rapid succession, with tiny precise micro-movements of the gun in between. Three head shots, and each of the ferals dropped almost immediately to writhe and die on the ground. The sound of the shots echoed through the canyon, and the deer, confused by this new threat, scattered. A moment later, they'd vanished.

Allie got up and brushed herself off. She'd been lying next to a tree, prone, waiting. Three years along, and she looked different, too. Her eyes were sullen and hard; her face was seasoned and burned by sun and wind, daubed and smeared with red mud and feral blood to camouflage it. Her hair was cut short, hacked off, so it wouldn't get in the way. She wore layered camouflage gear and had machetes and several pistols holstered and sheathed to her belt line. She was muscled, even more so than she'd been as a lacrosse player, her body lean and lithe, and she moved with a careful determination, not a step wasted, always aware of her surroundings.

Her dirt bike was farther back in the trees, branches draped over it to keep it hidden. It was a CRF450 with the handlebars and engine and gas tank painted over in camouflage, the chrome and metal of the wheels and fork first spray-painted a dull gray and then smeared and caked with mud to keep them from glinting, and with a Q-Stealth Silencer muffler she'd salvaged from a ruined bike shop and installed herself. One of a thousand new skills she'd had to learn since the world had ended.

She slung her rifle on her back, cleared the branches off the bike, straddled it, and rode down to see the dead ferals.

———

The shots were all dead center to the head. She couldn't afford to lose her touch, not with the world the way it was now, not with ferals everywhere. Hard to believe they had once been someone's brother, someone's husband, maybe even someone's father. Out here, when she was hunting them, seeing them as the predators they were, it was sometimes hard to think of them as ever even having been human. Her own father came to mind, and she shook her head, trying to push the memory back down. She didn't want to remember the creature he had become at the end. She wanted to remember how he was earlier— teaching her to bat, testing her reflexes by throwing a tennis ball at her, encouraging her in his own rough way—but every time she thought of that ball speeding toward her face, she couldn't help thinking of his fist pummeling her mother's head. And her mother, holding down her real-estate job but always with time for her or her sister when they needed her, living her life masterfully until, from one day to the next, she was dead, gone.

Allie shook her head. That was the past; the past was dead and gone and better left alone.

She unwound the hook and chain from the bike's back fin. Choosing the largest of the ferals, she pushed the hook up through his throat until she could see the tip of it protruding between his teeth. She could still feel the heat radiating off his skin. She turned and pulled the chain over her shoulder, beginning to drag him along the grass, until she reached a stretch of cracked and irregular pavement. He slid along behind, feet jiggling with the motion, the leathery skin below his jaw slowly tearing.

She dragged him to the edge of a parking lot and then into it, toward a ruined and deserted Target superstore. The glass entrance doors had been broken out, the letters torn from the façade as well, only the red bull's-eye remaining. She pushed her way through the entrance, eyes alert, and moved past the ransacked shelves, through a scattering of merchandise: women's shoes, racks of baby clothes coated in dust, children's bicycles, collapsed shelves of toys. She dragged him to the back of the store, to what had once been the sporting goods section. Here the shelves had been pushed over or cleared, leaving an open circle around a half-dozen lengths of chain suspended from the ceiling—where the heavy bags had once hung. The floor here was stained, reddish in some places, nearly black in others. Near the edge of the circle were a few cases of Mason jars, with rings and lids, as well as a dozen coils of rope.

Quickly and efficiently, she worked the hook out of the feral man's throat and lashed his legs together with the rope. Then, with the hook and chain slung back over her shoulder, she went out to haul in the other two.

By the time the light had started to wane, she had all three of them inside, their legs bound. She had to work quickly, before the blood coagulated. She strung the ferals up in a line, from the chains in the ceiling, until they were a good four feet off the ground. She arranged three Mason jars below each of their heads and then moved from one to another, slicing the ferals' throats with her machete and setting them swaying ever so slightly, so the blood drizzled into all nine jars.

She moved down the line, then returned to the start, watching the flow of the blood, nudging a jar a little. She watched, waiting, until the flow slowed.

When she was satisfied, she moved the jars, twisting the rings on tight until they were closed and the jars wouldn't leak. Then she went back and grabbed the first feral by the hair. Holding him steady, she slashed open his belly. His intestines slopped out, falling in a mess to hang over his face and pool against the floor. She tugged them until they were all out, then severed each end, leaving the man's guts in a heap below his head. The smell was pungent, but she didn't so much as wrinkle her nose, just went on to the next belly.

Nightfall found her in the back of the store, manipulating a series of steel chains lined up on the floor in an intersecting pattern. She nudged one, moved another slightly, until, satisfied, she got up and wandered to the front of the store to watch the last of the sun slip behind the horizon. *Here I am, alone at the end of the world*, she thought. She had moved the intestines there, slit them open, strung them in a long line along the entranceway, blood poured over and around them as a kind of scent barrier. She inspected her work there, too, and was satisfied by what she saw.

Using an LED penlight, she guided herself back into the darkness of the store. She passed chunks of wrapped and cured deer meat, passed her dirt bike leaning against the end of an aisle. A little farther along were supplies, a series of guns lined up and carefully arranged to allow for quick access. She went past that, working her way with great care through the pattern of intersecting chains to where, in the back, was a sleeping bag. The jars of blood were in a line beside these. Climbing into the sleeping bag, she opened the closest jar and pushed her hand into it, scooped out some of the gore, and smeared it all over her face, her arms, and under her shirt.

After screwing the lid back on, she lay down. She clicked off the penlight and closed her eyes, taking a deep breath.

A moment later, her eyes were open again as she fumbled in the darkness. She knocked against the jars, heard them clinking against one another, felt along the floor between them and the sleeping bag, then felt the floor on the other side. There it was: her rifle.

Holding it across her chest, one hand grasping the barrel, the other just shy of the trigger, she closed her eyes again and tried to keep them closed.

# Chapter Six

Morning found her a few miles away, in a small town built on the edge of a forest, less than an hour by dirt bike from where she had grown up. She was on the roof of a two-story home in what had once been a quaint community, sheltered behind the slope of the roof and a chimney. She had the rifle's scope to her eye and was staring through it, down at the streets below. She slowly combed through each of the suburban streets, passing over the houses that were still standing, over the piles of ash of houses that had burned down, over the dry, sparse lawns, dead in patches and four feet tall in others. Here and there, a desiccated skeleton, or remnants of something that had once been human. Bits and pieces of consumed animals, a swath of dried black gore on the concrete, midden heaps that ferals had left. The town looked a little as though it had been ravaged by a long-ago war and forgotten, she thought, dragging her scope down one street and up another. Like Viking berserkers had marauded their way through, chaotic and random, tearing some doors off hinges and leaving others intact, torching every third house, killing the inhabitants, and then leaving the bodies to rot. Middle-income houses, the kinds of places ordinary folk would occupy. The kind of place she used to live in. Some of the doors of the houses stood wide open; some had windows that were broken and shattered, old threadbare curtains furling out through the rotting frames. Others looked the same as they always had, as if the owners had just locked the doors and stepped out for a few errands and might be back at any moment.

She reached the end of her scan without seeing movement. Good. Might be a quiet day. She moved the scope back and wiped her forehead. The feral blood she was smeared with stank, but she'd grown accustomed to that, having no way to avoid it and still be safe. Also, it stung when it got into her eyes, and that was something she hadn't gotten accustomed to. She had to be careful not to wipe too much of it away—last thing she needed was for her scent not to be sufficiently masked when she was out on recon—but she had a pocket mirror and a half-jar of blood there beside her. It made her laugh to think of what passed as makeup for her these days. If she seemed to be losing that ruddy hue in the mirror, she'd just daub a little more on. Better to be overly cautious than to end up dead.

She turned and moved to the other side of the chimney, placed her eye against the scope's eyepiece, and stared out again. *One hell of a glamorous job*, she thought. *But somebody's gotta do it.*

She caught a flash of movement when she was almost past it. She stopped and went back, found it again, and held to the spot, reaching up carefully to twist it into focus. Eight ferals, about three hundred yards away, almost hidden by the edge of a house. A hunting pack. They were dragging two slaughtered dogs and a deer through the suburban streets. She zoomed closer in, looking at their faces, but none were familiar.

*New faces*, she thought. *Not good.*

They made their way through one of the broken-out windows into a house, dragging the deer and the dogs with them, leaving a swath of blood over a collapsing planter box. She stayed on them a moment, memorizing the location of the house, and then continued her scan.

Almost immediately she found another group, another hunting pack, though this one hadn't caught anything yet. They were still in stalking mode, fanning out in the street. A stray dog a little ways along had just noticed them, hadn't realized yet that it didn't stand a chance, that they already had it surrounded. One face she recognized, the rest no. More new faces. That was unusual, and not a good sign. She sighed and lifted the rifle off its stand, and then caught something with her naked eye and brought the scope back around.

Another group, this one even larger than the other two. What was going on? They almost never roamed in packs of more than four or five. Any more than that and there was too much jockeying for position among the betas, and they ended up tearing each other apart instead of hunting prey. Had something changed?

She crawled over the roof peak and turned to face the other way, staring back at the forest, taking inventory of that area as well. There was a dirt road, a sign posted next to it reading HARBOR AHEAD with an accompanying arrow under it. Over the arrow, people had scrawled ominous warnings: "Stay Back!" "Hell Ahead!" "The Docks of Death."

She paused on the sign a moment, not really looking at it, waiting. After a moment, she caught a flash of movement and scanned where she thought it had come from. A few more moments and she had it: a lone feral, stalking through the forest, on its own.

"Bingo," she said.

She held to him for a moment, considering. Yes, he was the one. Now all she needed was bait.

She let the scope wander out farther into the forest. She caught a shimmer and focused in, saw a small lake. Soon, a plan had begun to form in her mind.

# Chapter Seven

Kneeling at the edge of the lapping lake, rifle on the ground beside her, she splashed water over her face. It was ice cold, refreshing in a way that left you numb. She scrubbed her face, loosening the layers of dried blood, then washed again. When she looked at her face this time in her steel pocket mirror, there was a hint of the girl she had been, her freckles and eyes betraying the young, feisty athlete she once was that the hardness of her arms and the severity of her expression belied. She liked that girl still, but felt distant from her. That girl belonged to another world. Which was why she didn't mind using her as bait.

She unbuttoned and removed her camo pants and undershirt, stripping down to her bra and underwear. Kneeling, she scooped up more water, washing the blood off her arms and legs and torso, too. She waited at water's edge.

She picked up the rifle, nearly naked but not defenseless, and kept her eyes on the water. When she saw the surface of it smear, a wind moving toward her, she raised her arms, letting the gust of air rush over her, pick up her scent, and carry it away. Once the wind died down again, she tensed, her eyes slowly scanning the beginnings of the forest in anticipation.

For a long moment, there was nothing but the chittering of birds, and then that stopped and it was pure silence. She let out a controlled breath, and smiled. The birds knew when to stay quiet because a hunter was out. Now she knew he was coming.

A burst of movement, and the lone feral she had spotted earlier emerged from the undergrowth, barreling toward her. Allie held her ground and invited him in, not retreating, not even raising the rifle, never breaking his gaze. He came forward, then slowed about fifteen feet away, just shy of the last tree. He hesitated, as if he knew something was wrong but was unable to quite understand what. Was he capable of turning back? She'd never seen a feral run from the promise of easy prey before, but who knew? Maybe they were learning.

"Come on, you bastard," she whispered. "You know you want me."

She opened her mouth and gave him a radiant smile. That was enough. He let out that savage cry she had come to know so well over the last few years and rushed forward, passing under the tree.

There was a click and he was hurled into the air.

She dropped the rifle and quickly opened the jar of blood, smearing her arms and legs again, her face, too. All the while, the feral shrieked and struggled, but she ignored it. She tugged on her pants and undershirt, grabbed the rifle again, and approached the tree.

The feral was caught in a mesh of intersecting steel chains, a kind of fortified steel net, struggling to get free. When she prodded him with the rifle barrel, he swiftly grabbed for it. Allie pulled the gun back.

"No, you don't," she said. "I've got plans for you, bright boy. Big plans."

He gave a bellowing cry. She climbed the sapling that had sprung the trap and securely connected the rings at the end with a smaller chain, padlocking it shut, a kind of ball made of chain. Then she uncoupled it from the sapling and attached the chain she had used to drag the dead ferals.

She pulled her dirt bike out from where it was hidden beneath branches and hooked the chain to the back of it. She kicked it on, revved the motor.

"My place or yours?" she asked, and gunned it.


She kept looking back to make sure he was still in the chain net. He always was, looking confused and disoriented as the ball rolled and swung and he was sent skittering all around inside his spherical cage. She maneuvered the bike as quickly as she could through the landscape, staying to the scrub, avoiding paths that would take her between trees. A few times she caught a snag and felt it drag at her bike, but each time the snag let go before the chain did or before she was thrown.

When she hit the dirt road, the going got easier. The feral began to screech madly, bouncing up and down in his giant chain-link net as they rolled forward.

She was worried about what she'd see before she reached the end of the dirt road. She could only go so fast in the dirt, and a pack of four or five might manage to take her down before she could take them all out. She went as quickly as she could, clocking forty, bouncing the feral around behind her, and hoping both that he'd survive the treatment and, more important, that the net would.

The trees flashed by. The road curved and she leaned into it, felt the back tire slide a little, then some more as the tow line caught. She almost went down, and almost hit a tree correcting. There was a flash of movement, and she started to reach for one of the pistols holstered on the bike, but it was only a pronghorn. She breathed a sigh of relief, slowed down a little, kept driving.

She broke off from the dirt road before it turned into asphalt, taking back trails and open country—too risky to be on asphalt, particularly so close to the deserted town.

She had driven a good ten minutes and was getting close enough to home that she was beginning to breathe easy when she heard it: over the sound of the feral's own bruised shrieks, over the roar of her own engine, another penetrating screeching sound.

She looked in her handlebar mirror and saw there, behind her, emerging from the shadows, a pack of feral males. The bike was going forty, and she tried to push it higher, but the drag of the net prevented this—they were keeping up with her, maybe even gaining a little.

She cursed, opening the throttle as wide as it would go. The needle stuck at forty and wouldn't go beyond it.

The largest one was nearly to her now, running insanely fast, mouth split in a snarl. His face was taut, his gaze fixed on her. Again she was struck by how handsome they looked and how quickly that shifted as soon as the rage overwhelmed them. He bayed at her, and came closer and closer still. He was reaching out to try to swipe her off the bike when she unholstered the pistol and shot him.

He fell back, tripping one of the others up. The remainder scattered for a moment, away and out of range, and then came back, running strong, still in earnest pursuit. The one she had shot was back up and running, too, though slower now, and with a little luck, she'd hit something important and he was running dead.

She steered with her right hand, keeping the gun at the ready with her left. They were getting closer again. If they figured out they could grab on to the net and pull her to a stop, she'd have to make a stand. Six against one. Maybe five and a half, considering she'd already shot one. The packs were getting bigger, were becoming more than she could handle, and for a moment she felt a trickle of fear. She made a rapid tally of her weaponry. Not impossible—she might survive—though also far from desirable.

One was almost even with her and she shot it, this time going for the legs, to cripple it, slow it down. She hit it, but it kept coming, now a little slower, beginning to drop back.

And there, at last, there it was before her.

She holstered the pistol. Thumbing her radio on, she brought her lips close to it and spoke.

"I'm coming in," she said. "Bringing guests."

"Roger," said a staticky voice back. "Any chance of taking them on a circle around before coming in?"

"Fuck, no," said Allie. "No chance at all."

There was a long pause. "That close, eh?" the staticky voice returned.

Allie gunned the bike, crouching, trying to make herself as aerodynamic as possible. The needle buzzed at forty, made it just past. She swerved onto the asphalt and it climbed a little more, the chain net sparking now against the road.

Up ahead was West Staten: a sprawling farmhouse on several acres of land, with several smaller structures adjacent. The property was surrounded by a twelve-foot-tall steel-fortified fence topped with ribbons of barbed wire. Several crude but sturdy crow's nests had been built onto the roof of the main house, providing lookout balustrades and gunner perches. An alarm was going off inside. She saw a flurry of activity as people rushed to their positions.

The remaining ferals were less than ten yards behind, but the fence was coming up quickly. Could she swing wide and draw them out a little longer, let the others get into position? No, she didn't think so, not while dragging a feral in the net. Up above, shooters began clambering into one of the crow's nests to man the guns.

The gate wasn't open, not yet, but the light was blinking, which meant it was opening, or almost. She couldn't slow, not if she hoped to get through before the ferals got her. She'd just have to ride forward and hope.

And indeed it did open, sliding sideways electronically at the last moment, then slamming swiftly back into place, the balled net scraping the sides, just squeezing through. She passed a technician—her friend and roommate Holly—frantically pressing a switch, trying to get the gate locked, and then heard the ferals slam into it and their screams of frustration as it held.

A moment later, they were clambering up the fence, as Allie kept driving. The guns had already started to fire, and three of the remaining ferals were torn to shreds by the gunfire and didn't make it across. The last two, though, were up and over, still in pursuit of Allie as she rode toward the main building in a slow curve. They followed quickly, taking the most direct path; she'd slowed down so it would seem as if they had a chance of catching her. They ran madly after her, shrieking all the while, and a moment later both exploded in a ball of fire. Land mine.

Allie slowed her bike, stopped it in front of the main building. She unhooked the net from the back. The feral inside was bruised and bloodied, barely conscious, but still sullen.

"What do you have to say for yourself now?" Allie asked. And when the feral hissed, she said, "I thought so." She grabbed a shovel from the side of the building and slammed the chain net once, and then dusted herself off and went inside.

## Chapter Eight

# Dr. Zeman

## 1

With some reservations, I've begun to keep this record in addition to my lab notes, which remain in electronic format. Perhaps I've simply become less rigorous in my old age. Perhaps I feel that an electronic record is simply no longer enough, that it's too easily corrupted or lost in a power surge or when our generators die. Or perhaps it's that I still believe that I might not be the one to finish this work, that if it is finished at all it will be by one of those women who are just girls now, who still have many years to live, and that this record, in combination with my lab notes, will help somehow.

So far our progress has been . . . no real progress at all. Experimental subjects do not respond, or respond not enough to be of much use. You would think, considering the amount of time I spent at Arcon, I would have a better idea of how to take apart a virus someone else put together, but it's not so easy. Viruses mutate by nature, that's just the problem, and this one had done exactly that: it mutated without our realizing it. Besides, I wasn't in that unit. Not the one involved in weaponizing the virus, anyway. I don't have their lab notes, don't have their informal record (if they kept one). All of that was lost in the fire that unleashed this plague on the world.

What caused the fire? I've wondered, but I can only speculate. Human error, is my guess. Somebody underestimated the strength of the subjects with the virus, one got free, something got turned over, a Bunsen burner was turned on by accident, and first a room and then the whole place went up, and apparently a few vats of the virus along with it. Or maybe someone was sloppy and it jumped to a human subject. We know, from having fought for our lives out here for the last few years, how that can go, the way it makes men feral. Get one man in a lab infected and things go way the hell south pretty quick. Once the fire started, the virus was airborne.

Relative to the multimillion-dollar equipment I used to work on, I've got what might be described as a high school chemistry lab—quite literally, since most of our chemistry supplies are things we gathered from the ruins of one of the local high schools.

Allie Hilts brought me a new subject today. "Try not to kill this one as quickly as you did the last one," she told me.

"I'll do my best, but I can't promise anything," I said.

She just nodded and went out.

I can't read Allie exactly, never quite know when she's putting on a front and when she's saying what she really feels, but I suppose that's a function of the kind of life she's had. She's withdrawn, never seems to open up fully, not even to her sister. She never lets her guard down for an instant. But, to be honest, that may be what makes her so good at what she does. As soon as she and Kim showed up, Allie seemed eager to get out again. I think, if it weren't for Kim, Allie would be just as happy to be on her own out in the wild, killing ferals for what they must have done to her and her family, fighting them until she died. Because, if she was alone, she would eventually die. We need her strength, but she needs us, too. Not that she'll ever admit it, but I'm fairly certain she knows.

We lost three scouts before her arrival in a matter of months, each of them making some fatal mistake, one of which led a whole bunch of ferals back to us. That's how we first met Allie—she was killing them from the outside, picking them off one by one while we shot at them from inside the fence.

She wouldn't come in that first time, but one of the girls on the roof would see her from time to time, lurking around the camp, watching us, judging us. That went on for some months, and then she just showed up one day at the gate and begged to audition (Is that the word? No doubt Jacky would curl her lip up at it . . .) for the position of scout:

"I can run, I can ride a dirt bike, I know how to hunt," she said, "I know how to track, and I'm totally careful."

"But you're, what, eighteen? Nineteen?" I said.

"So?" It wasn't lost on me that she didn't tell me exactly how old she was, which meant I must be guessing high.

"You're just a child," I said. "How can I in good conscience—"

"In good conscience, how can you not?" she asked. "How many more scouts have to die before you realize I'm the best one for the job?"

"You're welcome to join us," I said. "Come on in and be part of our community. We'll find a place for you. Maybe as a scout, maybe as something else."

She shook her head. "As scout," she said. "And you have to make a place for my little sister, Kim, too."

I threw up my hands and sent her over to Jacky, our head of security. I don't know what Allie did to prove herself, but it must have impressed Jacky, and I have to admit grudgingly that she's not easy to impress. Before I could blink, both Allie and Kim were living with us, and Allie was our newest scout.

And, indeed, she's taken the challenge on and surpassed even my own hopes. Before, getting a live subject was exceptionally problematic, to say the least, and we'd often lose either someone who was trying to bring a feral in or the feral itself. But Allie's not only brought me a half-dozen subjects: each time she brings me a subject, she brings him in a new way, devising some new system or trap.

"Why not just stick with what works?" I ask her. "Just choose one collection method and stick with it."

"'Collection method,'" she says, and wrinkles her delightful little nose. "Doc, you make it sound like I'm gathering butterflies."

She never does try to justify herself. If she doesn't like a question, she just ignores it. That's how she is. My guess is that she gets bored, that she's trying to distract herself, and the appeal of trying something new outweighs in her mind the risk of an untried method. But, with Allie, we'll never know unless she tells us, and even then we won't know if she's telling us the truth.

## 2

What's fascinating is that we've managed to survive as long as we have, in particular that we managed to survive those early days. I'm hopeful, optimistic, and I do a lot to buoy up the other women, to make them feel like they're living a decent life instead of just surviving. With each month, it feels a little more like that, but it's something of an illusion, too. We won't be endlessly able to find propane for the generators, for instance. Every day brings us closer to running out of things. But even I can see we've beaten the odds, at least so far. Above all, I think, we were just plain lucky individually for the first month or two after the end of the world, and then, somehow, we found one another, and then were luckier still and managed to find the farm and ready supplies and dig in before they came for us. For a while, women trickled in, refugees who had managed to avoid being slaughtered, but over time that slowed and eventually stopped altogether. Allie and Kim were the last to come. There are other communities like ours out there—we pick them up sometimes on the radio; Jacky and Allie and some of the other scouts have even visited them—but we're the exception, not the rule. Most women who were alive three years ago, maybe even 99 percent of the women who were alive three years ago, are now dead. Not just here, but everywhere the virus has spread. On this continent certainly, maybe in the world as a whole. Many of the men are gone, too, either dying because their bodies got burned out by the infection or because a woman packing a pistol shot them or because they tore one another apart. The worst areas, so I've been told, are the cities—nothing but mass graves, some of them, thousands of dead, riddled with disease and infection, reeking of death. No, at least out in small towns or the country the population was low enough that you're not shoulder to shoulder with dozens of ferals.

# 3

We keep them confined. We have a line of six cages strung along the back wall of the laboratory, made of strong sturdy rebar scrounged from a construction site, frequently cross-braced. To administer the serum, we used to sedate them and then haul them out and strap them to the table. We'd bind them in place with leather straps, but their response to sedation is irregular. One feral broke through a strap and tore out Cynthia's throat before I managed to shoot him in the head. I still see her gasping on the floor, looking up at nothing, with the air coming from her open windpipe spraying a fine mist of blood. I watched her die, my hand pressed to her throat, unable to do anything. Since then, I've made sure that I work in the lab alone. I don't want to go through that again, or to have anyone close to me go out that way if I can help it. If anyone is going to die because of these experiments, let it be me, and me alone. Please, don't let it be like Arcon.

Now I use a tranquilizer gun—one of Allie's best looting victories, as far as I'm concerned. She seems capable of finding almost anything, and, more important, of living long enough to bring it home to us. Now we can inject the feral with the serum from a distance. Perhaps not the soundest method scientifically, but certainly the safest for us. We take blood samples forcefully, with a needle on the end of a stick, and get skin scrapings in a similar way. True test subjects, once they're in a cage, never leave.

The conditions here are primitive, nothing like what I had at Arcon. There's only so much I can do, and all of my test subjects will die, and not die pleasantly. That's one of the hard facts of my job. I haven't found a cure, but I've managed to make it so each new serum kills them less quickly than the one before, and I suppose that's a sort of progress. I tell myself on optimistic days that it is, but on the other days it seems like a standstill. Trying to deploy gene therapy in a place like this is marginal at best, kind of like trying to build a functioning rocket ship out of a banana. I keep trying, keep working, keep killing the subjects, and with each one I kill I learn a little bit. At least in theory. Some days, all I learn is that I don't know anything.

# 4

The genetic engineering techniques used at Arcon were very sophisticated. When we were manipulating the twenty-third chromosome pair, tinkering with the XY designation that determines male gender so as to create those faster, stronger primates meant to be weapons of war, we not only added a second Y-gene. We also, as my experiments on the most recent subjects have suggested, diminished the role of the X-gene in these primates. When the virus jumped to humans, the same thing happened to our men. It's not quite so simple as this, but, in layman's terms, I not only have to get rid of the new Y, but also stimulate the X. The extra Y-gene caused an overproduction of testosterone and adrenaline, giving the males extraordinary strength and speed as well as destroying certain areas of brain function. Broca's area, in the frontal lobe, wastes away, leading first to decay and then to dissolution of the ability to speak. The regulatory capacity of the hypothalamus is compromised in a way that makes it impossible for a feral to calm its own anger effectively. But I believe that it is the diminished role of the feminine X-gene that makes the feral males particularly violent and makes them want to kill us. They'll of course kill one another as well, but that's largely to assert dominance or jostle for position within the pack structure. Or, in some circumstances, if they get too hungry. But women they'll attack on sight without fail. If we can strengthen the X-gene, perhaps their murderous impulses will diminish enough that we don't have to be fighting constantly for our lives. Diminish enough for us to build up a real laboratory and sort out a real cure.

And so this is the dilemma for me. Do I go after a real serum, one intended to make men what they once were? Or do I try for a short circuit of some kind, a way of shifting the X enough to make the current males less harmful, less aggressive, to buy us some breathing room? Jacky has reached the point where she's reconciled to it, where she's moved on from the idea that men could ever be back as part of society. She seems to thrive in this new society of women, arguing that it functions better than the patriarchy we had before. "What the hell do I care if you find a cure?" she told me the other day, in her own inimitable Jacky way. "Men are gone and there's no going back. Good fucking riddance, I say."

But I do care. I haven't given up on men. Yet. I still hold out hope. Call me biased, but the extinction of the human race would not be a good thing. As they are now, with two Y-chromosomes, these subjects—these *ferals*, as we've come to call them—do not produce normal sperm. The ferals we see are all due to mutation; I can't even imagine what their offspring would be like, but since the gene is dominant, I can only imagine they would be as bad as the ferals, or even worse. Unless I can figure out some way for a female egg to imitate a sperm and make another female egg believe it has been fertilized (and, believe me, I'm working on that project as well), we need men. And so we need to find a serum to return these ferals to the men they once were.

But, the cynic in me wonders, what if it's too late? Who is to say that modifying their DNA again will get us back to where we started? There's no guarantee they can return to being healthy, no guarantee they will suddenly be capable of producing normal sperm again. And the longer we wait, the less likely it'll be that a woman among us will be young enough to be able to reproduce.

It's an uphill climb, with despair on every side, but what can I do but keep climbing?

# 5

The latest subject. Allie caught him by coaxing him into a pit, but how she got him out of the pit and into the straitjacket that he was wearing when he came in, I have no idea. He can't tell me his name, so I have given him one, as a way of humanizing him a little, of reminding myself that there was once a man within what's now a monster. I've done that with the others as well, though I mostly kept the fact of doing it to myself. Allie Hilts got it out of me at one point, and at first I thought she'd use it against me, mock me, and, well, yes, she does a little. But she takes it seriously, too, sees it as a kind of ritual. She remembers the names better than I do, and remembers, too, the histories I give them: a name is a good start, but it's not enough to humanize creatures this monstrous. Sometimes the history is short, sometimes longer, depending on how much weed I've smoked and how rushed or despairing I feel at the moment, but it's always something.

When Allie brought him in she said, "Who is he, Doc?"

I thought about it for a moment. "Carlos," I finally said.

"With that blond hair, I would have thought Sven would be more appropriate," she said.

"All right, Sven," I said.

But she shook her head. "No," she said. "You already said his name. You can't change it." She takes the naming seriously. Even her objections and teasing are a built-in part of the ritual.

"What's he like?" she asked.

I looked at the feral gathered like a coiled spring in the back of the cage, regarding us with his dark, angry eyes. "He's a . . . mechanic," I said. "Self-taught, but very good at it, or good, anyway, with certain sorts of cars. He has a knack for fixing old VW Bugs."

"Not too many of those around anymore," Allie said. "He's going to be out of a job soon."

I nodded. "Lucky for him, the world ended before he was."

We were both silent for a moment. "What about his one thing?" she finally asked.

"His one thing . . ." This was another part of the ritual, the one thing that made the man behind the feral stand out, particularized him, made him different from all the other VW mechanics named Carlos out there. I sat down at the table and took a long hit from the bong. Self-medicating. Allie just waited, arms folded.

"Why don't you pick it?" I said to her.

She shook her head. "Not my job," she said. "I just bring them to you."

"All right," I said. "How about this? Carlos likes Buster Keaton movies. Loves them, in fact."

She nodded slightly, and went out. I can't tell if she even knows who Buster Keaton is. If she doesn't, she's probably too proud to ask.

So I was left alone with Carlos, the VW mechanic who loves Buster Keaton movies, and whom I was about to slowly and painfully kill.

# 6

What level of pain must they experience? The way they bellow after being injected, the speed with which they dart about the cage, unsure of what's happening to them, like wounded animals. Do they even have consciousness anymore, at least as we understand it? Some cognitive scientists used to believe that consciousness was a kind of evolutionary accident, and that it perhaps gets in the way of the instincts that keep us safe. Perhaps these are creatures of pure instinct, who have shed that evolutionary accident to become something altogether different. They're highly developed specimens physically, but something is no longer there upstairs, and it was that something that made them human.

# 7

There is a moment, always a moment, when I think that something is happening, when I feel that, yes, this time, perhaps we have something. The subject's face clears a little, the heat of the skin diminishes, the muscles relax. For a moment—a moment I've come to despise—I feel hope. But then the skin becomes even hotter than before, the bloody flux that characterizes the first onset of the virus returns, and there is nothing to do but wait and watch them, see if they exhibit any new symptoms before they die. Their bodies prefer destroying themselves to getting better. We are just a few days into Carlos's moment of glory, and he is already on the wane.

## 8

A careful charting of symptoms, charts comparing Carlos's decline to what his brothers, further along in their treatment, are suffering. The new serum is, well, a little better. Or different, anyway.

Have I learned anything? Have I made any progress? Yes, probably, but it may take me weeks, if not months or years, to understand what it is exactly that I've learned. There may be something there that I'm just not seeing. There may be something there that I might never see.

## 9

Allie is gone for several days, venturing out alone—"prowling," as she says. There are moments when I worry about her out there, though I hardly have the right—she's not my responsibility, never has been. And I should know by now that if anyone can fend for herself, it's Allie.

Indeed, she does come back, arriving this time in grand style, roaring through the gate on that bike of hers, dragging behind her a feral she's captured, in a sort of homemade metal sphere, a kind of giant badass hamster ball. She brought a few loose ferals in behind her as well, which meant we wasted precious ammunition, even wasted a land mine blowing the last two to kingdom come. Allie, dear Allie, your boldness might well kill all of us one day.

I lecture her as usual, scolding her. She ignores me as usual, just waits me out. She's confident that she knows exactly what she's doing, that every movement she makes is planned out in advance. She's like any young person that way. She turns to leave and makes it to the door before turning to ask:

"What's his name, Doc?"

I don't answer her. Instead, I take a three-by-five card and scribble on it, then tape it to the outside of his cage. "See for yourself," I say when I'm done.

She walks up, looks at the card, then taps it with her forefinger. The feral in the back of the cage eyes her, alert. For a moment I think he's going to spring, rattle his cage, but whatever treatment he received at Allie's hands on the way to the camp has made him wary of her, gun-shy. Being dragged around for miles inside a metal ball might well do that to a person.

Oh, look at me. Thinking of these test subjects as people. That's the effect of naming something, I guess.

"Jacob Roman," she says. And then says, "Good name."

I raise my eyebrows, waiting for her to tease me. "You think so?" She doesn't know who Roman Jakobson is, probably, or his ideas concerning communication functions. She doesn't know, in other words, that I'm cheating a little, giving him the mangled name of a theorizer of something on my mind at the moment; but who am I to disillusion such a lovely young girl?

She nods, then says, "What's his story, Doc?"

I'm already back at the microscope by the time she asks this, looking at a tissue sample from Carlos, who is in the cage at the far end, slowly dying. As are we all, I suppose. Eventually, I'll take the card taped to his cage and place it in the drawer of my desk, filed up against the cards of all the other subjects that have passed through here. Allie doesn't know that I do this, and if she did I wonder what she'd think. *Getting sentimental in your old age, Doc?* she might rib. She'd really be surprised if she knew that sometimes I get the cards out and thumb through the names again and try to remember not the ferals in their cages but the men whose faces I saw hidden behind them, and whom I often felt I caught a brief glimpse of coming to the surface again right before they died, in their last second or two on earth.

I keep looking through the microscope. Nothing surprising here. The latest serum hasn't gotten us as far along as I would have hoped. Allie is still there, waiting to hear what I will say.

"Jacob had a ... thorny start," I say. "His parents were long-suffering, unemployed alcoholics. Jacob fought to be everything his parents were not. He succeeded. He never touched the sauce, and graduated magna cum laude with a degree in graphic design. He became an award-winning, highly lauded, highly paid book-cover designer. His style was akin to Abstract Expressionism." I'm acutely aware that if I were to change the gender, replace "graphic design" with "human geneticist," and tweak the last two statements to allude to my role in the fuckup at Arcon, this would be a description not of Jacob Roman but of me.

"His one thing?" asks Allie.

I don't look up. "Jacob looked to the skies but saw something different than most, Allie. He had little faith in life but believed supremely intelligent life existed in other solar systems."

I don't hear her go out. But when I draw away from the eyepiece of the microscope she is gone, the door left slightly ajar.

I sigh and get up to close the door. When I come back, I approach Jacob Roman's cage and take a closer look at him. Does he look any more human now that he has a story? Not really. But his having a story makes *me* more human. Or at least makes me *feel* more human.

But I will always be, first and foremost, a scientist. If I can learn something by killing him, I'll kill him.

We regard one another warily. "Well, Mr. Roman," I finally say to him. "We have a lot of work to do. Shall we begin?"

## Chapter Nine

Reentry was hard for Allie, as always. When she was out there, on her own, responsible only for herself, life was exhausting but exciting, a constant adrenaline rush. There was nothing except her and the ferals, each hunting the other, never a moment when she could let down her guard. At West Staten, though, she had to think about other things, had to wonder how she fit into this community exactly, and if she really did at all. Sure, they needed her—without her, Dr. Zeman wouldn't have a steady supply of test subjects, after all—but that didn't mean she fit in. She didn't need their affection. She just needed them to help keep Kim safe. Doc called it herd protection, but Allie wasn't content to sit here and wait to be prey.

And what about Doc Zeman, anyway? The thing she always thought about, the thing she couldn't help thinking about when she brought Doc a new test subject, was that even though Zeman was maybe part of the solution now, presenting herself as a kind of relaxed hippie doctor with aspirations to make things right, it hadn't been all that long ago that she'd been part of the problem. She'd worked for Arcon, for God's sake. Not just worked at Arcon—she'd been basically part of the team of geneticists that had caused this to happen in the first place. Allie liked her—it was hard not to like Doc—but did she trust her? Well . . . what choice did she have? There was no one else. It was Doc Zeman or no one.

That was part of the problem: she could never bring herself to let her guard down. Maybe that was a result of all the time she spent outside, too. If she stayed here in the community for a few weeks—a month at a stretch, say—rather than going out prowling every few days, it'd be different. But even then, she was pretty sure, she still wouldn't quite fit in.

It was different for her little sister, Kim. She was in the heart of the community, in the center, much loved by the other women, many of whom had lost daughters or sisters and were happy having someone to look after. Now, standing there in the back of the main farmhouse's common room, watching her sister, Allie felt torn.

When she got off her bike, Kim had been nowhere to be seen. Allie was surprised not to find her waiting when she roared through the gates: often she was. Perhaps Kim had been assigned a task, was on latrine duty or doing laundry or down getting dinner ready. Or perhaps she was simply in a part of the compound where she couldn't see Allie coming in. But she'd heard, of course—you couldn't help hearing, with the alarms going off, the land mine and gunfire. That usually brought people out.

The head of security, Jacky Barnes, had been there, though, freshly down from one of the towers, pumped like she always was after a firefight. With her help, Allie had taken the feral over to Doc, then gone to her room to put her camo and other gear away and take a quick cold shower. When she got out, she'd slipped into jeans and a T-shirt—not wearing camo around the camp was about as close as she could come to making a concession to the rest of the community.

She found Kim in the large common room. There her sister was, standing on a makeshift stage that hid the fireplace, a red-cheeked, blonde twelve-year-old, happy. The room was filled with women, some sitting, some standing, watching the performance, forty or so of the forty-eight that comprised the camp, most of them smiling. A castle had been made out of cardboard and painted pale gray and lavender, and Kim was wearing a costume dress, all ruffles and frills, with glitter spread along the collar. At her feet, prone, was another young girl, this one wearing trousers and a red jacket trimmed with gold brocade. Her hair had been tied back, and she was sporting a plastic mustache. Allie couldn't tell if the girl was supposed to be asleep or was pretending to be dead.

Allie nudged a woman near her, Karen. "What is this?" she asked.

"'Sleeping Beauty,'" Karen whispered back.

Allie nodded. She turned and watched a moment more, her brow slowly furrowing, until she realized what it was that confused her.

"I thought the prince was supposed to awaken the princess in 'Sleeping Beauty,'" whispered Allie.

"Artistic license," whispered the woman. "We can't teach them to wait around for men to wake *them* up, can we?"

*No*, thought Allie, *we probably can't. Or shouldn't, anyway. Still, maybe we should just let the prince stay asleep. Not give false hope.*

On stage, Kim dropped to one knee and drew the sleeping prince's head into her lap. Bending over, she smacked a kiss on the sleeping prince's brow, and the latter stretched, yawned, and said, "Is it morning already?"

The audience laughed and applauded. Abruptly, the play stopped. "That's all we've got so far," said Kim to the audience, and there was more laughter, more applause. Kim and the prince stood hand in hand and took a bow, as other, younger children, who must have been in the play before Allie arrived, quickly rushed out from the side of the stage to join them.

Allie, in the back, clapped halfheartedly and slipped away.


A few hours later, darkness having fallen, she found herself in the back of the common room again, standing by herself. The makeshift stage had been pushed to the side, and on the mantel now was a CD player, blaring music from the 1980s, from back before Allie was born, stuff her mom and dad liked to listen to. Of course, a lot of the women here were the age of her parents, so maybe it made sense. But it was just one more reason to feel like she was at the edge of the group.

All around her, women were drinking, dancing, talking. They mingled, cavorted, touched one another lightly on the arm, the cheek. It wasn't for her. It all seemed so fake to Allie, like people trying to pretend nothing was wrong when, in fact, everything was wrong. Like fucking while Rome burned. How could they act like the world was normal? How could they have a party in the ruins and pretend things were fine?

She was here because she had promised Kim she would come. She was here for Kim. And in a few minutes, once Kim had seen her, spoken to her, told her she was glad she'd come, she'd make a surreptitious exit and go out and down the hall and up the stairs to their room.

Someone turned down the music. She heard a rattling sound as someone else struck a glass with the handle of her spoon. And then Doc Zeman was there in the center of the room, with a circle clearing out around her. "Excuse me!" she said. "A toast to our young women for their fine performance!"

Everyone got quiet. The music was turned the rest of the way down, and conversations finished and folded up as people turned toward Doc and raised their glass or searched for a glass with something in it so they could join the toast.

Dr. Zeman just stood and waited, in no rush or hurry. She wore thick reading glasses, peering over the top of them unless she was looking at something right in front of her, and had on a dress with a floral print. Her brown hair was braided and had a streak of blue running through it. She wore around her neck a man's tie, loosely knotted, the whole of her outfit looking thrown together, quirky, and yet perfectly expressive of her personality. Doc was smart, Allie knew, incredibly so, but she didn't have that Asperger's quality that scientists seemed to have, at least in the movies. She had a softer side, an interest in poetry, in music, which offset her more clinical and rational side, probably something she'd had to develop to have a smoother ride in a predominantly male scientific field.

*But,* thought Allie, *maybe if Doc had had that Asperger's thing after all, the virus wouldn't have made it out. And, however smart Doc was, she hadn't gotten very far with her serum.*

Seeing people attentive, Doc raised her glass.

"Some say the difference between humans and animals is the ability to see beauty, and to make art," she said. "To our girls—for keeping culture alive. It could be easily forgotten here, at a time like this. Keep up the inspiring work. You are my heroes. Bravo!"

"Bravo!" echoed the crowd, and glasses were touched to lips. Kim and the other girls from the play stepped forward and bowed again, and there was a smattering of applause. Doc was all smiles, proud of the young girls, and the girls were allowed to bask in their fifteen minutes of fame.

*Good time to get out*, thought Allie, and started to edge for the door.

People were starting to turn, breaking back into their smaller groups, but before they could get far, another woman stepped forward. When Allie saw who it was, she stopped moving toward the door: Jacky Barnes. She was tough and feisty. Though she had a military background, she didn't wear it on her sleeve—she seemed streetwise and irreverent. *No, Jacky*, she thought. *Don't, don't, don't.*

"Just one more," said Jacky.

*Oh hell*, thought Allie.

Jacky lifted her glass, a big angular beer stein brimming with a dark home brew.

"One more toast," Jacky said, nudging Doc slightly out of the way. Jacky and Doc were like that, always getting in one another's way just a little. "To badass Allie, who had another successful hunt!"

"To Allie," they rumbled around her, and Allie nodded, flashing a brief smile. For a moment, Jacky just stood there, and Allie wondered if she was expected to come up and say something herself, but then Jacky started talking to someone near her, conversations rose, the music was turned up again, and Allie decided she was safe.

She was almost out the door when Kim stepped in front of her.

"You're not going already, are you?"

"Whatever gave you that idea?" asked Allie, her voice sarcastic.

Kim put her hands on her hips. "But you promised!" she said.

"I . . . thought it was winding down," said Allie.

"Yeah, right," said Kim. "Anyway, we need you."

"We?" asked Allie, and then noticed the two six-year-olds huddled to one side of her sister.

Kim gestured at the twins. "Lola and Stephie don't believe me that before infection women and men used to kiss."

Allie felt something break inside of her. She had to resist breaking out laughing, but was worried that if she did it would quickly turn to tears. Is that all it takes to lose a sense of how the world used to be? Just a few years?

She deliberately made her eyes wide and unblinking. She nodded seriously up and down.

"Did you ever kiss one?" Stephie asked.

"There was this game we used to play," Allie said. "It was called 'Spin the Bottle.' All the boys would sit in a circle, and you'd put this bottle on its side in the middle and spin it, and whatever boy it pointed to when it stopped you had to kiss."

The twins made gagging noises, squinching their eyes shut.

"Why would you play that? Weren't you scared?" asked Lola.

"It was different then," said Allie. *For one thing, the boys weren't trying to break your skull back in those days*, she thought.

The twins stared at her for a long moment, and when she didn't say any more they scampered off, pushing each other a little as they went. Kim, though, stayed where she was.

"So?" said Kim.

"It was good, kiddo," said Allie. "I like that they made Sleeping Beauty a man."

"My idea," said Kim, suspiciously. "What?"

"It's just . . . I just wonder if you're spending too much time on all this. You should be training more. That's what's important."

As soon as Allie said it, she regretted it. *I'm right*, thought Allie. *But I shouldn't have told her at her celebration party. That was wrong.* She was just opening her mouth to apologize when Kim turned on her heel and left.

"Kim," Allie called after her, but her sister didn't stop, didn't slow.

She cast another anxious glance around. The others were still mingling, still talking. Some had done more drinking than others—not just the home brew but two bottles of Johnnie Walker Black that Allie had scored a few runs back. People had begun to let down their hair. Jacky was in the corner with her current flame, Emma: short black hair with a lot of curl to it, skin a little lighter than Jacky's, tank top, camo pants. Doc Zeman was dancing with several of the younger girls, a martini balanced in her hand, the liquid sloshing higher up the side of the glass with each step. Allie had had a close call getting that bottle of Bombay Sapphire that Doc kept all to herself for her martinis.

Sure, fine: everyone in her own way was having a blast. That was great. But someone had to stay sober and remember how hard that liquor had been to get.

Allie left.

# Chapter Ten

Ten minutes later and she was high in the air, pushing open the trap-door in the floor of the highest crow's nest and climbing up onto the observation platform.

The guard there, a thirtyish African American woman named Kayla who had a shaved head and a nose ring, removed the night binoculars from her eyes long enough to see who it was. "What's up, Allie?" she asked.

"Nothing," said Allie. "I just thought . . . Go enjoy the party, Kayla. I'll take watch for a while."

"Yeah?" Kayla said. There was reluctance in her voice, as if she thought there might be a catch. She and Allie had never completely trusted one another. "I'll owe you."

Allie gave a noncommittal shrug. "It's fine," said Allie. "There's a good bottle hidden under the stairs by the east entrance. Check behind the cinder block with the broken top corner."

Kayla nodded and handed the binoculars over. She stood and made a show of stretching, then made her way down the ladder and out of sight.

Allie took a deep breath. Here, in the open air, alone, she could be doing something, be on the hunt. It kept her from thinking too much.

It had been a long day. She deserved to treat herself.

She took out her rolling papers and tobacco and rolled a cigarette, lighting it and letting it hang from the side of her mouth. Still smoking, she raised the binoculars, eyeing the grounds, scanning the forest beyond the fence. After a moment, she spotted something that Kayla seemed to have missed: movement. She focused, zooming in on a small group of ferals, and watched them.

They were circling West Staten at a distance, staying back in the cover of the trees, moving slowly around the perimeter, without attempting to come forward. That was strange, more controlled than ferals usually were. One of them, she realized after a moment, was holding the others back, directing them, controlling them somehow.

This leader was tall, incredibly large and statuesque, even for a feral, his face a mass of crisscrossed scars. She'd seen him before, and she'd come to call him Scarface. He didn't have just the simple aggression of the others: he moved in a way that suggested intention and foresight, even cunning. It wasn't what she'd come to expect from a feral, and that bothered her. Before he appeared, she'd only ever seen five or six ferals to a pack, max. But him she never saw with fewer than ten.

Keeping her eyes on him, she stubbed out the cigarette and put down the binoculars, groping the sniper rifle off the rack behind her. She brought it to her shoulder, sighted, steadied herself. But before she could take careful aim, Scarface and his pack scattered, scurrying off into the darkness. Almost as if they knew they were being watched. Though Allie knew that was impossible.

At least, she thought it was.

Thoughtfully, she lowered the rifle. Maybe next time.


She still had the rifle in her hands, ready at a moment's notice, when the hatch opened and Holly climbed through. She was wearing a revealing dress, low-cut at the top and riding high below. She was gorgeous, with curling dark red hair and green eyes. She had narrow cheekbones and full red lips.

"I knew I'd find you here," she said.

"Looking for Kayla?" asked Allie, beginning to stiffen up again.

Holly laughed. "No, you. See any motherfuckers out there?" she said.

Allie could see Holly was buzzed again, but she couldn't hold it against her. There were names she still shouted in her sleep most nights, though the booze helped. They all needed something, but Allie couldn't let her guard down. For Kim's sake. She needed to stay sharp, and deadly.

She gestured out over the fence. "He's out there again," she said. "Scarface." Her voice changed, becoming almost reverential, though there was an undercurrent of fear in it, too. "You know, he's smarter than the others. He knows not to climb the fence because of the mine-field, and somehow he's taught the others not to climb it, either."

"Come back inside—have a drink," said Holly, reaching for her hand. "You've been out there for days—let's celebrate your return. Come on!"

Allie stared at her for a long moment, avoiding her reach, but said nothing. After a while, she turned, looked back out. Holly came a little closer, leaned toward her, hooking Allie's arm in her own.

"Sometimes I wish that you and I could go down to the harbor," Holly said. "Hop on a boat, and sail off into the sunset."

"Do you even know how to sail?"

"Sure," she said, and shrugged. "Sailing, motoring, tides, currents, all that. My dad used to pilot the ferry. He'd let me sit up there with him sometimes and showed me how to run it. I miss it."

"A ferry's hardly the kind of boat you'd sail off into the sunset on."

Holly shrugged. "Any port in a storm," she said. "Any boat will do."

Allie turned and looked at her, her expression level, deadly serious. "Good plan if you want to commit suicide. The harbor is hell—the beehive."

Holly unhooked her arm, moved back a little. Allie could tell by her face that her feelings were hurt. For a second she felt a twinge of regret, but quickly choked it out. "Jesus," Holly said, "I know that. I was just dreaming. Sometimes I don't know how to talk to you, Allie. You're just so damn . . . angry."

Allie frowned, irritation thrumming in her voice. "Every male is infected and we are outnumbered. You have no idea. None of you do. You're happy to sit here and drink and mess around until they kill every last one of us. I'm not going to let that happen."

"You don't have to—"

"Life ends when the young ones get old and die. Not just for you and me, for everybody—the human race. What is there to be happy about?"

For a long time, Holly was silent, her face looking as shocked as if she'd been slapped. When she spoke, her voice was subdued. "How can you not be happy?" asked Holly. "At least you managed to save your sister." She turned and faced Allie. "That's exactly why I need to dream," she said. "To imagine a world in which we could get on a boat and sail away. But you never let me or anyone else do even that."

Allie didn't bother to respond. She raised her binoculars and looked out, catching glimpses of the same group of ferals, circling like a pack of dogs out there in the shadows.

## Chapter Eleven

# Kim

I never thought my sister was wrong about the way she did things, at least not at the time. Not right exactly, but not wrong, either—she did what she had to do to steel herself to keep going. Almost everyone else tried to find little moments when they could pretend that life hadn't changed that much, that the important things were just as they had been before. I tried that, too. And when that wasn't enough, we dreamed, thinking about life as it had been before the ferals, thinking of our parents, of outdoor barbecues, convenience stores, proms, imagining what we'd be doing now if Arcon had never existed. But Allie, she lived in the moment. She was always present in the moment, and *just* in the moment.

I think, if anything, she'd been forced to grow up too fast. She felt the weight of that more than she should have. After all, all of us had been forced to grow up too fast, not just her, but she took it personally somehow.

I saw what Dad became, felt him hurt me, but I didn't see him kill Mom. I was unconscious for that, knocked out by the thing my dad had become. Allie wasn't. I didn't have to kill Dad. I knew it happened, knew those facts, but I could still, with an effort, remember my parents as they were, could still take a ton of joy from the family photographs that I'd tacked up beside my bunk in our room. Allie for some reason couldn't. She couldn't even look at those photographs, and some days I imagine it took all she had to keep her from telling me to tear them down. Everything, every bit of the past, hurt her. And so she avoided it. Lived only in the present. Told herself that she needed to stay focused, that if she let her attention wander even for a moment—had a trivial conversation, accepted a drink or two, relaxed a little, laughed, took a night off—we might all die. It was no way to live—it was a way of not really living, in a sense, of always being so tightly wound you were in danger of breaking—but it was the best she could do at the time. She was deeply wounded, deeply fucked up, though I think that she wouldn't have admitted that at the time, and probably wouldn't admit it still, even today.

Or is that all bullshit? Just a way for her not to engage, not to feel? The coward's way out? Sometimes I think one thing, sometimes another.

Allie thought of herself as isolated, alone, even though we all had gone through the same or similar experiences. These other women, they'd had to kill husbands, brothers, lovers, others they were close to, as a way of staying alive. Nobody had it easy. They told themselves that, no, they hadn't killed their loved one, not really—they'd killed something that had taken over the body of their loved one, destroyed him. That it was something they had to do. But only the rational part of them believed this, and there's so much more to us than that. And it was hard to stay isolated when you lived in a communal order, where everyone was the same, where we had no real leaders, where we all pitched in and shared. Some cooked, some cleaned, some stood watch, but we all understood that we were in it together, that we were a community. All of us, that is, except for Allie. She liked to think she was only there for my sake.

## Chapter Twelve

Allie woke late. Or, rather, she pretended she was still asleep while the other three in her room—Holly, Kim, and Kim's friend Beth—got dressed and prepared for the day. She watched her sister, Kim, through veiled eyes, thinking of how much she'd grown, how much she'd changed since that day three years ago when Allie had kept her from dying. She'd lived more than a thousand days of keeping her from dying since then. So far, so good. But every day was a new day.

Kim came over and stood beside her bed, looking down at her. Allie didn't move, continued to regard her through the veil of her eyelashes.

"Come on, Allie," said Kim. "We're going to be late for breakfast."

She didn't say anything, still didn't move, until, with a snort of exasperation, Kim turned and went out.

Once all three girls were gone, she got up, got dressed. She stopped for a moment near Kim's bunk, staring at the pictures tacked there. The four of them, the whole family, all happy and laughing at a skating rink. Allie dressed in her lacrosse gear, her father in the background smiling proudly. Kim and their mother sitting at the kitchen table, scissors and glue and cut-up pieces of construction paper all around them, working on some sort of school project, their heads bent toward each other and nearly touching.

She stood there staring, counting under her breath, drinking it all in.

And then she turned away.

One minute of the past per day. That was all she allowed herself, all she could bear. All that was safe.

Most days, even that was almost too much.


When she got to the common room, the food was nearly gone already. She took a couple of forkfuls of scrambled eggs made from eggs collected that morning, a scoop of oatmeal, a piece of the dense bread that Carla baked and the recipe of which she always claimed to be "tweaking," even though it always tasted exactly the same.

When Allie turned to look for a place to sit, there was Holly gesturing at her. She ignored her and looked for Kim, found her sitting at a table with kids her own age or younger. No free spots at the table. She looked for other possible places to sit, but the tables were largely full. Finally, she walked back and sat next to Holly, who smiled at her luck. Allie didn't smile back.

She ate quickly, shoveling down the food, listening to the conversations going on around her without joining in. Even when Holly addressed her directly, she answered as unresponsively as possible. As soon as she was done, she stood and cleared her plates and those of the others. She felt Holly's eyes on her back, watching her go.


An hour later found her down in the basement, surrounded by treadmills and weight benches in the makeshift gym, mostly stuff that Allie had scavenged with a great deal of trouble. Many of the women of the camp were there, with the exception of the women on watch and Doc Zeman. Most of them were working out like they were training for the Olympics: pumping iron, running on the treadmills, wrestling, jumping rope. The air, steamy and hot, was full of sweat and adrenaline, the women all clearly warriors, their bodies lean and strong, unashamed of showing their battle scars. Allie had noticed that the women sparred hard after a party, as if to make up for a night's laxness with increased vigilance the next day. They pulled their punches less. They got bruised, and that was good—they needed to be reminded this was more than just playing around.

Allie, in torn sweats and a ripped T-shirt, was doing pull-ups. She was intensely focused: for her, this was another way to forget, one of a series of daily tasks that would direct her from morning to night and help her through the day. "A substitute for therapy," Doc had called it once. *No,* she had thought at the time, *exercise is better than therapy.*

She felt something, sensed it, and so, never slowing her reps, began to look around for what it was. Jacky and Emma were wrestling on the mat not far from her, the two of them evenly matched. They were paying attention only to one another, to the battle between them. Same with the other girls and women—they were all engaged with each other or with the machines they were using. Until, that is, she saw Holly on the treadmill, caught the surreptitious glance she cast, and realized that was what she had been sensing.

She closed her eyes and tried to shut Holly out. She kept churning out reps, one after another, after another, after another. A few more and she'd find someone to hit.


Two hours later, she was at the rifle range they'd built just inside the camp's fence. In front of her was a line of fifteen young girls, including Kim. Each girl held a rifle to her shoulder and was shooting at one of the targets thirty yards away. Allie paced behind them, watching, offering corrections of posture and stance as well as an occasional word of encouragement. When she came to Kim, she hesitated, stopped.

"Lock your shoulder, Kim," she said. "No, lock it. Is that what you think locked is? How many times do I have to tell you?" She roughly adjusted her sister's stance and posture, then turned and strode on, speaking loudly now, addressing everyone.

"Listen up," she said. "There's going to come a time when you'll be out there without their blood to mask your scent. You shoot like Kim's shooting here and the motherfuckers will find you and kill you. Learn to protect yourself. You can't always rely on others."

# Chapter Thirteen

## Dr. Zeman

### 10

I watch him writhe about spasmodically within his steel cage. They say that psychopaths have a memory problem, that they can't learn from something that happened to them just a few minutes before. If it's in the past, it's not connected to them, can't possibly have anything to do with them. You can administer an electric shock to a psychopath and then tell him a few minutes later that you're going to deliver a shock to him, and his heartbeat will hardly even accelerate. Do that to a normal person and the experience of waiting for the shock is almost worse than the shock itself. They anticipate it, dread it.

Ferals are like psychopaths. They don't learn, don't become wary of something that hurts them. Or, no, not that exactly: they do become a bit wary, but their anger, their rage, outweighs their wariness. So they might hold back, might resist for a little while, but before long they will rush in even when they know they shouldn't.

Except for one. Allie calls him Scarface, and he is a leader, a thinker, at least as far as such a thing is possible with ferals. I'd love to capture him and get inside of his head, but Allie hasn't been able to manage that yet. He is accompanied by ferals that follow his lead, far more of them than we normally see following an alpha. He seems to control them by a gesture here, a squeal there. It's the first clear indication we've had that they might use a sort of language.

Is Scarface an anomaly? Is there a chance that there has been a mutation of the virus somewhere, that there are ferals out there who have more control and more brain function than we have hitherto seen? That's at once very good news—a serum might work on them that wouldn't work with the others—and terrifying news—the simple traps that we use to take out the others, the simple ways in which we avoid them, might not work on someone like Scarface. Could his cunning even be a sign that his dormant X-chromosome is waking up? Jesus, how terrifying would it be if bringing back the X-chromosome at this stage would make them sharper, more dangerous but no less murderous?

One of the reasons we have survived the ferals to this point has been their predictability. You sow a minefield and they'll run right into it, even if they've seen a few of their fellow ferals blown up just a couple of seconds before. What does it matter? It's not them that's been blown up, the tattered remnants of their mind must think, they'll be okay. But if they're becoming unpredictable, we're screwed, really screwed.

Of course, I won't say that to anybody. How can I? I'm the good doctor, the one who gives them hope, the one who tries to keep life and culture functioning here. If the good doctor gives up hope, then what will the rest of them do?

# 11

Earlier today I was in the lab, surrounded by beakers and vials, by the medical machinery we've appropriated over the last few years from hospitals and clinics that Allie manages to find, bringing back one item at a time, or two—I'd trade it all for the contents of one room of Arcon's gene therapy complex. Just an ordinary day for me: work on a new iteration of the serum, fail to make significant progress, smoke a little weed, lather, rinse, and repeat. I was listening to the low hum of the generator and observing our remaining ferals. Jacob Roman, crouched in the corner of his cage, stared out at me with those haunted and haunting eyes. I was observing him and he was observing me. Thomas Spareto (a baker whose fingers had been burned so many times he could now remove the bread from his oven with his bare hands) is the one writhing in his cage, the painful struggle between him and the virus almost at the turning point where the virus will win. The blood-flecked white pus that started leaking again from his eyes, ears, and nose a few days ago has become simply crimson blood. The third, whom we called Norman Gass (a lover of fly-fishing whose one thing was that he didn't believe in God but still went uncomplainingly to church every Sunday with his staunch Baptist wife), appeared sickly, gaunt, as if his body was slowly starving itself to death. The last one, Carlos, is dying. He bleeds out, lying on the floor of his cage. It won't be long now before all that's left of Carlos are a few cross sections of tissue on slides. In a manner of speaking, Carlos is already dead: he just doesn't know it yet.

At times, no matter the project, no matter the challenge, you find yourself staring at your subjects, or your notes, or your data, and wondering: *Is it all worth it? Am I going about this in the right way? Is it something even worth going about at all? Am I wasting my time?* You pore over your notes, searching for something, trying to figure out if something is there, staring you in the face, that you're just not seeing. You're looking for that moment of revelation, that moment when everything shifts slightly and clicks together and suddenly makes sense. You're looking for the key that'll make that happen. It's bad enough if you just can't see it yet. But if there's nothing there, really nothing there, well, then, that's much, much worse.

This was one of those days. It did not feel worth it. It felt like I should just pack up all the lab equipment and go fall on a land mine. But I was struggling, trying to make it feel worthwhile, so I didn't notice that Allie had come in until she was standing beside me.

"You startled me," I said, almost dropping my pad, heart beating fast.

She didn't reply, didn't nod or smirk or anything, just waited.

"Everything okay?" I asked.

"You called me in, remember?"

I sighed and got right to the point.

"It's Kim," I began, and then saw her bristle, saw the way she was trying to keep a look of fear out of her eyes. I waited for her to prompt me, and when she didn't I went on. "No, nothing has happened to her, if that's what you're thinking. She wants to quit my theater group— she said she needs more practice on the gun range."

Allie's expression didn't change. "She does need more practice," she said.

"She needs to continue with the theater group," I said. Allie wasn't going to understand this, not ever. "It feeds her soul. It's good for her development as a complete person."

"We're not complete people anymore, Doc. None of us."

Was this Allie being vulnerable? Or just Allie trying to win the argument? It's so hard to tell sometimes. I reached out to touch her cheek and she flinched, pulled away.

"Allie Hilts," I said, "as strong as steel and as fragile as a rose. We have to keep trying to be complete in this incomplete world, Allie. It's our duty."

She shook her head. "Our duty is to stay alive," she said. "Or you'll have plenty of corpses to play Sleeping Beauty, and no one left to wake her up."

We stared one another down, a forty-year-old woman and a girl around twenty years younger, neither of us willing to accept the truth of what the other was saying, neither willing to admit that *her* truth was only part of what *the* truth really was. We might still be there staring, neither of us willing to look away first, if it hadn't been for a rustling coming from Carlos's cage.

I turned. Allie did, too. Carlos had risen to one knee. His chest was slick with blood. He peered at us. We peered back.

"You know," I said, speaking softly so as not to alarm him or the others, "just before they die, something happens in their eyes. You have to look closely to see it. But it's there, just for a nanosecond. They almost look like they used to. At that moment, I mourn the loss of them all over again. I live for that moment, but I resent it, too. It's the only thing that keeps me going, but sometimes that's more of a curse than a blessing."

We held his gaze until, without closing his eyes, he tipped slowly to one side and fell.

I approached the cage. The muscles of his face had relaxed. His eyes had begun to cloud over.

"He's dead," said Allie.

"Yes," I said.

"I didn't see it," she said.

I was silent for a long moment, weighing my words, considering what I could say. Nothing came to me.

"No," I finally admitted. "Neither did I."

## 12

There was a different world, and we lost it. I had a husband in that life, a fellow researcher—we'd met in graduate school and he'd followed me to Arcon when I took the job there. His name was Richard Zeman. He liked to be called Rich. His one special thing was that if you said a sentence to him he could repeat it backward. Exactly, intonation and everything. You could tape-record him doing it and then play the recording backward and you'd swear you were hearing yourself say the original sentence.

He was one of the first ones to go—the only thing left of him now is his last name, which I took when we got married, against my better judgment.

I don't know if the virus jumped from the apes directly to him or if it passed by way of someone else, but if he wasn't the first he was close enough to the first for it not to make a difference one way or the other.

Where it did make a difference was in our knowing what was happening to him, understanding the symptoms. We'd seen it in the primates, and we knew where it would take him, and how quickly. We had at least a few lucid seconds, with him aware that he was infected and me aware that there was no way out, none at all. He asked me to kill him, and I, being a good wife and a good scientist, understanding what was to come, did. I filled a syringe with a gram of pure morphine and injected it into his arm. Later, when I thought he was dead but realized pus was still oozing from his eyes and that he was beginning to wake up, that he was still shallowly breathing, I realized it was not enough and gave him another gram, this time in his carotid artery, at a point just above the clavicle. That was enough to be the end of him.

We had a son, too. That was a little more difficult. He didn't understand what was happening to him, and I was in lockdown, in the basement of a house I'd broken into a half mile from Arcon—I probably would have died there if Jacky hadn't just happened to be hunkered down on the same street. Got to give her that: she rescued me. But my son, I had no way to get to him. We spoke on the phone as he went up and down and the symptoms grew worse. I tried to explain to him that there was no cure, and if he didn't take his own life, he'd end up taking someone else's, but how can you explain something like that to a thirteen-year-old? What a terrible feeling of helplessness. And to think I was part of the team that did this to him, did it to everyone. I was still trying to talk to him after he lost his power of speech and dropped the phone. I don't know what happened to him, if he's still alive or long dead. I probably will never know.

I'm not going to share his name. And I'm going to keep his one special thing just to myself.

All that seems so long ago. Can it really only be three years? I don't think of them often—it's too painful, and I've accepted that my life will be different now, that there will be no more men in my life. Even if I do find the cure, I have spent too much time staring at these ferals, considering their pathology, trying to imagine them back into being human men, ever to be comfortable in the arms of a man again.

I don't think of them often, but I do think of them whenever one of my test subjects dies. I do remember Richard's eyes, the way they had begun to change, the way the realization that I had done as he asked, that I was killing him, brought them back to being what they had been, at least for a moment.

But that moment was over far too soon.

## Chapter Fourteen

## Jacky

So—it's just me and my girl, Emma, manning the store. HQ is really a garage, an old tractor storage shed, but we've tricked it out and made it one real badass security center. We've got an armory—nothing high-tech, because high-tech just breaks. This is all good kickass gear, stuff that'll outlast us. Ferals don't have the patience for guns—they like to get up close and personal—so we've assembled an arsenal. Land mines, grenades, shotguns, you name it. There is no shortage of gun and liquor stores just down the road, and basically that's all the shit we need to stay alive.

Can't stand looting, though. The ferals are bad, but I can protect myself from those motherfuckers. No, it's the little things that get to me. Like, last time I was in town, I'm creeping down Main Street, all smeared in the motherfuckers' blood, and I step on a branch and snap it. Only it's not a branch but an arm bone, the thin one in your forearm. Some woman, dead and gnawed, a wedding ring still on the hand at the end of the arm—probably given to her by the same guy that ended up killing her. I step wrong, even today, and I can still hear that arm crunch. No, thank you. I'll leave the looting to Allie whenever I can. She's a natural.

We've got battery-operated military-grade radios, enough for every member of the camp and then some, all charged and carefully arranged for quick access. Shit, Emma and I both know how many steps the radios are from the door in case we got to get them in the dark. Batteries are starting to be a problem. We've got rechargeables and the propane generator, but that's not going to last forever. Fuck it. We'll learn smoke signals if we have to.

We've got maps, too, and some survival packs if we get swarmed and have to make a quick departure—but that's mainly for show, to make the biddies feel safer. We get motherfucking swarmed and ain't nobody making a departure unless it's the kind where you leave your body and your soul either gets stuffed into an animal and comes back to life again or is sent to some country-club-style heaven to retire. There's some disagreement on that score. Personally, I think that when you're dead you're dead, and no part of you is going anywhere else.

We're there, and, well, you know, we are girlfriend and girlfriend, and so maybe we're playing it a little unorthodox, getting a little friendly, so to speak, but then Emma's patting me on the back, calling my name, trying to get me to stop. So I pull away and say, "What, what is it, what the fuck?" and she just points, and there, behind us, is Allie.

I give her a look. "Girl, don't you believe in knocking?" I say.

"Here to debrief," she says.

Emma and me, we straighten up and give each other looks that promise we'll get back to it later, first opportunity. We're a good fit that way.

We all three sit our asses down at the war table. Allie's on one end and I'm on the other. Emma's on the side in the middle, and she's got the pad and pencil. She'll keep track of the intel, collate it later with what we already got.

"So debrief already," I say to Allie.

She nods and launches in. "I ran into three ferals on the north hill," she says. "I found six deer carcasses not far from there, torn up and torn open, most of the meat left to rot. It pissed me off. That's our food, not theirs."

"Damn straight," I say, and Emma smiles. "How many of the motherfuckers did you kill?"

Allie shrugs. I get a look from Emma: *Don't push her.* My girl can cram a lot into a look. She's deep.

"All right," I say. "Your next run will be in a couple of days. No stepping out of the fence before then. You have to promise this time."

Allie hesitates, then nods. "All right," she says.

"When you go, we need batteries, more propane, and—"

"One more thing," says Allie, interrupting. That's not protocol, but we've never been all that big on protocol. We go with what works rather than by some shit rules written by some man decades back, and that's kept us alive a few times when going by the rules wouldn't have. "I saw a bunch of ferals yesterday that I didn't recognize. Coming up from the south, by way of the Bayview Bridge. All new faces."

I shrug. Who cares? One feral is pretty much like another. I'm surprised she's paying attention to their faces at all. And we've always had stragglers and wanderers, lone wolves passing through, or a small pack low on food and looking for a new hunting ground.

"So?" I say. "A couple of travelers. What's the big fucking deal?"

She gives me a cold, level look. She wants me to take her seriously. "This is the third time in two weeks that I've seen newbies," she says. "All big groups. All coming from the southern end of town. I don't know what they want, what they're looking for, but I'm seeing a pattern."

And, simple as that, the girl has my full attention. Shit, last thing we need is a mass migration, dozens of ferals coming up into our neck of the woods. And worse than that, this isn't something they've done in the past. The ferals changing, reacting differently: that's something to really get freaked about.

"You sure about this?" I ask.

"I know every feral who lives within a fifteen-mile radius. I'm sure."

I nod. This girl doesn't play games. If she says she knows, she knows. Time to gather a little backup intel.

I pick up one of the nearby radios, key in another camp.

"Huguenot," I say. "Come in, Huguenot."

I let go of the switch. There's static for a moment, and then:

"This is Huguenot. Go ahead."

"Huguenot, this is Jacky over at West Staten. Who's on duty there?"

"This is Naomi. Everything okay, or is this a social call?"

Damn—Naomi. She and I had a little thing once, long time ago, but hard to keep that kind of thing flying once you land at different camps. She started at West Staten, but then some folks from what would become Huguenot showed up, trying to get some advice on how to make their camp safe, and she waltzed off with them. Probably just as well, since we'd been cooling for a while. In fact, maybe that's why she went. Did I tell Emma about it? Probably not—it was before her time, anyway. But she'll still be pissed if Naomi starts bringing up fond memories of old times. Emma's got a hot streak.

I keep my voice as neutral and noncommittal as possible. "We're good," I say. No banter. "Quick question: you seen any new faces coming into your area lately?"

"One of our scouts reported some newbies a week or so ago," says Naomi. "Why? What's up?"

"We're seeing new faces here, too. Coming up from the south—we don't know why. Nothing to be alarmed about at this point, but more than normal. Keep an eye out and we'll do the same."

"Roger that," says Naomi.

I wait for her to add something. When she doesn't, I say, "Just watch for any new motherfuckers near you, and stay vigilant."

I click off the radio. I look at Allie.

"Jesus. May have to have you break your promise and step out over that fence and observe the motherfuckers after all."

She nods. "I'll go out every day and monitor."

I nod back. "Track any newcomers. See where they're going, why they're coming here. No point getting the whole compound in a tizzy. Keep this on the DL between us until we know if it's something we need to worry about." I lean over the table, toward her, making my voice quiet and steady. "But let's pray it isn't," I say. "More of those motherfuckers here ... Not only do we starve quicker, our threat increases tenfold."

## Chapter Fifteen

She crouched between the husks of old cars, windows broken and paint peeling off now. There were hundreds of them, raggedy lines and clusters of vehicles that had been abandoned in gridlock the day the world changed. She was in full battle gear again, wearing camo and smeared all over with feral blood. From where she was, she could see from one side of the suspension bridge to the other. The sun hanging above her shimmered off the water below.

She'd been stationed there for several hours now, just waiting, eyes slowly scanning back and forth except for the moment when she had opened a can and wolfed down some cold chili for lunch. She was more comfortable out here, despite the risk, than she ever was back in the compound with the others. Here, alone, on the hunt, she felt good, right. Like she was doing something rather than burying her head in the sand.

She had a way of turning her mind off, just letting her eyes roam and her body take over. It wasn't really zoning—her body was more aware than it was when she was fully directing it. It reminded her of those moments playing lacrosse when she'd just let go and stood back amazed by what her body could do. Here, even though she was motionless, she felt the same, like her body would know what to do and would take her along.

Maybe that was why she liked it, because part of her could be absent in a way she never could be when surrounded by the others back at camp. Where did that part of her go? She didn't know. It didn't think, exactly, didn't accomplish anything. It was as if it found a door in the back of her skull and went through into a darkened room and then just sat in darkness, in nothingness, and felt nothing, *was* nothing, just looked out at a distant world through a tiny window, until her body knocked on the door and called her back.

Which it did now. Movement on the bridge.

She raised her rifle, brought the scope to her eye. After a moment, she found the movement again and settled on it. A mangy horse scrounging for food, moving slowly through the cars, rooting at grass near the side, making its way across the bridge. Not a horse that grew up wild, but a domesticated one that had somehow broken free before being eaten. Now, swaybacked, coat patchy, it was keeping just one step ahead of its own death.

*Like us*, thought Allie.

She heard a piercing feral moan and flashed the scope away from the horse, scanning urgently along the bridge until she found them: a group of ferals, just coming onto the bridge from the southern side. How many? Six, she thought at first, and then realized: no, seven. All new faces. She watched as they began to run toward the horse, which was already in full gallop, moving rapidly away from them.

Scooping together her gear, she got ready to pursue them. Too many new faces. She had to see what they were up to, had to figure out what had brought them here.

The sick horse galloped down the side of the highway, dodging through the peppering of cars disabled there as it moved toward open ground. The ferals were right behind, in hot pursuit, slowly gaining. Allie remained crouched, tracking them from the other side of the road. She stayed hidden, moving slowly, watching from behind cars.

The horse might make it, she thought. If it could get to open ground and go into an all-out gallop, the ferals would probably give up the chase in favor of easier prey.

Suddenly, sensing the ferals too close behind it, the horse veered down and into the median, which was bowed enough to take it out of sight. She cursed under her breath. The ferals would follow it, and she wouldn't be able to see where they were. She'd lose them.

She'd already lowered her scope when the horse galloped up out of the median and onto her side of the highway, barreling almost straight at her.

She backed away, still trying to remain as inconspicuous as possible, glancing behind her, looking for refuge. What was there? Cars, plenty of them, but with the windows broken out. No way she could hold out in a car against seven ferals—too easy for them to come at her from all sides at once. Besides, there were bodies in some of those cars.

She kept looking, scanning, all the while moving swiftly backward. There, just off the road, an old gas station. Good.

She rushed toward it.

Once there, she peered in through a still-intact tinted window. She saw nothing she could make out—the tinting was too heavy. She tried the door handle, found it unlocked.

She slid inside, shut the door, and hid beneath the window. A moment later, she raised her head to peek out as the horse thundered by. She ducked down again, and heard the screeching of the ferals growing louder, coming closer. The sounds grew nearly deafening, and then they were crashing through the tall grass right outside, the slap of their bare feet on the broken remains of the pavement. And then they rushed by, still in pursuit, the sounds receding. They hadn't smelled her.

Close call. A little *too* close.

She rose slowly and looked out the window, making sure all the ferals were past. No sign of them. Good. Maybe she should just wait a little bit and see if there was anything useful in the gas station. Later, she could still follow their track and figure out where they were going. A group of seven was likely to leave a pretty discernible trail. She wanted to follow them, but she didn't want to confront them. She didn't like those odds.

That was when she caught the reflection of movement in the window glass. She froze. Something behind her, coming out of the back room of the gas station. Human in shape. A feral. She held perfectly still.

It drew closer, approaching her from behind, looming larger. The familiar web of scars become clear in the ghostly reflection in the glass. Even in that partially transparent reflection, Scarface was the most terrifying thing she had ever seen.

*Holy shit.*

She was trembling now, fighting the urge to run, and he, he was only a few feet away. *He can't smell me*, she realized. *I'm masked by the blood and he doesn't know what to make of me.*

She still had a chance.

He was only a few feet away now. He leaned forward, very close now, and she felt his hot breath, the heat radiating off his body. He sniffed her neck. Slowly her hand moved closer to her gun.

And then, suddenly, catching a hint of her scent below the smeared blood, he apparently *did* know what to think of her. He opened his mouth and let out a deafening howl of rage.

Her body took over. She spun and raised her gun to shoot and was swatted across the room by his swinging forearm, the bullet thumping harmlessly into the wall. She landed in a heap, striking her head hard, a dull burst of pain obscuring her vision.

The last thing she saw before losing consciousness was Scarface, face pulled back in a snarl, stalking slowly toward her.

## Chapter Sixteen

She awoke to the feeling of light coming and going, spattering past. She managed to open her eyes and saw nothing in focus and then closed them and opened them again and this time saw above her leaves, trees, patches of light and shade. She felt pain in her neck and shoulders, could hear a scraping sound in the back of her skull. It took her a moment to realize the sound was coming from her being dragged along the ground, her head jouncing along in the dirt. It took a moment more to realize that, if she was being dragged, it meant that someone must be dragging her.

She forced her neck up off the ground and saw, holding her legs, Scarface and another feral, an additional feral to either side of them. He chittered at the others, seemingly talking to them. They moved almost as if in a trance, as if he was controlling them.

*How am I still alive?* she wondered. They should have torn her to bits by now. They should have killed her long ago.

Before even realizing she was doing it, she was struggling, lurching, trying to pull away. Her captors, much stronger, ignored her, simply tightening their grip on her legs. When she kept it up, Scarface hissed and the other two ferals each grabbed an arm. They lifted her up and spread-eagled her, immobilizing her.

They carried her along a dirt path, the trees less dense here, the sun now blinding. There was the sign reading HARBOR AHEAD with its warnings scrawled beneath. Shit, they were taking her to the beehive. She gave a scream of pain and frustration, and the feral to her left gave a warning tug, nearly tearing her arm out of its socket.

And then she heard a thwap, loud and wet, and saw something flash through the feral's back and out again, metallic and gleaming. Only after it was gone and blood was spurting from the wound and the feral's breath was whistling out of its back through its punctured lung did she realize it had been a machete. Another wet sound and she turned her head to see the blade sunk into the stomach of the feral on the other side and out through his back and then gone again, a brief glimpse of the hand holding it this time. The ferals were screeching now, all four of them, a high-pitched panicky sound different from any she'd heard before from them. The two ferals swayed and let go of her arms, and she fell, hard enough to knock the wind out of her. By then they'd fallen, too, their heavy bodies sprawling across her own, but not before she caught a glimpse of one of the ferals in front of her holding his hand to his neck as blood pumped through and down his bare chest, and of Scarface himself grabbing at the machete stuck in his own thigh and tearing it out and dropping it, and then turning, fleeing, disappearing into the trees.

She lay there beneath the bodies, feeling the hot, sticky blood oozing around her, masking her scent. For a while she pretended to be dead, her ears pricked and attentive for any sound or movement, and when, after several minutes, there was none, she worked her hands free and managed with great effort to roll the bodies off of her.

She examined the wounds on the dead ferals. Good, clean cuts—by someone with a very sharp machete and a lot of strength who knew what she was doing. But where was Machete Girl now?

The three ferals were dead. Scarface was gone. She was still alive, but with no idea of who had helped her, or of why, after she had done so, she had fled. Maybe she'd gone in pursuit of Scarface, hoping to finish the job.

Who could it be?

She waited, listened, but there was no sign either of Scarface returning or of her rescuer coming back.

*I'm alive*, she told herself. That was the important thing. She shouldn't be, but she was.

She got up and limped back up the path, away from the sign for the harbor, back toward the camp.

Chapter Seventeen

# Dr. Zeman

## 13

Allie showed up at the gates this evening, dazed, without her weapons, and soaked in fresh feral blood. There was so much blood on her that it took us a while to realize she had a deep gash on the back of her head as well. I wasn't there when she arrived, but I saw her shortly after, when Jacky brought her to me to see what I could do for her.

Though I'm a doctor, I'm not that kind of doctor. I'm a Ph.D., not an M.D. Still, I do have some basic medical training and some textbooks with pictures as well, and over the past three years I've come to be pretty handy with the needle, if I do say so myself, simply because someone had to. So, while Jacky and Allie were debriefing, I cleaned the wound and then sutured it shut. She didn't even wince. Eight stitches in all, and there'd be a bruise for a while. I checked her eyes for shock, then told her she shouldn't sleep for at least six hours, just in case of concussion, although a real doctor would know better than I if that was really necessary. Better safe than sorry.

"What happened?" I asked as I was putting in the sutures. "It's not like you to be caught off guard."

Usually Allie is pretty mum about things, so I was surprised when she started talking. Once I finished the stitches, I just settled back and listened.

"I don't know why they didn't kill me," Allie was saying. It wasn't the first time she'd said this, but she kept coming back to it. It still didn't make sense to her why she was alive. Nor, frankly, to me or Jacky. And her story didn't add up all the way. I couldn't help wondering if there was something she wasn't telling us.

"They had every chance to," said Allie. "And in normal circumstances, they couldn't have held back. But they were clearly keeping me alive and dragging me toward the harbor for some reason."

Jacky furrowed her brow but didn't say anything at first. Neither did I. What was there to say? We were as confused as she was.

"Why didn't they kill me?" asked Allie again.

Jacky shook her head. "I've never seen or heard of something like this before. They kill on sight. It's what those fuckers do."

"Not anymore," said Allie.

Jacky looked at me, concerned, and I gave her the same look. Neither of us wanted to say what was on our minds.

"So who the hell saved you, Allie?" asked Jacky. "And why'd she run off?"

"No idea."

"Was it someone from camp?" I asked.

"No," said Jacky. "Not fucking likely. Allie was the only one outside the perimeter today. And why would they just take off if they were from our camp? We can check in with the other camps, see who had people out and if one of them might have wandered over into our territory for some reason, and if any of them were handy with a machete." She turned to Allie. "In any case, you keep an eye out for her. She's a good person to know. We'll need her once Allie manages to get herself killed."

Allie grinned.

After irrigating the wound, I cut a gauze pad and applied it over the cut, taping it down on all four sides. And then offered a little small talk, something to get her to let her guard down. "Should heal nicely as long as you keep it clean. Nice straight cut. What did it?"

"I don't know," she said. "Something that I hit on the way down after Scarface hit me."

And then I dropped it on her. "Why were you out there anyway? There wasn't any reason to be. You just returned from a supply run two days ago."

I watched her eyes flick over to Jacky, but I wasn't quick enough in raising my own gaze to see how Jacky's face responded. When Allie looked back at me, it was clear she was going to do the thing she always did with unwanted questions: just ignore them.

So I looked to Jacky instead. "Well?" I said, as imperiously as possible.

For a moment, Jacky hesitated, and I thought she was going to refuse to tell me anything. I just held her gaze. Finally, she sighed and started talking. We haven't got a great relationship, Jacky and I, all the usual sparring for authority that you get when two strong people are co-running the show, but we're both committed to West Staten and the people in it, both striving for the same goals, and we always, in the end, work together, even if it's a bit grudging. "We've been seeing groups of new motherfuckers coming up from the south," she said. "Lots more than normal. I sent Allie out to monitor this."

I winced inside at the word "motherfucker." I hate it—it feels to me like a relic of patriarchal oppression, though my guess is, Jacky doesn't even think about what the word means. And since Jacky had been pretty good otherwise today about keeping her potty mouth in check, I tried not to let my wince show. Besides, I was much more interested in the substance of what she had just told me.

"The other camps are reporting the same," said Jacky. "An upswing in numbers. Or they were, anyway. They've been difficult to hail for the last twenty-four hours. Probably just technical difficulties with the radio, but . . ." She let it hang, leaving the alternative to my imagination.

"Why wasn't I informed?" I asked.

We had an agreement that Jacky would keep me in the loop, no matter what. What else had she been hiding from me?

And, just like that, Jacky was up in my face, the veins on her neck standing out. She sneered. "What the fuck!" she said. "Are you my goddamn boss now?"

*No*, I was tempted to say, *I'm the only hope you have of getting the world back to normal.* Instead, I just ignored her outburst and blocked her out, turning fully toward Allie.

"Allie, if you don't mind, I'd love to know what's going on," I said.

For a moment more, Allie held out, and then she sighed and began to talk.

"I saw another large group of unknown ferals making their way over the bridge. Seven, I think. Fourth large group in two and a half weeks. Way more than usual."

Not good news, not at all. I tried to keep my face the same, relaxed, when she said it. But I could tell from the way Allie was looking at me that she could tell how worried I was.

And still am.

## Chapter Eighteen

# Allie

I'm lying awake in my bed, my head aching dully, a persistent throb. That's enough to keep me from going to sleep. Besides, I'm not supposed to sleep for a few hours more, just in case of concussion. Kim spent the early part of the evening clucking over me and my head wound like a mother hen, which felt weird—I'm the one supposed to be watching over her, not the other way around. She insisted on going with me while I went to the armory to replace the weapon I'd lost, then kept me up and talking as long as she could. Eventually, she faded and drifted off, and I let her. Now she and her friend Beth are sound asleep in the bunkbed on the other side of the room, but Holly, in the bed next to mine, is not. She's propped up on her elbow, facing me, her expression hard to make out in the darkness.

We've been talking about what happened to me, about my little encounter with ferals and the mystery woman who saved me. It feels good to talk about it, and I'm liking the attention from Holly, the way she gasps when I give her the breakdown. Maybe it's just that, after coming so close to dying, I'm craving some companionship. Jacky probably doesn't want me to tell anyone, but since Jacky doesn't know the full extent of what happened anyway, she doesn't get a say. I'm not Jacky's bitch—I'm here for Kim's sake, and that's the only thing that matters. I've sworn Holly to secrecy, and I've whispered the story so that there's no chance Beth and Kim will overhear. And of course, just like with Jacky, I don't tell her the whole truth, either.

In the version I make up for her, there is no Scarface, just me and one hidden feral, just me getting struck and nearly knocked out and then coming conscious just in time to catch a glimpse of someone slicing the throat of the feral who intended to kill me. I need to tell that part, the part about the unseen Machete Girl, because it still seems so weird. I need to talk it out with someone. Holly's here, she's convenient, so it gets to be her.

And there's another reason to tell it, too. I almost died today—it could have happened, and it's only sheer luck that it didn't. If it does happen, what happens to Kim?

We've gotten to my debriefing with Doc and Jacky, and I'm having to do more verbal acrobatics than I'd realized to make this version of the story work. I don't want to worry her, don't want to scare her by giving her the impression that the ferals are massing to wipe us out, which they obviously are, so I'm focusing on how Doc and Jacky act with one another, the way they always jostle up against one another like two dogs vying for the alpha spot.

"Why do they hate each other?" she whispers.

I think about this. They don't hate each other, exactly—they just have very different ways of thinking about the world, ways that are not really compatible, are maybe even diametrically opposed. They respect one another, but each of them is sure that she's the one that's really right. It's like how a religious person and an atheist can have a grudging respect for each other but still believe the other one is totally misguided. "Jacky wants to kill them all," I whisper back. "Doc wants to cure them."

There's silence for a long while, and for a moment I think Holly's fallen asleep. But when I look over she's still there, propped on her elbow staring through the dark at me. So I get to the point.

"Holly," I say.

"Yeah?"

"I almost died today. If anything happens to me . . . will you look out for Kim? Keep her safe?"

"Sure," she says. "Of course."

"It might mean leaving here someday. West Staten may not last forever. If push comes to shove, are you up for it?"

She doesn't say anything for a moment. I wonder what's going through her head. I need to know that Kim will be safe if next time Machete Girl doesn't show up out of nowhere to rescue me. I need to know we have a backup plan.

"Have I told you how I got here?" she asks.

Has she? I don't think so, but I don't think I've ever asked her. I shake my head, but then realize she might not see it in the dark. "No," I say.

"Things started getting weird, boys acting weird at school, and I wasn't sure what to do. I had a woman teacher, Mrs. Stocks, which is probably what saved me. When she started to hear the shouts and the screams out in the hall, she thought it was a terrorist attack, and so she barricaded the door. For a while it seemed like we were safe, and then one of the boys, Kyle Moran, started to, like, change. He started leaking blood and pus from his eyes and ears and nose, and when Mrs. Stocks got close to him, tried to help him, he just went berserk. He threw her through a window. Then the other boys started changing, too.

"My friend Anneke and I had been hiding behind our desks, but when Kyle broke the window with our teacher we both dashed for it. Anneke took maybe an extra two seconds getting out—she was worried about cutting herself, maybe, or wanted to make sure the fall wasn't too far. I, on the other hand, just leaped out the window head-first. Of the two of us, only one survived, and it wasn't Anneke."

"How'd you manage?" I ask. "Where did you go to ground?"

"I was on my own on a boat for six months before I came in from the cold. Living on fish and whatever rainwater I could collect. It was a lonely life, but I made it through."

She creeps out of her bed, tiptoes across to mine. She sits on the edge of the mattress. "Sometimes I think you underestimate me," she says. "Sometimes I think you underestimate all of us. Everybody who's here, everybody who made it to West Staten, is a survivor. We've been tested. Any of us are capable of looking out for Kim, and all of us would."

"I'm not asking about everybody else," I say. "I'm asking about you."

"I already told you," she says. "I'll take care of her."

"I just," I say—even though I know I shouldn't be saying it, that I should let it go, "I just need to know, if West Staten collapses, is she your first priority?"

She hesitates a moment. "Sure," she says. "I told you."

*Good*, I think. That's all I need to know.

And then, after a moment, a little scared, she adds, "Do you think that West Staten could collapse?"

I reach out and touch her shoulder. "I hope not," I say.

And that, I figure, is the end of the conversation. I let my hand fall and turn away. But before I know it, she has pulled back the sheets and climbed in with me. I don't stop her, though I don't encourage her, either. She spoons up behind me, embraces me.

"Please be more careful, Al," she says. "The thought of losing you is too much. I want to thank the girl who saved you."

She settles in, tightens her embrace. Her body is so warm, her skin smooth. She's wearing just a half T-shirt and panties, and I can feel the smooth fronts of her thighs against the backs of mine, her body snuggling to fit better against my own. It feels nicer than I want it to feel.

And then, I'm not quite sure how it happens, she's not exactly spooning me anymore. I'm not on my side anymore but flat on my back, and she's looming above me, leaning over me. I see the glints of her eyes disappear as she closes them, then watch her head dip down toward my own, her lips parted, her breath hot and sweet. Not sugary sweet: softer than that, like she's licked a knife that was used to spread honey. It's like I'm hypnotized. I watch her lips until I can't see them anymore and then I feel them touch my own lips, moist and warm. It feels so good. Almost involuntarily, I let my own eyes close, and feel my lips meeting hers, kissing her in return.

It goes on like that for a little bit, the kisses lengthening, her tongue in my mouth and my tongue in hers, my nipples hard and sensitive against the fabric of my T-shirt, until my breath and hers are coming fast and our mouths are even wetter.

And then, suddenly, in my mind I'm seeing Jared and me kissing, watching it like I watched Brit and Damon on that iPhone video all those years ago, the footage grainy. I can't figure out what's going on for a moment, and then I realize it's him and me. He's grinding up against me and I'm damp now, and ready, his lips full and moist as he kisses my lips, my throat, my breasts. And then he lifts up and says, "Are we gonna fuck or what?" and as I watch, his face begins to leak a blood-flecked pus and the purple veins begin to throb on his temple and I know that any moment he's going to kill me.

Holly's still kissing me, her tongue deep in my mouth, her hand stroking the top of my thigh, but I'm pulling away, pulling back, sitting up, covering myself, bringing everything to a stop.

"What's wrong?" she asks. Her eyes are open and shining in the darkness; her breath is ragged as she crouches there, over me, unsure of what she's done wrong. She hasn't done anything, it's not her fault, I should be able to relax and enjoy myself, it's not like I think it's immoral or anything, but I can't, I just can't. Every time I try to let go, the past comes rushing back to me. And in this case it's not even the real past: it's twisted, deformed.

"I can't do this," I say.

"Why?" she asks. "What did I do?" She's talking louder now, and I'm worried she's going to wake Kim. Last thing I want to have to do is explain to my sister why Holly is straddling me in bed with both of us breathing heavy. I reach out and put my finger to her lips.

"Nothing," I say softly. "It's not your fault. I just can't. I'm sorry." She opens her mouth to say something else, but before she can, I say, "Please, leave me alone."

She just looms there over me for a long moment, hurt, stung. Then she stands, retreats. I expect her to go back to her own bed, like she's done the couple times this has happened in the past, but I let it go a lot further this time, and maybe that's too much for her. She heads to the door and goes out, exiting the room, leaving me with my aching head, my throbbing body, and my awful dreams of the past.

## Chapter Nineteen

Morning found her once again on the northern expanse of the bridge, the metal of the span and the windows of the cars glittering under the diffuse light. She was in battle fatigues, smeared with blood, hunkered down between cars, scouting for new ferals. She needed to be out here, needed to prove to herself that yesterday was a fluke, that she could do this. If she didn't get right back on the horse, it'd get harder and harder with each passing day. She kept raising the scope to her eye, scanning the area—more frequently than she needed to, probably. Come on, she told herself, relax.

No movement, nothing at all.

Lowering her rifle, she checked her watch. Two hours in, and nothing, not a peep. Maybe her encounter with Machete Girl yesterday had changed something, had redirected the newbies.

She reached up and touched the bandage on her head, winced.

*Who was it?* she wondered yet again. No word from the other compounds—Jacky had tried to check in with them, but radio contact was still down for some reason. With Huguenot, too, now. Surely, there had to be some way of finding out who the stranger was, of making contact. But Allie had managed to see no more than a flash of her hand as it swung that machete.

Perhaps there was something at the scene, something she could start with, a clue of some kind, or a trail she could follow. Even as she thought it, she knew there probably was nothing. She'd have noticed it yesterday, despite her dazed state.

Still, maybe it was worth a try.

She spent another hour waiting, scanning the area. Still no movement on the bridge. She became increasingly restless, partly because it was frustrating to be sitting still, partly because she was wondering how the next encounter with a feral would go. Had her luck finally run out? Maybe, but she had to go back to the place where she had been attacked, look for a trail. She knew whatever trail there was would only get harder and harder to follow the longer she waited, but still she hesitated.

Finally, she packed everything up and set off.


From the slope of a hill, lying in the damp loam of the forest floor, she looked down at the place where Machete Girl had slaughtered the ferals. The corpses of the three ferals were there, just as she had left them, untouched.

Why hadn't they killed Machete Girl? Was she really that good?

She waited, watched, directing the scope slowly through the vicinity, looking for any sign of movement or presence, anything out of place. Nothing.

She panned back to the three dead ferals, increased the magnification until she could see the flies crawling in and out of their mouths. She examined the bodies closely, dragged the scope along every inch of them. Nothing unexpected. She sighed. She reduced the magnification again, began her movement out once again, slower this time.

Even so, she almost missed it. She'd been looking lower, near the ground, but this was higher, affixed to a tree. Because of her angle, it was lost among the leaves—if she'd been standing on the ground directly below it, she couldn't have avoided seeing it. She increased the magnification, but the paper was flapping and torqued, partly blocked by leaves. She couldn't read it.


*I'm not an impulsive person*, Allie told herself. *I'm careful, precise. I only take chances when they're chances worth taking.* Was this a chance worth taking? Yes, it was. She kept telling herself this as she stood up from her place of concealment and boldly walked down the hill.

It was a single piece of thick, creamy paper, slightly dirty, with a crease threatening to become a tear at the place where it had remained folded for a long period of time—years, maybe. It had been skewered on a broken branch, pushed down deeply enough to make it unlikely to blow away. She moved closer, examining it, then stood on her toes and snatched it off the branch.

One side was blank. The other read simply:

*You OK?*

She examined it. It had been written in black pen. The handwriting was messy, no doubt written in haste, a scrawl.

Machete Girl had saved her life. Surely she deserved an answer.

She reached into her bag, searching for a pencil or pen, something to write with, found only a piece of chalk she'd used to mark trees when taking a new path through the forest. She was just considering heading back to the dirt bike to see if there was anything in the saddlebag when she saw it: a pen lying in the nook of the tree, left just for her. She smirked when she saw it, then bent down and picked it up.

She tore the paper along the crease, pocketing the half that had the note written to her on it. The other half she pressed against her leg so as to write on it, and then paused for a moment. How long had it been since she'd left a note for someone? Had she even written a note to someone since the world ended? No, she hadn't. High school? Maybe something slipped into Jared's locker between periods? Or something to Brit, folded up and passed from desk to desk until it reached her in math class? Or maybe something simple to Mom or Dad, explaining why she wasn't home—"at mall," that sort of thing.

*Meet here tomorrow. Noon.*

She wrote this and then affixed it to the branch before scurrying back up the hill.

## Chapter Twenty

# Allie

When I get back to the farmhouse, Holly's packing. I haven't seen her since yesterday, have no real idea where she's been, where she spent the night last night. I'm tired, still in my fatigues, and covered in feral blood. I want to rinse off and be alone for a while, but I stop anyway.

"Hi," I say.

Holly doesn't say anything back.

I watch her for a moment, waiting. When she doesn't speak, I sit gingerly on the edge of my bed.

"Moving out?" I say.

She still doesn't say anything. In fact, she turns away a little so her back is to me.

"I'm sorry about last night," I say, and see the muscles in her back tense. "It wasn't about you." For a moment she stops packing, just holds whatever shirt or pair of socks she has in her hands as if it's a precious thing. And then I say—I can't help myself—"You'll still look out for Kim, right?" and she starts packing again.

"For God's sake, Holly," I say. "You don't have to move into another room. Let's just talk it thr—"

And with that she zips up her bag and exits. She's trying to show that she doesn't need me, that she doesn't care, that I'm not worth her spending even another second of her time on, but she's showing something else entirely. She's ashamed, I know, but she shouldn't be. Probably I'm the one that should be, for not shutting it down sooner. She's also clearly heartbroken, and I should be ashamed to say that I'm not.

A moment later, Kim appears. She comes in, glancing back over her shoulder, and when she looks at me there's a question in her eye.

"Where's Holly going?" she asks.

"We had a fight. It'll be fine."

She looks over at Holly's bed. It's stripped bare, all of her gear gone.

"Doesn't look fine to me," she says.

"We had a fight," I repeat. "She'll come to her senses. Eventually."

Kim looks at me in a searching way, but when I don't volunteer more, she finally shrugs. "Whatever," she says. Then she changes the subject. "I was practicing my shooting all day today."

"Good," I say. "You need it."

Her brow furrows a little at that, but she chooses not to rise to the bait. "Any sign of Machete Girl?"

"How do you know about that?" I ask. Holly must have told. Or maybe it's not as big a secret as I thought, and Doc or Jacky or both are letting people know.

"Everybody's talking about her," says Holly. "Are you going to bring her here? Can I meet her?"

I open my mouth to respond to this, to tell her about the note, to tell her that the girl is fine, that *she's* worried about *me* being okay, and then I think better of it. I haven't held a secret for so long, I've forgotten how sweet it can taste.

"I don't know how to find her," I say.

She nods, then wanders back out. As soon as she's gone I stand up, lock the door, and sit back on the bed. I take out the note and look at it. "You OK?" I trace the handwriting, feel the paper, try to imagine the hand that wrote it, the same hand that held the machete, the hand that saved me.

## Chapter Twenty-one

She had stationed herself near the bridge again to watch, to wait. The whole morning, she wondered whether Machete Girl would show up. And then, as the time drew closer, she began to get nervous, wondering if she herself should just take off, if it wouldn't be better to leave things as they were and never meet her. She'd built the woman up so huge in her mind that if and when she actually met her how could it be anything but a disappointment?

In her mind, Machete Girl was much like Allie herself, a lone wolf. But she'd taken it one step further—she was living alone in the woods, killing ferals one by one, long after Allie had retreated into West Staten. Allie daydreamed that it'd be up to her to coax Machete Girl into the camp, get her to help. Maybe with her help they'd be able to keep the ferals at bay long enough to build a real fortress, something impregnable rather than makeshift, and fill it with all the medical equipment they would need to bring men back.

She shook her head to clear it. Maybe she was still a little lit up from the other night with Holly, even if she'd been the one to bring things to a stop.

It was a gray, foggy day, with clouds threatening rain, a dull thunder occasionally rolling across the sky. At 11:45, she left her post and made her way back into the forest, toward the rendezvous site. By 11:56, according to her watch, she was there. She looked through the scope at the tree. The note was gone, but nobody was there. She watched until 11:58, then moved forward and to the tree, looking all around it for a sign that the paper had blown off rather than being removed. No sign of that, no sign of anyone.

For a long moment, she stayed staring up at the tree and at the place where the note should have been. Then she sat down at the base of the tree, broke down her rifle, cleaned it, and put it back together. When Machete Girl still hadn't shown up, she broke it down again, just for the practice.

An hour later, she was still waiting. It was raining now, sheets of it scouring the landscape. She stayed huddled in the shelter of the tree, damp but not soaked, still stubbornly waiting.

She checked her watch, and when she saw how much time had gone by, her face crumpled. *I deserve it*, a part of her told the rest of her, *for how I let Holly down. Now it's my turn.*

She'd just picked up her bag and was getting ready to stand when she heard the sound of a stick breaking. She froze, suddenly alert, rifle in her hands, a smile on her face. She caught a flash of movement at a little distance and raised the scope, hoping to see the familiar machete.

But what she saw was something entirely different. Ferals.

She caught four or five in the scope right away, stalking quietly through the forest. Very quickly she picked out another five. By the time she was done, she was sure there were at least fifteen, an enormous group, the biggest she had ever seen. It didn't make any sense that this many of them would be together outside the beehive. And all of them, she realized, were newbies.

Quickly and carefully, she sought shelter behind a tree. The rainwater, she suddenly realized, had washed most of the blood off her, but there was enough rain still in the air to keep them from smelling her from where they were. Otherwise, she'd already be dead.

She watched them closely as they continued moving. They weren't hunting, she realized, but moving forward with purpose, going somewhere.

When they finally disappeared deep into the brush, she slowly let out her breath. She checked her watch again. Too late—Machete Girl wasn't showing up.

But it was in checking her watch that she saw it, just behind the tree where she'd been hiding, partly covered over by dead leaves. It must have blown off with the storm, the wind. She wouldn't have seen it if she hadn't had to hide from the ferals.

She picked it up and read it.

The paper was a little wet, the ink a little smeared. She read:

*Come alone!*

The words were followed by an arrow. She turned the paper over and saw a hand-drawn map with a route marked on it, smeared as well, but still readable.

She smiled. The mystery girl hadn't stood her up after all.

## Chapter Twenty-two

The map led her over to a neighboring town, a town that she hadn't spent much time in before the virus struck, and not at all since. She walked down the once-quaint Main Street replete with shops, restaurants, an old two-screen movie theater. The shopfronts had been broken out, the cars overturned. There were scatterings of human and animal bones, spatterings of dried blood, and bits of deer hide.

She was soaking wet, the feral blood certainly all gone now. She had some back at the dirt bike and should have gone to get it before coming here, but she'd been worried that it would take too long, that the girl would have given up by then and be gone. Too late now; if worse came to worst, she'd find a feral to kill on her way back. The bottle of blood in the bike was getting old anyway. The blood lasted for four, maybe five days, tops.

She consulted the map. Yes, this was where she was supposed to be. She stood in the center of the street, motionless in the pouring rain, and waited.

After about thirty seconds, she was sick of waiting. What was this, some sort of game?

"Hello?" she shouted.

There was no response, just her voice echoing through the dead town. She waited, then waited some more. As hope began to ebb, anger steadily rose within her. *Fuck it*, she finally thought, and turned on her heel to leave.

"Wait," a voice said.

Allie stopped dead in her tracks, hard rain pounding on her face, which had suddenly taken on an expression of incredulity mixed with hope and fear because of what she thought she'd heard in the voice.

She was afraid to turn around. "Say that again," she said, and held her breath.

There was a long hesitation, and then the voice said, "Say what again?"

She let her breath out all at once, feeling floored. She was sure of it. The voice was male.


Slowly, she turned. Behind her, through the downpour, she saw a man in his early twenties, alive, able to speak, *normal*, standing in the center of the street no more than ten feet away from her. He was wearing camo and was heavily armed. He had long, dirty, matted hair. A thick, unkempt beard covered the bottom half of his face. He seemed jumpy, nervous. His expression was taut, intense, haunted, not unlike Allie's own.

"You're not real," she said.

"I'm real," he said. "I'm definitely real."

"I dreamed you up," she said. "I got hit harder on the head than I realized. I'm lying on the floor of the gas station, waiting for Scarface to tear my fucking throat open, and I've just imagined you into existence as a way of saving myself from the truth."

He shook his head. "I'm real," he insisted.

She nodded. She wiped the rain from her eyes and then, suddenly, whipped her pistol up and targeted it at him. But his gun, a Desert Eagle Magnum, was up just as quickly and pointed at her face. They stood there, aiming their weapons at each other, expressions steady despite the rain, neither pulling the trigger.

Finally, he spoke, his voice wavering nervously. "I'm not infected," he said. "If I was, I couldn't talk. I could only howl and kill. If I was infected, you'd be dead."

"Or you would," said Allie.

For a moment more, they held one another in the sights of their weapons, and then, slowly, Allie began to lower her gun. Shortly after, the man lowered his as well. They stared at one another, hardened, battle-weary, worn down by this new world.

After a moment, Allie took a deep breath. She smiled a wavering, vulnerable smile and began to move tentatively forward through the rain, extremely slowly and without any threatening movements, as if she were approaching a cornered and potentially spooked animal. She was on edge, her hands shaking.

He watched her come, gawking at her. When she was just a few feet away, he asked, quietly and hesitantly, "What—what's your name?"

Allie didn't answer. A million questions were rushing through her head, so quickly that she could settle on none.

When he got no answer, he offered, "I'm Sam."

Allie swallowed. "Allie," she managed. She reached out a hand toward him, withdrew it before touching him. "How?" she asked.

"How what?" he said.

"How are you like this?"

Sam looked down at his body. "You mean not infected?" he asked. And when she nodded, said, "Genetically immune, I guess." He shrugged. "I don't know."

"Any others like you?" Allie asked.

Again Sam shrugged. "I haven't seen any," he said.

She stared, agape, unable to take it all in, unable to take *him* in. It had been three years since she had seen a man that she could call a man. It seemed impossible.

In front of her, Sam lifted his hand toward his face, and Allie, lost in her thoughts, just caught the flash of movement—immediately her gun was up and pointed unerringly at his face. Just as quickly his was, too, pointed at her. They stood there, staring at one another, neither gun barrel wavering.

"I was just wiping the rain out of my eyes," said Sam. "See?" He lifted his hand again, carefully, and repeated the gesture.

Allie hesitated, looked uncertain, relented. Slowly, she let her rifle fall again. Sam did as well. After a moment, she smiled, let out a whoop. He smiled back. This was what she'd been waiting for, hoping for—this man, this Sam, was the key to a cure, he had to be. Now Kim would be safe. Now, someday, everything could go back to normal.

"Okay," said Allie. "You need to come back to my camp. We have a scientist. She—"

But before she had finished, Sam's smile had faded. "No. No. No." Sam was shaking his head furiously, speaking over her. "That's not happening. Nobody can know about me. No one."

"What do you mean, nobody can know about you?" said Allie, irritation creeping into her voice. "This is huge—"

Sam's voice was more irritated still. "If they know about me, they'll take me and we'll all die . . . we'll all die together."

Allie looked at him in astonishment and confusion. "What do you mean? What are you talking about? It's safe. You have to come back with me—"

"There's no fucking way I'm coming back with you," said Sam angrily. "You'd be dead if it wasn't for me. You owe me. So do not tell them about me!"

"That's crazy—"

"If I even *feel* like you told them, you'll never see me again."

Allie frowned. "First guy I meet in three years, and it turns out he's an asshole. Come on, right now, let's go," she said, and reached for his arm.

Before she could take it he had grabbed her by the wrist, twisting it hard. She growled in pain but didn't give in, instead butting him in the nose with her forehead. Blood sprayed out, over his beard and her face, and he let go of her wrist. She'd taken a step back when his fist shot out, struck her hard in the jaw.

She dropped to her knees, her vision starting to go dark, but then she shook her head and lunged forward, grabbing his legs, biting his thigh. He howled and fell on top of her, using all his weight to grind her down, elbowing her at the base of her skull.

Ears ringing, she punched and scratched, hardly even aware anymore whether she was landing blows or not. He hit her hard in the side of the head, twice, and when she still didn't go down, the blows stopped. *I'm winning*, she thought, and then felt the muzzle of the gun pressed just behind her ear.

"Enough," Sam said harshly, the uncertainty that had been in his voice a moment ago now completely gone.

He took a step back, weapon still steady. Allie stayed on her hands and knees for a moment, panting hard; then she wiped the blood off her bruised face and stood up slowly.

Her fingernails were broken, her knuckles skinned and bleeding.

The wound on her head throbbed, and probably the stitches holding it together had been torn free. Her ribs felt bruised as well, and her eye was almost swollen shut. Sam, across from her, didn't look much better. She'd managed to tear out a chunk of his hair, and blood was dribbling down one side of his face. His nose was puffy and swollen; his eyes were already going black-and-blue.

"Can't even win a fight with a girl," she said, needling him.

"This was a mistake," Sam said. He seemed almost to be looking through her as he said it, as if he were speaking to himself. "I shouldn't have done this. So stupid, I'm so stupid. I should've kept going." His eyes narrowed, and suddenly it felt like he was looking at her again, coldly judging her. He motioned with the gun. "Get the hell out of here," he said.

Allie hesitated. She'd pushed him too far, she realized, but the idea of just leaving, never seeing him again—maybe never seeing another normal human male again—was too much for her to get her mind around. She looked around, trying to buy time. But before she could figure out what to do, there was a rustle of sound in the near distance. Maybe an animal, but just as likely a feral.

She could tell by his face that he'd heard it, too. When he spoke again, his voice was quieter, barely audible.

"Move," he said. "Now."

She nodded absently, a million thoughts still swirling in her head. "I don't understand," she said. "I have so many questions, I—"

And that was the moment when he cocked the gun. She could tell by his face that he was serious, that he'd shoot her if he had to. Reluctantly, she turned to pull herself away. After about ten steps, she turned back, just to get one last glance. But he had already vanished.

She stood there, thunderstruck. Had he even been there to begin with? She turned around and walked back, saw the signs in the mud of their fight.

Yes, he had been there. There was still hope.

## Chapter Twenty-three

## Allie

What do you do when everything you thought you knew about the world suddenly changes? When you'd pretty much resigned yourself to the idea that humanity was going to die out and then you find, no, there still may be hope? Okay, I didn't get off on the right foot with him, I didn't find out anything about him, and I may never see him again, but still. There's hope. At least, I hope so.

I need to bring him back, I need to show him to the others. We need him. Why won't he come help us? What's wrong with him?

What if he's the only one? He can't be the only one, can he?

I run through the rain, hurrying back to my bike as quickly as I can and still stay safe. How can I find him again? How can I convince him to trust me?

And do I trust him?

## Chapter Twenty-four

She arrived back just after dark, soaked to the skin from the rain. She moved absently through the main farmhouse, distracted, feeling conflicted inside, wondering if she should tell or if she shouldn't. Why was Sam afraid of the camps? Was it fear that made him threaten to disappear if she told anybody about him? And he did that even before they'd had their knock-down, drag-out fight. Now maybe he'd just disappear, no matter what. Maybe he was already gone.

She was so distracted, so involved in her own inner discussion, that she managed to turn the corner and run smack into Jacky and Emma.

"Whoa," said Jacky, catching her and steadying her. "Where you headed in such a rush?" And then she noticed Allie's bruised and bloody face. "Shit, girl," she said, "what the hell happened?"

For a moment Allie didn't say anything, her mind racing. The image of Sam kept coming back to her, and his promise to disappear forever if she told. She wasn't exactly superstitious, but she still couldn't quite believe it had happened, and she didn't dare do anything that might jinx it. No, it was better all around if she didn't say anything. Or was this just cover for her wanting Sam all for herself?

"Took a fall on my bike," she said.

"Bad fall. You okay, honey?" asked Emma. "How did it happen?"

Allie felt herself flare up. "I was out there gathering supplies to keep you all alive, traveling on roads that have been falling apart for three years. How do you think it—"

"Any more new motherfuckers?" interrupted Jacky icily.

Allie turned. "Don't interrupt me. I was—"

"You start saying some shit that's worth saying and I won't. Until then, fuck you, acting like it's Emma's fault that you got yourself in over your head."

"And you," said Allie. "The ferals out there are changing, and what are you doing about it? Just recording how many of them I've seen

every time I come back from a run? What good is that going to do you
when dozens of them swarm over the wall?"

But Jacky had her by the arm and was propelling her fast across the
room, and Allie was too surprised to resist. "Spoiled little girl," Jacky
was grumbling, "thinks she knows everything." She dragged Allie to a
door in the back of the security center and kicked it open, thrust Allie
through the doorway.

Allie had always assumed it was just a closet, but the space inside
was bigger than she'd expected. Inside were a few small stacks of land
mines, a case of hand grenades, three oil drums, and a few cases of
Ivory soap. "That's what I'm doing," Jacky said. "You're not the only
one going out hunting for supplies, and my shit's a little harder to
come by than booze."

"Like soap?" asked Allie. "What, you going to wash the ferals into
submission?"

Jacky growled. "Allie, fuck, I like you, but you're making me not.
Don't take your bad day out on us. Cut it out or I'll fucking clock you."
She let go of her arm, took a deep breath. "Maybe I'll clock you even
if you do cut it out."

"The Ivory soap is for basic napalm," Emma said from behind
them, her voice calm. "Shred it and mix it with gasoline and it does
wonders."

"So," said Jacky, "we're fucking getting prepared, too. Want to start
over? Any new motherfuckers coming up from the south?"

"A huge group," Allie admitted, chastened. "The biggest I've seen.
Fifteen."

"Fuck," said Jacky. "And I'm still not hearing from the other camps.
I'm starting to wonder if there even are other camps anymore."


Allie continued through the camp, lost in thought, passing others as
if in a dream. She was trying not to think about Sam, but she couldn't
help it. If she'd been out scouting, she'd be making mistakes. *Should
I tell someone?* she was wondering, part of her almost unable to resist
sharing it, part of her holding back at all costs. If she told, Jacky would

form a search team and rush to find Sam, and he'd for sure run and disappear forever. Shouldn't she keep the information to herself until she figured out a way to coax him in?

And, it's true, she liked having a secret, especially one this huge.

After a while, she found herself in front of the door to Doc's lab. She would talk to Doc, just talk to her—not about Sam, at least not at first. But she'd talk to her and decide whether to say anything, and when. The door was half open and Doc was inside, her back faced away from the door, smoking a joint. She had her pad open and seemed to be analyzing data of some kind.

For a moment Allie considered going in, even raised her hand to knock, but then she hesitated. Doc would question her about her injuries, and she had just enough actual medical knowledge that she might be able to tell they hadn't come from a spill off her dirt bike after all. No, before she went in, she had to know for sure if she wanted to tell.

She stayed there a moment, watching Doc, watching the ferals left in their cages, one active and aggressive, the other in the last stage of the sharp decline to death. Strange to think that they had once been like Sam—it was hard now to believe they were even the same species.

What could she do with Sam but take the direct approach? Go back and stand there at their meeting spot until he showed up. Was there really any other alternative? After all, she could hardly wait for him to come to her.

Doc was too smart, she told herself. Doc would be able to tell that something was wrong, maybe even make a stab at what. No, better not to talk to Doc at all.

Still she lingered, still she hesitated, almost convincing herself to go in. But by the time Doc sensed something and turned around, Allie was already gone.

A few minutes later, she was at the threshold of her own room, staring in. The room was empty except for Kim, who sat on her bed, alone, holding a rifle. She had it locked to her shoulder—*Just*, Allie thought, *like I told her to do. Finally.* She was practicing lowering it and then bringing it up again. The large gun seemed incongruous in her delicate hands. Even more so because she had varnished her nails a bright pink.

*It doesn't have to be like this*, a part of Allie thought. *The world can be different for her. It can be more like it was before.*

Was that true? She didn't know exactly, but what she did know was that all the answers, if there were any, were to be found by bringing Sam into the camp.

## Chapter Twenty-five

She was up at the crack of dawn and out the gates, telling Jacky that she was hoping to pick off a few ferals, to reduce the odds a little. But all of them that she saw were in groups, large ones, too dangerous to mess with. By noon, Doc had contacted her on the radio with a list of supplies she wanted for the new serum, and a few minutes after noon, she had a penlight between her teeth and was rummaging through what was left of a pharmacy in the back of a drugstore, filling up a backpack she'd taken off a tipped-over rack on the way in. She looked for rolling papers and tobacco as well, but couldn't find any.

As soon as she was done, she didn't even pretend to patrol, just made a beeline for the place on Main Street where she had met Sam.

She parked her dirt bike a few hundred yards away and then walked into the square on foot, through the scattered carcasses and bones, the broken glass and rubble. She circled around, careful where she stepped, until she found a spot that felt right.

"Hello?" she called out. She raised her hands above her head to demonstrate that she wasn't armed.

There was no answer.

"Hey!" she called. "Hey!" Louder this time, but, she hoped, not loud enough to attract ferals—to convince Sam to come out. She had left her weapons back with the bike. Except, of course, for the knife in her boot.

Today it wasn't raining. The sun was harsh and hot, beating down from above. She felt like she was on the set of a Western on the verge of a high-noon shoot-out. She looked all around, waving her hands in the air, turning in a circle, to show there were no weapons on her. Of course, he could be miles away, but she had the feeling that he was watching, that this meeting place was close to where he habitually went to ground.

"I came alone!" she cried. "I won't stop yelling until you come out!"

No response. *How many more times can I yell before the ferals start to hear?* she wondered. She waited, spirits sinking, her eyes darting around, and then, suddenly, there he was, at the mouth of an alley. He stopped there, waited.

"Quiet down," he said. "You're going to get yourself killed."

"I'm sorry about yesterday," said Allie. "It was just . . . just so unexpected. I need to talk to you."

"So—talk."

"Look," she said, her voice softer now, so soft he could hardly hear her. "You're right. I get it. I can't imagine what you've been through the last few years. But I've thought up a plan."

"A plan," he said.

She nodded. "Yes," she said. "Can't you give me just a few minutes?"

He hesitated. Finally, he said, "I'm listening."

"Can I come a little closer?"

"No," he said.

"What, you want me to yell my plan? A minute ago you were saying it'd get me killed."

Sam thought a moment. "Stay right there," he said. "Hands in the air. I'll come to you."

She raised her hands. Sam drew closer. When he was just a few yards away, there was a click and a flurry of metal and Sam was yanked up into the air.

She nimbly climbed the tree that had served as the tension spring and strung a chain through the opening, padlocking him in. Then she let the metal ball fall with a clang to the ground. She climbed down herself and squatted near the chain sphere. Sam was awake but seemed befuddled, as if he'd been dazed when the mechanism went off. But maybe he was only pretending to be dazed, so as to buy a little time.

"Gotcha, you son of a bitch," she said. Sam just groaned.


But by the time she had attached the sphere to the back of the bike and was getting ready to pull it, Sam was awake and seriously pissed.

"I should have seen that coming" was the first thing he said.

"You sure should have."

FERAL                    133

"You've had your fun. Now get me the fuck out of here."

"No," she said.

"I saved your life and this is how you repay me? Goddamn it, Allie, I thought I could trust you."

She didn't bother to answer.

He shook his head within the sphere, the chains clinking against one another. "I'm caught between women and ferals," he said. "At least I know not to trust a feral. . . ."

"Screw you!" she said. "I need you. You're the ticket back to a normal world."

"You're killing me. Do you know that? That's what you're doing."

"How? How am I killing you? Don't you know how important you are?"

"Of course I know!" said Sam from within the sphere. "I'm not an idiot, Allie. I've been in a camp already. I know the drill."

Allie opened her mouth and closed it again. It was not the answer she'd been expecting. He'd been in a camp already? Why? Which camp? Why wasn't he still there?

"Let me out," he said. "Please."

"I'm taking you to West Staten."

Sam held his head in his hands. He crouched within his sphere, trying and failing to get comfortable. "You're all alike," he said.

This made Allie even more angry. "We're not all alike," she said. "I'm different."

Sam shook his head. "Not so different, when push comes to shove," he said. "None of you are. Not a one. And, as it turns out, not all that different from ferals, either."

"Fuck you," she said. She crossed her arms and stared at him.

"I don't want to die with the rest of you," he finally said.

"Die?" she said, surprised enough to forget her anger. "Who said anything about dying?" She waited, but he didn't answer. "What the hell happened to you, Sam?" she asked. And when he still didn't answer, more gently this time, "Please, what happened?"

———

"After the infection hit," he began, "I waited to get sick. I'd been going to State. I was a freshman, living in the high-rise dorms, when guys were catching the infection and going berserk. All of them were getting it fast. Over the course of a few hours it became a madhouse, but they didn't pay any attention to me, which made me think I must already be infected and symptoms hadn't started to show. I figured that any minute I'd be next. But I was wrong. Didn't happen.

"I told myself it was only a matter of time. I didn't dare go home and try to find my mother, not even to say good-bye, for fear that I'd turn feral while there and tear her apart. I called her on the phone, while the phones were still working, and that was the last time I heard her voice. Days later, I decided I might not get infected after all and went to the house, but I found her dead, her body mangled and mutilated."

"What about your father?" asked Allie.

"I . . . My dad left my mom when I was five. I never really knew him. It was just me and my mom, just the two of us. Once she was gone, that was it.

"I isolated myself, deep in the woods, living like a hermit. I was just counting down the days until I became feral, hoping that when the change started to come I'd recognize it and have the strength of character to kill myself. The ferals mostly left me alone, though if I got in one's face he might challenge me, even attack. I confuse them, somehow: as an uninfected male, I don't inspire the rage that women inspire. I don't smell right. I waited, tried to avoid them, slowly taught myself to kill them. Days went by, then weeks, then months, and I was still waiting to turn. Only gradually did I begin to think, *Wait a minute, it might not happen after all.*

"There was a camp—an old schoolhouse that a couple of women had found just a few weeks after the collapse. They barricaded themselves in, and then gradually started to make a fortress for themselves. I kept my distance from them, too—superstitious, maybe, that if I got too close that would be enough to turn me feral. But I watched as they forayed out and came back with more survivors and weapons. I watched them build a fence around the schoolhouse, then watch-towers on the roof, and then I watched more women stream in. A few times, the ferals found them, and I thought they might not survive, but they always managed to pull through.

"So, when I finally became fully convinced that I was normal, I walked out of the woods and into their camp. I wanted to help. I thought they would be happy to know that there was at least one male out there with some sort of immunity, that I could help them. That we could help each other.

"But things had gone too far already by that time. They were traumatized, mistrustful. They could hardly believe that I was still alive, and they couldn't convince themselves that I wasn't really sick after all—maybe I just hadn't manifested symptoms yet. They just couldn't believe the evidence of their senses."

He stretched in the cage. "Can't say that I blame them," he said. "Every other male they'd met for the last six months had tried to slaughter them. That doesn't exactly give you tons of confidence in the gender."

"So they wouldn't let you in?"

"They let me in." Sam gave a bitter laugh. "And they locked me up. When days went by and I didn't get sick, they decided maybe I wasn't infected after all. Then the testing began."

"Testing? What kind of testing?"

"I was drugged. I don't know what they were doing to me—it's all hazy—but I can see." Within the cage, he pulled his shirt off over his head. Underneath it, his bare torso was riddled with incision wounds, needle pricks, scars. He looked like a strange medical experiment.

Allie couldn't help thinking ashamedly of the similar marks on Doc's ferals and of how she herself had captured them and brought them back and how they'd been poked and prodded and drugged and finally killed. It was different, she tried to tell herself: they were ferals—they were animals—and he was a man, and what Doc had been doing was for the good of the human race. It was different.

"When they couldn't figure out some sort of serum, they decided to do 'whatever it takes' to ensure the survival of the human race. I might have been able to understand, even come around eventually to the idea that this was the best way to ensure the continuation of the species, but they kept me in the cage. They'd drug me, and then I'd wake up strapped down.

"Sure, I could talk just like them, but they only saw the monster in me. They couldn't get past the idea that I was less than human, a sort of tame feral."

For a moment he stopped, just staring out through the crisscrossed chains that formed the cage. No, Allie thought, no, it would be different at her camp. Doc wasn't that sort of person: she was smart and compassionate, she gave the ferals names. She'd treat Sam differently. She'd treat him with respect.

"Then it happened," Sam continued. "The camp was attacked. Overrun by an army of ferals. Not just one or two packs, a whole army of them, moving like a coordinated force, a military unit. Totally unlike anything I'd ever seen during my time outside. Everyone was killed. They got overrun. I'd still be in my cage if someone hadn't let me out before she bled out on the floor. I guess at the last moment she had a change of heart."

"It would be different at my camp."

"What, nobody would open my cage when the ferals come?"

"No, I mean—"

He cut her off. "I've seen you capture a feral. In this very same trap, in fact. Tell me, what did you do with him when you took him back?"

"But I . . ." And she stopped, not knowing what to say, how to justify herself.

"No. It wouldn't be different," he said. He shook his head. "Look. I know what I am. I know that I represent a hope that you can't bear to surrender. I don't want you to surrender it. And I plan to suck it up and go to another camp. I have to, for the sake of humanity. Just not to West Staten. Or any camp up here."

"Why not?" asked Allie. "I don't understand."

"That attack wasn't a random feral attack. If you bring me to your farmhouse, I'm going to die with the rest of you when they come. And, trust me, they are coming. You've seen them."

"Bullshit," said Allie. "You're lying." But what about the radio silence from the other camps nearby? she wondered. Maybe they weren't even there anymore.

He shook his head. "Haven't you seen the signs? New ferals everywhere around here . . ."

When he saw the expression on her face, he nodded. "You've seen them," he said. "But you can't accept what's going on, can you? Come on, give me a chance to help you. Let me show you what I'm talking about."

"Show me what?"

"Let me out of this trap. We'll have to do some traveling. It's a half a day away from here. You can keep your gun trained on me the whole time."

For a long time, she just stared at him, considering.

"How do I know you're not trying to trick me?" she finally asked.

He shrugged. "You don't," he said. "But in case I'm telling you the truth, can you afford to say no?"

## Chapter Twenty-six

She undid the padlock and let him out, wondering the whole time how big a mistake she was making. She was careful to keep him in her sights, and careful not to let him get too close.

"This is why I decided to make contact," he said in explanation. "After I'd watched you for a while and saved you from the ferals, I decided I had to let someone know, had to try to give your camp the chance to get away before it was too late."

Only after he said that did Allie realize with a pang that she'd been holding out hope that he'd had a more personal reason for making contact with her. But of course not: the world was much more pragmatic now. What room was there for feelings?

Walking about three yards in front of her, he took her down an alley and to a garage that was closed and still relatively intact, the outside of the door smeared in feral blood. He raised the door and invited her in.

The garage looked strange to her inside, and it took her a moment to realize why: it was clean. It was empty except for a five-hundred-gallon propane tank that ran the whole length of one wall, and, closer to the other wall, a four-seater quad ATV. It had been souped up, the engine replaced by something larger, one bar of the frame cut out, and another, curved, put in its place to accommodate the larger thing. On the back was a smaller U-shaped propane tank, bolted in place.

"Nice ride," she said, half mocking.

"Thanks," he said, not rising to the bait. "I like to think so."

The seats and floor space were filled with supplies, except for the driver's seat. He had to restack some things, leave a few boxes in the garage, to make enough room for Allie to slip in. They climbed in, him in the front and her in the rear. She kept the muzzle of her weapon trained on the back of his head.

He drove the quad well, and she was surprised, once they were out on the road, how fast it could go. Pretty quickly, he had it up to fifty.

Like her bike, it had been modified, a silencer added in addition to the muffler. But it also had a lot more storage space than her bike. A side panel covered with webbing held tools of all kinds. The back of his seat had a med kit strapped to it. The seat next to him was stacked high with two large tins that read SURVIVAL BISCUIT, a can opener taped to the side of one of them. On the seat beside her were an inflatable raft and a pump, a tire patch kit, a Sterno stove, a box of matches, and a flare gun. The floor well below it held a pile of blankets, a rain slicker, and a camp shovel.

"You always keep it crammed with so much shit?" she asked.

"Yes," he said.

As he drove, she looked around the vehicle's interior, scrutinizing the instrument panels, imagining how the leather wrapping of the steering wheel would feel. She looked at him, too, sneaking glances. After a while, she moved the gear around and shifted to the other side of the back seat so as to have a better view of him. She was still awestruck by his physical presence, an uninfected male—by the way he didn't look like a monster when you got close, just looked more and more human. His long, callused hands worked the clutch. She stared at his bearded face, trying to imagine the features that must be hidden beneath. When she caught a flash of his tormented eyes in the rearview mirror, she felt like she was looking into her own eyes. Before long, she began to regret that they hadn't taken her dirt bike: it would have been nice to have his chest pressed up against her back. Nice, too, to be the one driving.

*Steady, Al*, she told herself. *Keep your mind on the game.*

Sam seemed to be sneaking glances at her, too, catching sight of her in the rearview mirror, checking her out. He was impressed by her, by her beauty and her strength, by her smarts. Impressed, too, and a little ashamed, by how easily she had managed to catch him. It'd been quite some time since anyone had managed to get the better of him, and now this girl of—what, eighteen? nineteen?—had. Attractive, too, with a beautiful face and high cheekbones under that toughened exterior. Once or twice their gazes met, but Sam would quickly flick his eyes away, pretending that he hadn't been looking at all.

And then she saw him staring hard in the huge jury-rigged rear-view he'd bolted in.

She turned and looked back over her shoulder. There it was: a lone feral, just out of the bushes and keeping pace with them, perhaps even gaining slightly. As it eyed Allie, the creature began to salivate.

"May I?" said Allie.

"Be my guest," said Sam.

Keeping her rifle aimed at Sam's head, she broke the pistol from the breeching holster at her side. Coolly, she aimed and fired at the sprinting feral. The creature's chest exploded mid-run, and it went down in a tumbling heap. A second later, the pistol was back in place.

"Left-handed?" asked Sam, obviously impressed.

"Yup," said Allie, deadpan. "I had to keep the gun in my right hand aimed at the more dangerous male."

## Chapter Twenty-seven

They arrived late in the day, after flying down a long, desolate country road flanked by fields. Unlike most of the other roads, Allie noted, this one had been cared for: someone had moved the wrecked cars aside and made sure plants didn't crack through and break it up, even repaired a pothole or two—or had cared for the last few miles of it, anyway. At the end of the road was a long fifteen-foot-tall wall, ribboned on top with barbed wire. Behind it was a building. Only the top of it was visible from the road, but that was enough to tell her it was large.

Bodies were hanging strung on the barbed wire, and as they drew closer she could see that they were ferals. Over a dozen of them, riddled with bullets, the corpses starting to decay. More were slumped in heaps at the base of the wall.

Sam slowed and stopped the quad near the wall. He climbed out; Allie followed his movements with her gun before climbing out herself. She scanned the area for danger, simultaneously tracking Sam.

"Follow me," said Sam. "There's a hole in the wall over here."

She followed him along the curving wall, stepping carefully, staying alert. When he came to a crumbled breach in the wall, he stopped and waited, making sure that she was there with him. *I should trust him,* a part of her thought. Another part of her thought, *He waited for me just to try to make me trust him so that he could trick me later.*

Sam peered through the rift.

"Clear," he said. And then she thought maybe he hadn't been waiting for her after all. Maybe he was just waiting to make sure no ferals were there. In that case, both parts of her had misread him. He waved her forward. "Let's go," he said, and went through.

He shinnied through the small opening, and after a moment she followed. He stood well back from the opening on the other side, so as to give her space. Allie worked her way through. When she got to the other side, she was shocked by what she saw.

"Christ," she said. "What happened here?"

Behind the wall was an old brick public school. JOHN MUIR MI, it read on the façade. Other little signs—turrets on the roof, the refortification of the doors—made it clear it was a camp, not unlike Allie's own.

Or had been a camp. The place had been destroyed. Half of the school was now a burnt-out skeleton. The other half had been riddled with bullet holes, the bricks pocked and flaking, nearly completely destroyed in spots. She was surprised that it was still standing.

In front of the building were dozens of corpses, the stench nearly unbearable. Maybe as many as forty women, some of them hideously mangled, and another four dozen ferals, most riddled with bullets. It was an awful, gruesome bit of devastation. And it hadn't happened that long ago—a month, maybe, or even less.

Sam stood a few feet away, watching her reaction. Despite what she saw, the gun didn't waver, remaining trained on him.

"A war," he said. "A war is what happened."

She eyed the gun turret towers on the roof, ran her eyes over the thousands of shell casings that littered the ground. Then she turned to Sam.

"These women were well armed," she said. "It would have taken hundreds of ferals to do this."

Sam nodded. "It did."

Allie shook her head. Her gun had begun to fall, the barrel moving slowly down his body. "Ferals don't travel in packs that large," she said.

"At least, they didn't use to," said Sam.

Her eyes caught on five piles of dirt at a little distance. Crosses constructed from sticks had been placed atop the mounds. Graves, she realized. She gestured toward them.

"How?" she asked. "Survivors did that?"

"Not survivors. There were none," said Sam. "I dug them. For the youngest ones I found dead here."

Allie stared at him.

"Was this the camp you were at?" she asked.

Sam shook his head. "No. That camp was hundreds of miles west."

Allie forced her eyes to pass over it again, to take it in, remember it. Then she turned to him, anger in her eyes.

"Why are you showing me this?" she asked. "What does this have to do with you coming to my camp?"

Sam remained calm, unemotional. "Look here," he said.

He reached to take his pack off, and she swiftly raised her gun.

"Give it a rest," he said. "What are you going to do, shoot the only nonferal male within a thousand miles?" He slowly removed the pack the rest of the way, watching her as he did so. He reached in, pulled out a map. He opened it and spread it on the ground, smoothing it flat with his hands.

It was a truck-stop AAA map of the region, covering a half-dozen states. There were over a dozen large handwritten X's across it, marking locations along a linear path.

"So?" said Allie. "It's a map—so what?"

"This X is this camp," he said, pointing. "Those other X's are the remnants of other camps I've come across since I survived my own massacre."

"The X's mean they're gone?"

"All of them," Sam said. "Destroyed by ferals." He gestured at the destruction all around them. He turned and looked her in the eyes, his gaze sincere, serious. "Life in the northern states is over, Allie," he said. "I've seen it with my own eyes."

Allie stared at the map. There were dozens of X's, she realized. So many. She thought of the radio silence, of Jacky's worry. It was all so much worse than they could have guessed. All that death and destruction reduced to little marks on a map. She looked around her, imagining a row of two or three dozen camps just like this one, stacked end to end, filled with the dead.

She reached out and touched the X closest to West Staten. "What's that one named?" she asked.

"Huguenot," said Sam. "It just fell."

"No," she said, little louder than a breath. Jacky had been right— Huguenot was gone. Kim was even less safe than she'd thought.

"Thousands upon thousands of ferals are coming up from the

south," he said. "Some kind of mass exodus. I know you've seen them. Some of them almost killed you."

"But why?"

"I think it has something to do with their body temperature," Sam said. "The fact that they run hot all the time. They need colder weather. Otherwise, they burn out."

Allie was nodding. "That's why they spend so much time down at the coastline, in the harbors, by the water. It's cooler there. Like now. In summer."

"Exactly," said Sam. "Here it's cold much of the year. This is, for the most part, a much better climate for them."

"My God," said Allie. "They're migrating."

Sam began folding up the map again. "Like birds but in reverse," he said. "The ferals who live down south are coming up here. Before long, there will be too many of them throughout the north. Women won't be able to survive here anymore. West Staten is one of the last camps standing. It's just a matter of time before it gets hit."

*It's just as I feared*, Allie thought. *I've seen signs of the migration myself, all the newbies appearing. I've known for a while something wasn't right. And West Staten isn't prepared—not for that many ferals. We're still thinking in terms of dozens when there are probably hundreds, maybe thousands.*

"And if I take you back to West Staten, you're either going to die when the ferals attack or starve to death in a cage after we've all been killed."

Sam slowly nodded. "Exactly," he said.

She tightened her grip on the rifle. "So I'm just supposed to let the only nonferal man I've seen in the last three years, maybe the only one in existence, walk?"

"If you value my life, yes, I'm asking you to save it. Let me get to a safe, secure camp down south. Ferals hunt by scent, and since I'm male they don't know what to make of me, so I'll be okay traveling alone. I'll get there. But it's too dangerous for me to be near your camp, you women, this region."

Allie frowned. "And we die."

Sam didn't respond, which, Allie realized, was answer enough. Yes, in his opinion, they were doomed.

"But ..." she started. "I don't understand. Why did you get involved? You could have just let them take me. Why be a hero then but run now?"

For a long moment, Sam just looked at her, and then he looked away. "I was running then, too," he said. "I'd seen you before. I saw you trap that feral. I saw how you handled them, how good you were, and it was like I knew you. Still, I might have left anyway, but then you were captured and, almost without thinking, I went in after you. After that, I couldn't leave without telling you what was coming. I thought you had a right to know."

Her heart, she realized, was beating faster. Her mind was trying not to read too deep a meaning into his words. If it hadn't been her, if it had been someone else, would he have told?

"I hope that wasn't a mistake," he continued.

She stared at him for a long time. Could she really let a nonferal male go free? Wasn't he their future? But that had to be balanced against the X's on the map, against what she had seen here. Why risk the future of the human race on the chance that they'd be able to withstand an attack? Wouldn't humanity stand a better chance if Sam were down south and safe? Wasn't it selfish of her not to acknowledge this?

Slowly, her gun lowered; then, after a moment, she gave a deep sigh and holstered it. Sam nodded, a subtle thank-you, and she could see in the crinkle at the corners of his eyes that he was happy that he'd guessed right about her, happy to know she was the kind of person he had hoped she was going to be. She nodded back, thanking him for the warning. She was now doubly in his debt.

"Look," said Sam. "You need to leave West Staten before they come. Do what I'm doing—head south."

Allie snorted. "We have forty-eight women, some old, some young. How, Jet fucking Blue? Oh, wait, their last scheduled flight departed three years ago. It's impossible. You said it yourself. We wouldn't stand a chance."

"That's not what I meant," he said. "You're good. You can make it. Alone."

Allie shook her head. "No deal. My sister's in that camp," she said. "I have to look out for her. I love her. No way I'm leaving without her."

Sam opened his mouth to speak again, then thought better of it.

"It's getting dark," Allie turned and started back toward the rift. "I have to tell them what's going on. I have—" But once she passed through to the other side, she saw the sun was already setting. "Shit," she said.

"It's too late." Sam was shaking his head. "We have a five-hour drive back. It'll take us well into the night to get there, and by then it won't be safe." He gestured at the school. "I have food. Gear. Since they've already attacked this place, they won't be back. Let's hole up here and leave in the morning."

Chapter Twenty-eight

# Allie

He's right—ferals are always thicker in number and more active at night, when it's cooler, and I don't have enough feral blood with me to risk the trip back then. Besides, it's not like he can just drop me off at my front door, and no doubt Scarface and his crew will be wandering around the perimeter of the camp, and then where will I be? No, we'll have to spend the night inside the school.

This is not exactly how I thought it would happen. There used to be a time I refuse to think about when I expected that I'd be wined and dined a little first, and I definitely didn't think I'd be wearing camo and have a couple of guns laid out on the floor beside me. Instead, once we're inside and have picked a good room, one that's relatively clean and has a window as far away from the dead bodies as we can get, I get a hunk of beaver tail that Sam chars with a blowtorch and which I have to eat with my fingers, and then a tin cup of water that has the coppery taste of iodine. I brought dessert: deer jerky from a buck I shot and cured myself. Sam rustles up a few candles from his supplies, and we set those up, so at least it's a candlelight supper. He's got a spare sleeping bag for me, too. A good Boy Scout, he came prepared.

We don't talk much at dinner. I eat and he eats, and from time to time we glance at one another, wondering what's going on in the other person's head. Or at least that's what I'm wondering. I can't say for sure about him, since I'm not in his head.

Apparently, what he's thinking is: *This beaver tail tastes awful.* Because, after the first bite of it, he digs into his bag, finds a saltshaker and douses his hunk with it. He tosses the shaker my way, and I catch it almost without looking at it, just like I used to do with Dad, and I douse my meat as well and toss it back. He's a decent catch, too. If we were outside, we could almost be camping. Is this what camping was like? Hard to remember.

After dinner, leaning against the wall, I find in my own supply kit my tobacco and roll myself a cigarette. I offer it to Sam, but he says no by shaking his hand, and so I take it for myself.

It's my one vice, and one I indulge in only on special occasions. One's enough, usually, but there's something about sitting and relaxing, giving yourself over to something that isn't about keeping the camp safe, is just about you, that's satisfying. I suppose that's how the other women must feel at parties, or with girlfriends, or with their plays or poetry. Like Jacky said: there's a time for fighting and a time for ... you know. I'm talking about s-e-x. Don't be a fucking prude about it.

Sam is just sitting there, also leaning against the wall, looking around him. He has a good profile, and I have to admit I'm watching, soaking him in, so that I can remember him after he has gone south.

He's looking around, lost a little bit, his lips moving. "Yes," he mumbles, "she really is." At least, I think that's what he says.

"What?" I say.

Sam startles. He looks over at me, confused.

"You said something," I tell him.

"Shit," he says, surprised. "I wasn't talking to you."

"No? Well, who the hell were you talking to, then?" What's that, Allie? A little jealousy creeping into your voice?

He's blushing. For a long moment he doesn't say anything, and then he offers, "Sometimes ... sometimes ... I talk ... to myself."

"Out loud?" I say, before I can stop myself.

"Yes."

"And you don't even know you're doing it?"

He shrugs halfheartedly. "I guess not," he says. "Not always."

"I talk to myself, too, but I do it inside. Internally," I tell him. "Especially when I'm around other people."

"I do externally," he says. Then adds, "I'm not around other people much."

I nod. The cigarette is nearly gone, so I stub it out on the floor.

We sit there, backs against the wall, in the glow of the candlelight, in silence, not talking to each other or talking to ourselves.

I'm zoning a little, thinking it might be time to crawl into my sleeping bag and say good night, when he says, "I named her."

"Who?" I say. I'm unsure where this story is going. But if it's about some past girlfriend, I'm not sure I want to hear it.

"The person I talk to. Belle," he says.

"Nice name," I say, and then hope that he can't detect that hint of jealousy hiding behind the words. It's crazy to be jealous of a girl he's invented so as not to feel alone, a girl that exists only in his own head.

"I know I'm really talking to myself," he apparently feels compelled to explain. "I'm not crazy. But pretending to talk to someone else makes me feel like I'm not alone all the time."

I say the only thing I can think of to say: "I understand." And I do. The only reason I haven't invented an imaginary boy to talk to is that all the boys I know are monsters. Literally, monsters. And, besides, the women at the camp already think I'm weird enough. Add talking to myself to that mix and they'd probably kick me to the fucking curb.

"You always like this?" I ask. "Even before the virus hit?"

"Weird?" he says.

I shake my head. "Not what I said," I tell him.

He shrugs. "The last few years haven't helped."

He casts me a look that almost drags my soul out through my throat and wraps it around him like a blanket. He's the first person I've met in a long time that I feel I can relate to.

"You said, 'Yes, she really is,'" I say, and my heart's beating a little faster as I ask it. "What did that mean? What question did your friend Belle ask you?"

But I've gone too far, it seems, come to the point too soon. He looks away, mumbles, looks down. "I forget," he says, but I know he hasn't—he's just embarrassed to tell me.

The moment's gone.

---

But other moments always come if you wait long enough. There we are, leaning over his map, well worn even though it's made out of some sort of durable, tightly woven material. We have to lean in close to see, since all we have are candles. We're relaxing, loosening up a little, so much so that Sam's started showing me around his old haunts.

"I come from here," he says, gesturing to a dot on the map. "This was where I was going to college when the virus hit. This is where I hid out while I waited for the infection to manifest," he says, dragging his finger a little farther over, to a spot that's almost worn through. "This is where they kept me prisoner."

His voice trails off. He both does and doesn't want to go on with the story. Probably it's been years since he's talked about it. For a moment I just wait, silent, for him to go on, and when I see he's still struggling with what to say, I jump in.

I stab at my own former home on the map. "This was me," I tell him. "I couldn't save my mom—from my dad—but I stopped him from killing my little sister, Kim."

I hesitate, wondering if I need to spell it out, say more, but I see with relief from his eyes that he's rapidly filled in the rest, that he knows what I had to do to my own father. Thank God, I won't have to go into specifics.

"My father was a police officer and a hunter," I say, wanting him to see my dad's good side, too. "He taught me how to use a gun, how to fight, how to camp. I owe him a lot. Because of him, my sister and I were able to survive."

Sam nods. "I didn't have any survival skills going in. I thought I would get infected, so I holed up alone. Didn't want to hurt anyone. First few days, I listened to a radio, heard how it was spreading—everything collapsing. Then there was silence. I . . . lost hope."

He displays his wrists, which are ragged with old scars. "Couldn't cut deep enough," he says. "I didn't have the courage."

I stare at his wrists. I've thought of doing the same thing myself—and would have, if I hadn't had Kim to look after.

"I'm glad you didn't," I say. "I'm glad you're still alive."

It's probably time for us to catch some sleep, but neither of us is quite ready to say good night, so we continue to sit on the floor, facing one another, in the guttering candlelight. His face, which usually has struck me as being so hard, seems like it's softened some as we've been talking, as we've begun to open up.

"I miss playing lacrosse," I am saying.

"I miss hockey," he responds.

"I was damn good," I tell him. It's true, I'm not bragging. Or maybe I am bragging, but I have the rights.

"I was damn average," he says.

We're silent for a while, just thinking. I never do this. When the women back at camp do it, start laying out their memories like a hand of cards, I'm usually edging for the door. But for some reason, it doesn't seem so bad when Sam's the one egging me on.

"McDonald's," I say. "I'd give a left toe for a Quarter Pounder with cheese."

"I'm pretty sure they had toe in them," he says. "I was a Five Guys guy myself." He smiles a little. "I tried making a burger with raccoon meat once. I wouldn't recommend it."

"I've made deer burgers and rat burgers," I say. "I didn't mind the rat."

When he laughs I hardly recognize him, but in a good way.

"Running water," he says.

"We've got that back at the camp," I say. "Kind of."

He groans. "What I wouldn't give for a warm bath."

"Some tough guy," I say. "Getting my nails done."

"So girlie," he teases.

"Screw you," I say, and flip him off.

He runs his fingers through his tangled locks. "A good haircut," he says. "A good haircut would make me feel normal again."

"Oh yeah?" I say.

"Yeah," he says. "Definitely."

"Well, I can't get you a burger," I say, "but turns out I can make you feel normal."

Sam looks at me and freezes when he sees the Ka-Bar knife that's suddenly in my hand. I scavenged it off a corpse. It's sharp and nasty. I hope the smile on my face doesn't look crazy.

"Allie? You okay?" he asks.

"Yeah." I beckon with the blade. "Come here."

Which is how we end up with him sitting on a chair we yank out of the wreckage. His eyes are closed. I'm standing behind him, sawing his hair off with my Ka-Bar. It's a good thing I keep it as sharp as I do. Once I'm done, I'll have to sharpen it again. He's got a lot of hair, and it's been a long time since he's done anything to it: there's as much dirt in there as hair.

I'm running my fingers through his long, tangled locks, removing knots as I cut hunks away. Eventually, I have to admit it to myself: I may have slightly exaggerated my skills as a hairdresser.

And I'm having trouble paying attention, too. I'm spending too much time staring down at him, scanning every inch of his face—his delicately closed eyes, his nose, his scruffy beard. I'm just inches away from him. He can probably feel my breath against his skin.

And then he senses something and opens his eyes. And there we are, the two of us, just inches away, staring at one another, listening to one another breathe.

I'm waiting for him to do something, but he's in the chair, sprawled out, looking at me upside down. Probably I look weird. Probably having been held in a cage as a breeder means you have a bit to sort through, sexually. By the time I realize that I'm going to have to be the one to do something if something's going to be done, the moment's passed.

Two moments lost in one day.

I salvage a piece of broken mirror from near the wall and bring it back. I put it in front of him with a flourish, then raise it until he can see his reflection clearly.

"Worst haircut in the history of mankind," he says.

"So—normal, then," I say.

We both laugh.


It goes on like that for a while, something almost happening but never quite. Both of us are just a little too solitary, a little too gun-shy, to make a leap. And so we get close, circle one another, move away again. But each time we circle, we come away from it feeling like we know one another a little more, feeling just a little closer.

I'm exhausted. We're lying down now, on blankets we've found, on top of the sleeping bags, getting ready for sleep. The candles have gone out, but there's enough moonlight that we can still see a little bit. I know where Sam is and can more or less see him. And what I can't see because of the darkness I can imagine.

I'm tired. I keep drifting in and out, aware of him there next to me. I can tell he's aware of me, too.

"Is she cool?" he says suddenly, out of nowhere.

"Talking to yourself again, Sam," I warn him.

"I wasn't," he says. "That was what Belle asked me earlier. 'Is she cool?'"

I hold my breath. I remember his answer. "Yes, she really is." And then I think, *He's opened the door—this is the moment. If you want it, take it.*

And I do want it. I really do.

## Chapter Twenty-nine

The morning sun was streaming through the windows. Her head was on his chest, her ear taking in the sound of his breathing as he slept, as she slept. His arms were wound around her, holding her.

When her legs began to get hot from the sun, she opened her eyes. Or, rather, they were open before she realized she had opened them. She saw a bit of broken mirror, a pile of dirty hair. For a moment she was confused, disoriented, unsure of where she was, and then she turned and saw Sam's face.

Quietly, she extricated herself and then stood, beginning to gather her things. For once, she'd slept without knowing exactly where the pistol was, and she had to search for it. It was in the corner, still in its holster. She squatted over it and picked it up, hefted it.

If they'd come for her, she might not have been able to get to her weapon in time. She'd let her guard down too far last night; she'd gotten sloppy. There's a time for fighting and a time for, you know, she thought, but you can't mix the two. That's when you die.

"Hey," said Sam's voice from behind her.

She looked back over her shoulder at him. He was staring at her, intensely, like he was looking straight through her skin and deep into her. She met the look and held it for a long time. But in the end she was the one to break it.

"Come on," she mumbled, turning away. "We have to get back."


She sat in front now, beside him, no longer pointing a gun at his head, comfortable with him now, and uncomfortable with the idea of being separated from him soon. It was a long drive, and she couldn't help thinking that every mile was taking them closer to the moment after which they would never see one another again. A thousand things ran through her head to say, but she didn't say the most important ones.

Whenever she wanted to, she just looked at him, drinking him in. She was pleased when she caught him glancing at her.

Hours later, they pulled onto Main Street, stopping the quad where they had first met. Sam parked and turned off the rumbling engine. They both clambered out, each instinctively scanning the area to make sure it was clear.

He hovered around her as she walked to the back of the vehicle. Neither of them spoke as she pulled her backpack out over the roll bar, slinging it on.

They stared at one another for a long while.

"When are you leaving?" Allie finally asked.

"I have to stock up on supplies," said Sam. "Then I'm gone."

"You won't find anything," she said. "We've taken everything from this area."

He smiled wryly. "I'm a good scrounger," he said. "I'll be okay."

He would, too, she knew he would. The two of them stood awkwardly, neither of them quite knowing how to say good-bye, neither of them wanting to say it first. Allie found herself fighting an unfamiliar surge of emotion, and Sam seemed to be as well. Neither of them knew what to do with the other.

"Go south, Sam," she finally said. "Get to a camp down there. Whatever it takes."

"Okay, sure," said Sam.

They gave one another one last long look and then, feeling the tears about to start, Allie turned away and started off.

"Wait," called Sam from behind her.

She stopped, but didn't turn back around. She wasn't sure if she would be able to hold it together if she did.

## Chapter Thirty

She spent an hour lodged in the branches of a tree, hunting, trying to clear her mind, scanning her surroundings with the scope. But her mind kept wandering back to Sam. *Come on, Allie*, she told herself. *Stay in the game.* When she caught sight of a lone feral, she followed him and shot him in the back of the head. When she got to him, he was still alive, blinking and shivering, so she whipped out her Ka-Bar and slit his throat, letting the blood spray over her face and hands and chest for safety's sake. *Was Doc right?* she wondered. *Did they have a moment before they died when they were human again?* And then she pulled herself together, made a conscious effort to become the old Allie, and made her way back to West Staten.

The land in front of the main house seemed remarkably empty for a late afternoon, everybody off somewhere, nobody around except for the women on the roof and the guard manning the gate. *Where is everyone?* she wondered.

She stopped just inside the gates and surveyed the grounds. She remembered what the camp Sam had shown her had looked like and imposed that chaos and carnage upon this place, imagining what it would look like after they were all dead—the bodies scattered in front of the main building, the craters in the minefield, the dead ferals caught on the barbed wire or flopped on the ground, and all the women, skulls crushed, bones broken, all dead. Yes, she knew the ferals would be over the wall quickly. The land mines would stop some and their guns would stop more, but if fifty or sixty or a hundred more ferals massed, they would only be able to hold out for so long.

They had to move.

She swung off the bike and walked slowly toward the farmhouse. She went in the front door, meandered down the hall. The common room was empty. *Where is everyone?* she wondered again, and a moment later, nervous, she unholstered her pistol.

She crept forward, deeper into the house. She moved through an empty kitchen, down another hall, not quite sure what she was look-ing for, until, up ahead, she heard laughter.

It was coming from the rec room. When she reached the door she found a dozen or so women inside, chatting, laughing, a festive mood dominating. Some were playing pool, others Ping-Pong. Some lounged around and talked. Allie stayed at the threshold, just watch-ing, observing her sister, observing Holly, who was at the far side of the room, laughing with a pretty blonde called Dana. After a moment, she holstered her pistol. She cast glances at the others, wondering what she was going to tell them about needing to move, and how.

"Look who the cat dragged in," Jacky said, striding toward her. "What's the skinny on those motherfuckers?"

*No time like the present,* thought Allie, and when Jacky reached her she took her firmly by the elbow, pulled her just outside the door.

She spoke quietly but urgently, uncharacteristically dramatic. "We have to leave," she claimed.

"What?" said Jacky, startled. "You just fucking got here. I know you're a lone wolf, but even lone wolves need company sometimes. Why don't you come on in?"

"No," Allie said. "Leave this place, I mean. All of us. For good."

Jacky's expression turned serious. "What the hell happened? What did you see? Tell me."

"I've seen some more new faces," said Allie, "A lot more. They're massing. Something's going on." *I'm rambling,* she thought. *I sound hysterical, like I'm upset over nothing. But I can't tell her about Sam—I promised.* "I think we have to move everyone south soon. This area is going to be overrun."

She could tell by the way Jacky drew herself up that she was taken aback, unsure whether to take her seriously or see all this as a sign of panic. Probably the only thing keeping her from that was that Allie was hardly the sort to panic about anything.

"Slow down," Jacky said. "We ain't moving forty-eight women, Allie. That's impossible." She stared at her a long moment. "What the fuck's going on here?" she asked, eyes narrowing ever so slightly. "What's really going on? You never said it was this bad—"

*It's not working,* thought Allie, and in an instant was deadly serious, less emotional, more intense.

"Forget what I said before," she said. "I'm seeing a lot of new ferals, Jacky. A lot! Something's driving them into this area. If it continues at this rate, we won't be able to survive. So we better figure out the impossible, because I don't think we have that much time."

Jacky shook her head, unwilling to believe, but something was beginning to build behind her eyes.

"Hold on," Jacky said. "Just hold up. Maybe you're wrong. Maybe it'll stop. Maybe—"

"Shut up! I'm not wrong!" Allie yelled; but when she saw the women inside the rec room beginning to pay attention, she dragged Jacky closer and lowered her voice almost to a whisper. "You don't know what I've seen. We need to do something, and we need to do it quickly, or I swear to you we're all going to die."

"We've got napalm ingredients, we have weapons—"

"Not enough," said Allie.

"Not enough? How the hell do you—"

"I went to another camp," Allie said. "One of the ones you've had a hard time picking up on the radio. I saw what they did to it. They didn't leave anybody alive. We don't stand a chance."

"What camp? Which one?"

"Huguenot," she lied. It was the closest camp, the one Jacky was most likely to believe she'd visited, and she knew from Sam it had been overrun. This was a way of getting Jacky to believe in the danger without telling her about Sam.

She saw a wave of pain pass over Jacky's face. "Okay," Jacky managed. "I don't even know where to begin." She ran her fingers over her short, spiky hair. "I'll start thinking of ways to get us all out of here. You monitor what's going on out there and start looking for outs—roads they're not traveling on, vehicles, propane, anything." She rubbed her face with her hands, then looked Allie right in the eyes. "Christ. This is not something we planned for, Allie. This is our little piece of this sickened planet. We were never supposed to leave it."

"When do we tell everyone?" Allie asked.

Jacky ran her fingers over her face again, groaning. She turned and looked back through the door of the rec room, at the women inside: cheerful, happy. She turned back to Allie.

"We wait," she said firmly. "Until we have a plan, a good one. Maybe there'll be another solution in the meantime."

"What does that mean?"

"Word came from the lab that Doc's new vaccine is working. That's what this party is about. The girls are already talking about their fathers, boyfriends, husbands—how they'll find them and give them the vaccine and then everything will go back to normal again. I told them it was way too early to celebrate," she said, gesturing back at the rec room. "I hope to hell I was wrong."

"Progress? How much?"

"The latest inoculated motherfucker is still alive," said Jacky. "He's outlasted the others, has lived on about twice as long so far. He seems to be moving his jaws like he wants to talk."

"Maybe he's just hungry," said Allie.

"Maybe," said Jacky, levelly. She turned, to look furtively back over her shoulder into the rec room. "Listen, let them have their moment while I try to figure this out." She turned back to Allie and regarded her shrewdly. "Can I trust you?" she asked. "You won't say nothing until we have more to go on?"

For a long moment, Allie didn't move, then she nodded her head once, sharply.

"Good girl," said Jacky, patting her cheek, and then she hurried away.

## Chapter Thirty-one

## Jacky

Sometimes this job sucks ass. Instead of being focused on the honest business of slaughtering motherfuckers, you get all caught up in the logistical bullshit of how to get forty-eight women hundreds of miles away to safety. That's not what I signed up for. What I signed up for was killing ferals. I couldn't give a fuck if Doc finds a vaccine—never did have much use for men anyway, feral or no. This is the new world, and it's just us women now. We get a vaccine, bring men back or whatever, is that going to make it any better? No, it'll just take us back to the same old bullshit.

I mean, shit, having to decide if I'm going to risk the lives of forty-eight women on a cross-country death march because of what a nineteen-year-old claims. Sure, she's a very special nineteen-year-old, she's never led me wrong before, and I trust her, but still. She's always been a bit overvigilant—post-traumatic whatever. What if this time she's seeing more than is actually there? What if she's wound up so tight that she's broken her spring? I mean, we've got a lot of guns, a lot of bullets, ingredients for napalm. The motherfuckers have never been organized—they don't have the brains for it. It's not like they'll do a coordinated attack. Going out there day after day—seeing corpses and feeling the crunch of bone beneath your feet—is enough to make anybody a little crazy, a little paranoid, and, unlike the rest of us, Allie never takes a fucking break. Maybe she's letting the stress of it get to her.

Then again, what if she's not? What if everything she says is correct, and something is driving more ferals up into our neck of the woods? In a few days, a few weeks, there'll be so many that they'll just keep pouring over the walls, and no matter how many we shoot or how many mines they set off, they'll keep coming.

But if we try to head south, aren't we dead anyway? How do you manage to string forty-eight women across open country with all those ferals around? Wouldn't we be sitting ducks, or worse?

It's one of those dilemmas for which there's no apparent or obvious solution, like what the lovely Emma calls a "damdif" situation. As in, you know, damned if you do, damned if you don't. Or as in it don't make no *damn* bit of *diff*erence what you choose to do, you're fucked either way. If Allie's overreacting and I get forty-eight women on the road headed south, a good number of them are likely to be dead before we get anywhere worth getting to. Maybe not just a good number of them, maybe all of them. If I don't, and just write her off and stall, and the ferals do come swarming over the fucking walls, then it's even worse: we all die for sure.

So what to do?

The only way to handle a damdif situation is to prepare to do everything and then hope the sitch changes enough so you can see clearly which of your prepared paths is the least fucked. So—we quietly get ready to go, and also, simultaneously, continue to fortify and further entrench, prepare to stay. And hope we know which of the two we really need to do before it's too fucking late.

## Chapter Thirty-two

# Allie

I'm not sure what to think, can't tell how seriously Jacky's taking what I've been saying. I mean, sure, she's taking it seriously, she knows I feel serious about it, can tell by my tone, but is that enough to convince her that we all need to pack up and break camp? But if I tell her what I've really seen, and where I've seen it, and that I know dozens of camps have been overrun, she's going to ask, Where the fuck did you get that intel? And then: What were you doing up there, five hours away, when you were supposed to be on patrol? and How did you get there? and You couldn't have visited all those camps—who told you? and then it'll be lie upon lie until the lies break down enough that she figures out that there's something I'm hiding. Or someone, I should say. Sam. No, I can't say any more. I just have to hope what I said was enough to light a fire under her, that she won't just convince herself that Huguenot wasn't prepared and that we, since we're prepared, are going to be okay.

I'm watching her back, pondering my next move, what I can say or do to convince her, when I accidentally catch Holly's eye. Immediately she's on her way over, looking a little uncertain but smiling, or at least trying to. That's a good thing, right? At least she's talking to me. Or walking toward me, anyway.

"Hey," she says once she gets there.

"Hey," I say back.

"Listen," she says, "I don't want to lose our friendship over this. I just need a little time to get over my feelings. Okay?"

I smile, relieved. I'm thinking about Kim. Maybe Holly will still look after her as long as I don't sink things totally. Maybe we can be friends without it being too awkward after a while. "Okay," I say.

"Great," she says. Then she looks at me a little closer. "You look . . . different," she says.

I flush, thinking of Sam, but I'm sunburned enough from the quad trip yesterday that I doubt she'll notice. "Just tired, I guess," I say. "Just back from a day and a half of scout duty."

She looks at me hard, like she suspects I'm lying but she doesn't quite know how to put a finger on what the truth really is. Finally, she shrugs. Then, as if she's just remembered it, a real smile this time: "Hey, you hear about the vaccine?"

I nod. We share a smile, but hers is a little more genuine than mine. I'll believe it when I see it. I want to believe, for Kim's sake. I want her to be able to live in a world with hope.

"It's weird that things could turn around so quickly," I say cautiously.

She shrugs. "That's science for you," she says. "That's why they call it a breakthrough."

I'm still dubious but I don't want to burst Holly's bubble. Let her have her moment of hope. But hope—hope is a killer. It makes us let our guard down. It makes us soft. I'll do some real investigating on my own.

When I arrive in the lab, Doc's got Joni Mitchell's *Blue* on the boombox. It's on a song I know—I've heard it in here before—about someone on a plane. Doc is singing along to it.

She's hunched over her microscope, examining slides. She looks tired, her hair mussed, like she hasn't left her desk in days—which, knowing Doc, she probably hasn't. That, as much as anything, is a sign that she thinks something's up, that she's excited enough about whatever she is seeing through the microscope to not want to leave.

"Is it true?" I say, and she jumps, almost knocking the microscope off the table.

"Allie," she says, her hand fluttering near her chest like a wing, "you shouldn't do that. You scared me."

"Is it true?" I ask again.

"Yes," says Doc, then sings: "'Turn this crazy bird around.'"

I hate it when she drags things out. She doesn't mean anything by it, but it still gets on my nerves. "Stop it, Doc," I say. "What's going on?"

Doc smirks. She opens her mouth to answer, then closes it again. She stares at me, a mock curiosity displayed all over her face.

"Where's Allie? You're not Allie Hilts. You're not the cantankerous introvert with the perpetually pissy grimace who's lost faith in all and everything." She grabs me by the shoulders and shakes me. "What did you do with her? If you've harmed a hair on her head, by God I'll . . ."

"I know a troupe of eleven-year-olds," I say, "With acting skills like those, you'll fit right in."

But she's not listening. Instead, she's staring at me, seriously this time, examining me. She lets go of me and walks around me in a circle, eyeballing me up and down. It's making me uncomfortable.

"Doc—" I begin.

"You're glowing, Allie," she says. "Actually glowing. You have an actual aura around you. In medical terms, you look alive, part of the living world, for the first time since I met you. What happened to you?"

Doc's too smart. She's figured out that Sam . . . Well, I think she's figured out that something has happened with me. But I can't tell her about Sam, so I do what anyone else in these circumstances would do: I flat-out lie.

"You're high, Doc. It's just a sunburn. Come on, get serious."

She doesn't remotely buy it. "Nice try," she says. "E for effort. I'll stop hounding you, because I have work to do here, but one day you will tell me what happened to elicit this new physiological response."

"Whatever. What's going on, Doc?"

Doc returns to her desk, sits back down, massages her shoulder. "I made some tweaks," she tells me. "Did some fine-tuning, played God as best I could, and finally injected our man Jacob Roman—"

"—who believes in extraterrestrials—"

"—with a new serum." She stretches. "And, yes," she says, "there's been a slight change in his XXY genome: preliminary tests show that his new Y-gene is diminishing to resemble that of a normal male, and his X is growing." She gives me a stern look over the top of her glasses. "We're in early stages, though. Now I have to make sure it continues to develop. But these walls are paper-thin, and our fellow women like to talk."

I walk over to the cages, to the one marked JACOB ROMAN, and stare in. He's remarkably relaxed for a feral. He's not leaking bloody mucus, either, like all the others do as they approach death. That's an improvement, definitely. He's just sitting there, expression almost placid, anything but feral. I move closer to the cage, and his lips start to curl up, but I can't tell if he's trying to snarl or trying to grin. Maybe he can't tell, either, because after a few seconds his mouth relaxes again and he reverts to that same look of placid, vacant contentment.

I come back to Doc. "When will you know if it's for real?" I ask.

"It's a virus," she says. "Just like the one that started this trouble. It works its magic fast and furiously, so we will know, for better or worse or somewhere in between, soon enough."

"How soon is soon enough?" I ask.

She shakes her head. "I wish I knew, Allie," she says.

Will soon enough really be soon enough? I wonder. Depends when the hordes of ferals overrun our doorstep.

Doc's expression flattens out. Her voice turns serious. "At Arcon, the sciences failed us. Or we failed as scientists. Either way, the science and the scientist need to be right this time. This needs to work, Allie."

"Not a very scientific thing to say, Doc," I say before I can stop myself.

Her expression sags with guilt. I can't help noticing it. "The disaster's not your fault, Doc," I say, though I have to admit that, yes, part of me does think it *is* her fault. "No one thinks that." These aren't lies, exactly, but they're also not exactly the truth.

She reaches out and pats my cheek. "That's very sweet of you, young lady," she says. And then, almost to herself, "I just wish it was enough to let me sleep at night."

I ignore this. For a moment I consider telling her that we're about to be overrun, but then think, no, don't distract her, let her keep working on her cure. Maybe she's managed to make it so that we don't need to leave. "You need new ferals," I say. "You're running low."

## Chapter Thirty-three

# Allie

I'm on the roof, in the highest perch. I have a lot to sort through and don't want any background noise while I do so. Jacky seems to be digging in, still thinking she can outfight the ferals. Doc is making her big push for a cure, but is she getting anywhere? And even if she is, isn't that the very thing that should make me try my hardest to get her to a safe place as quickly as possible? And then there's me, pushing for a way out. The camp is being tugged in three directions at once.

If I leave, who can I safely take with me? Kim, of course—I can't leave without Kim. I'm responsible for her, I'm her only family. I'd take Doc if she'd go, but will she? Probably not. She's too close to a solution, so she thinks, and is too committed to figuring the vaccine out—she won't want to leave her lab behind. If I were to tell her about Sam, tell her the whole truth, it might be enough to get her to go. . . .

No, I can't do that. I can't just snatch a few women up and leave the rest of them to die. I'd regret it for the rest of my life. I'd have almost four dozen deaths on my head. I can't live with that. I shouldn't even be entertaining the idea.

So what do I do? Stay here and cross my fingers and hope like hell we survive?

After a while, Kim comes up the ladder. I can tell it's her by the way she breathes. She just stands there to the side of me, watching me look out through the binoculars.

"What do you see?" she asks.

"Nothing," I say.

"That's good, right?" she says.

I shrug. "It's not good, it's not bad, it's nothing." I hand the binoculars to her. "Here," I say. "Take a look."

She lifts them, begins to scan. "Slower," I say. "Relax into it."

"What am I looking for?" she asks.

"You're looking for whatever doesn't belong. You'll sense it more than see it. Then you'll just wait, stay attentive; and suddenly you'll see it."

She sweeps the binoculars slowly, then, just as slowly, sweeps them back.

"It's good for you to learn this," I say. "If something happens to me, then it'll be your job to—"

"Don't say that," she says.

"Don't say what?"

"That something might happen to you," she says. "Who says it will?"

"Who says it won't?"

"I just—"

"You have to be prepared for anything," I say. "If you're not prepared, you'll die."

She hands the binoculars back to me and heads down the ladder. She's pissed, I can tell.

"You have to be prepared for more than just the worst," she says, just before she disappears. "If you're not, why bother?"

"Kim," I say. "Kim!"

But she doesn't come back. Like hell if I'm going to apologize. Like hell if I'm going after her.


When evening comes, I'm alone and on my perch, staring out, just letting my thoughts wander around, hoping that something will suddenly sort itself out and reveal itself for me and I'll know what to do when I see it. But I'm not getting anywhere. I see movement out there, almost invisible in the darkness. I raise my binoculars and scan the tree line, slowly, patiently, until I catch sight of it again.

It's Scarface. He's alone—or, if the other ferals are with him, they're out of sight, deeper in the trees. He is staring through the fence straight at the farmhouse, eyeing it, considering it in a way that I didn't think ferals were capable of. In a way that I *hoped* ferals weren't capable of. He's special, this one, and not in a good way. What are you up to, you bastard? Just preparing to lead an army of hundreds of your deadly little brothers over our fence?

I need my rifle. If I was quick enough, I might get him this time.

He makes his way back and forth along the fence, looking at the farmhouse from different angles. I can tell he's limping from where Sam cut him with the machete.

Sam. I can't stop thinking about him.

Fuck Sam. He left. Scarface is there, skulking around. He's the only kind of man left in the world, at least in my part of the world. And he needs to be killed.

## Chapter Thirty-four

By noon, she was flat on the roof of an enormous home, overlooking a once-affluent community that was now destroyed. She had a map spread out in front of her and had been busy for the last forty-five minutes, at different places and on different roofs, crossing out streets and circling potential escape routes, noting all the ferals she saw and where.

Through the binoculars she was watching some of them, a group of about twenty, a large crowd. What do you call a group of ferals? she wondered, playing again with that pet question of hers. It was "a murder of crows," though "a murder of ferals" had a nice ring to it as well. Jacky would say "a motherfuck of ferals." Doc would probably call them "a skulk of test subjects" or something like that. Or maybe even Doc would agree with "motherfuck." "A fury of ferals?" That was pretty good.

They were feeding, feasting on a jumble of decimated animal carcasses. Fast food—but not fast enough. She watched them intently as they tore the carcasses open, swallowing down gobbets of flesh, lapping up the puddling blood, fighting over the scraps. None of them were faces she'd seen before.

She had put down the binoculars and was recording the group on the map when she heard a *crick* sound, not far distant. Alerted, she scanned the area. She spied a hint of movement on an adjacent roof, something so fleeting that she wasn't completely sure she had even seen it—or, if she had, whether it might just have been a bird. Though she kept her eyes focused on that rooftop for a long time, not moving her gaze, the movement didn't come again. She waited longer, but still nothing appeared, so she returned to her map, marking routes, charting possible paths of escape.

Later in the day, she had managed to trace one escape route as far as the local college. She had climbed up into the bell tower of the campus church and from there had a view of the entire campus, where she could mark possible obstacles or likely escape routes. The place was outside of her normal range: she hadn't been on the college grounds since attending a lacrosse camp there her sophomore year, back before the world died. Then the campus had been picturesque and well manicured; now it was overgrown, the plants beginning slowly to swallow the buildings.

The problem, she realized, was that she didn't know what might be inside the buildings, whether there were places the ferals might bed down. Places that looked safe now might look anything but a few minutes after dark.

She was scanning the area through her sniper scope, thinking, weighing the advantages of staying out after dark and seeing what changed against the dangers of being out in a relatively unfamiliar place on her own, when she came upon something in the scope that stopped her cold.

There, about seven hundred yards away, just past the end of the campus, the highway was teeming with movement. It was a group of ferals, a fury; the largest she had ever seen. They crossed the highway like a demonic parade. There were at least fifty of them.

*We're dead*, she thought. *We didn't leave when we had the chance, and now it's too late.* They were, as far as she could tell at this distance, all newbies. Now there were dozens—even hundreds—of new ferals in the area, swarms and swarms of the fuckers.

She had lowered the scope and was making notes on the map when she heard it. A clicking sound coming from somewhere below here, somewhere close. She leaned out to get a better view of the street and just managed to see, below, the front door of the church quietly closing. Something had just entered.

*Holy shit*, she thought.

Her mind began to race. Quickly she folded the map. She sheathed the sniper rifle on her back and took out her Ruger SP101, screwing a homemade silencer onto the end of the barrel. How much time did she have? Had it smelled her or just come into the church for some other reason, acting on some last, short-circuited bit of humanity?

She opened the trapdoor in the floor of the bell tower and climbed down as close to silently as possible to the floor below.

She moved slowly, stealthily, gun raised, ready to fire. She had to hope that the silencer would muffle the noise enough that the ferals out on the highway wouldn't hear this one die and get curious.

At the corner, she gathered herself and then quickly spun around it, ready to fire. Nothing. She continued along the hall, clearing the rooms to either side, until she came to the staircase.

She descended carefully, stopping every few steps to listen. Nothing. Very slowly, she made it down to the bottom and to the door leading into the chapel proper.

She eased it quietly open and entered. She had come out behind the altar, with good cover. Staying near the walls, where the shadows were deepest, she scanned the vast church. The light piercing the stained-glass windows cast shadows dyed red and blue and yellow. She looked around, looked some more, tense, alert.

It was too quiet.

Part of her wanted to make a break for it. Another part knew that she had to wait, play it out, carefully and cautiously. Time was on her side. Those two parts were arguing with one another within her when the floor behind her creaked.

She spun and fired a shot that went wild and buried itself in the woodwork.

"Hold on! Stop shooting! It's me, Sam!"

Allie froze. She looked for him, searching everywhere, seeing nobody. And then Sam stood slowly, emerging from between some of the church pews. He looked rattled.

They locked eyes. Her mouth was agape; she felt like she had just seen a ghost.

"Christ, Sam," she said, "I almost shot you. What the hell are you doing here? You should be gone already!"

"I was out looking for supplies," Sam claimed. "I saw you up in the tower."

He sidled to the end of the pew and came up the aisle toward her. Seeing him in the flesh was almost more than she could stand. And then something clicked.

"You've been following me," she said.

Sam refused to meet her eyes. For a moment he was speechless, red-faced, unsure of what to say. And then he nodded, and Allie's irritation diminished. Sam had been following her, trying to keep her safe. Of course, it was a misguided impulse—she knew how to take care of herself—and that was irritating. But at the same time, she couldn't help being a little flattered that the idiot hadn't gone south, that he'd stayed to look out for her.

"What the fuck, Sam?" she asked. "Shouldn't you be getting out of here before all hell breaks loose instead of stalking me?"

Sam still seemed awkward, not even trying to answer. But he did look up, finally, and meet her eyes, and there was enough in them to tell her that, no, he didn't feel like he had better things to do, that he felt this, right here, was the best thing for him to do.

"You're not in a hurry to leave, are you," she said.

He shook his head.

"Why not?" she said. "You sure as shit can't come into West Staten. That's a death sentence."

"I know."

"So—why're you still hanging around?"

"It's just . . ."

She waited for him to go on, holding his gaze a long time, intensely. He gave a big sigh, and then a tentative smile. Finally, he spoke.

"Come on," he said. "I want to show you something."


He led her across campus, both of them moving swiftly and silently, and into an athletics building. They crossed an indoor track thick with dust and entered a men's locker room, with windows shattered, the lockers broken, clothing scattered everywhere. In the back was a set of concrete stairs. He led her down them and into a long, narrow, dark tunnel, and when she hesitated, he took her hand and guided her forward.

At first, it was almost impossible to see where they were going, but then her eyes adjusted and she saw, at the far end, a dim light.

"Where are you taking me?" she asked as the light swelled.

He didn't bother to answer. They continued on. She could see enough to walk fine on her own now, but she didn't let go of his hand. The light, now that she could see, was an opening, and she caught sight beyond it of something metallic, and above that a hint of sky. The floor of the tunnel underwent a slight incline, which they climbed up to step out of the tunnel and into the light.

Allie's jaw dropped. "Holy shit," she said, and let go of Sam's hand.

She was in a stadium, a massive one, seemingly empty. The size of the place was breathtaking, maybe fifty thousand seats in all. The grass on the field was five feet high, shivering in the wind.

"Follow me," he said.

They walked along the ramp and toward the field. The stadium was completely empty except for a pack of dogs that was wandering the mezzanine, searching for food. Sam and Allie stepped out onto the field and into the tall grass, and were pushing their way through it.

They'd only gone a little way when Sam pointed to something on the ground, nearly hidden by the tall, thick foliage.

Though Allie looked, at first she couldn't make out what it was. She got closer, but it wasn't until she was very close indeed that she realized it was a series of musical instruments, covered over by grass as if they were small burial mounds. She and Sam began to root them out: brass horns, trumpets, tubas, snare drums, cymbals, more. There were dozens of pieces scattered about.

"Marching band must have been on the field when infection hit," she said.

He nodded. "Come on," he said.

They continued wading forward through the grass, stepping around the remaining mounds of instruments, as Sam led her across to the far side of the field. There he parted the grass and showed her a dilapidated sports-equipment bench. It was laden with lacrosse gear.

Sam took up a crosse. "Lacrosse team must have been practicing as well," he said. He turned to her, smiled. "You said you played," he said, and held the crosse out to her.

Allie accepted the crosse with a little bow. She stared at it, smiling. "I haven't held one of these since the day it all happened," she said.

She bent down and searched around near the base of the sports bench until she found a ball. She threw it up and caught it in the crosse's pocket, tossed it up and down.

Sam watched her, enjoying the way she was caught up in the moment, in the almost hypnotic movement of the ball. He turned and took up another crosse. A moment later, her concentration was broken when he snatched the ball away.

"Is that a challenge?" she asked, still smiling. "Really?"

"You claimed you were good," he said. "Bring it."

"You're really ready to have your ass handed to you on a plate?" she asked.

Sam's only response was simply to turn the ball deep into the pocket and run off into the high grass, baiting her. For a moment, she looked after him, amazed, and then her competitiveness kicked in and she took off in pursuit.

## Chapter Thirty-five

# Allie

He's fast, but not quite as fast as me, not when he has to break a path through the grass. He doesn't know the game like I do, doesn't know how to cut and double without losing his momentum. Though, I do have to admit, he's better than I thought he would be. There he is, hauling ass across the field, and I'm following him, letting him do all the work in terms of breaking a path until I'm just right directly behind him, watching his crosse, waiting for the right moment, the moment when I can leap and stretch and snatch the ball right out of it. For a moment, he doesn't even realize it's gone. When he does, he puts on the brakes and tears back around, but I'm already ahead, crashing through the long grass toward the overgrown goal. I'm smiling and he's smiling, and I haven't let loose like this in a long time, not since before civilization fell apart. He's there beside me, cutting his own path rather than following in mine, which slows him down some, but he's still getting ahead of me, trying to get well in front so he can defend the goal. He cuts in front of me and tries to take me down, but I use his chest as a kind of step and shoot over his head and score. He's on the ground, and I'm still on my feet, doing my victory dance right over him. It's been three years since I've done that dance, but it comes back without effort, like riding a bike. My body just knows it.

"Want another shot, sport?" I ask. "Or are you ready to say 'uncle'?"

He gets up, smiling. "Don't go easy on me this time," he says.

He jogs over to the goal and feels around in the grass until he comes up with the ball. I take up a stance mid-field, legs bent, and wait for him.

He comes at me slow and cautious, and he's better than I thought he'd be at not telegraphing his moves. He fakes cutting left and then accelerates right, around me, but is again soon plunging through long grass, and I just follow behind, slowly catching up. And then I—inadvertently, of course, I swear that was an accident, ref!—trip him and drive him hard to the ground. I growl at him—just showing him who's boss—and then am up and off, with the ball.

I'm running fast, back along the path we've already beaten in the grass, but then I can hear him too close behind me and I dive into the thicker grass and start weaving. I'm short enough that, crouched, he's going to have a hard time keeping a bead on me, and with a little luck I'll hit one of the trails we've already stomped before he catches me.

But just as I'm thinking this, I feel the breath go out of me as I'm tackled and knocked to the ground, grass whipping across my face and getting in my mouth. Not exactly legal, but what the hell—we're a little short in terms of team members, too, and usually you don't play in five-foot-tall grass. The ball pops out of my crosse, and the crosse goes flying, and there I am, grabbing for the ball, and Sam's grabbing for it, too. We're rolling through the grass, scrambling, knocking it out of one another's hands, grabbing, pulling, wrestling, until finally, somehow, I have it. Sam is on top of me, trying, it feels like, to walk up my body and get the ball. I hold it tight against my chest with both hands, and he's straddling me now, his hips against my hips, pinning me down, grabbing at the ball, both of us laughing, lost in the moment.

And then he catches my eye, and I see in his eye something that calls to me, to what I'm feeling beneath the roughhousing and playing, a warmth that I love. A warmth that frightens me. I stop moving and he stops, too, and we both stay motionless, breathing heavily. After a moment, he smiles.

"You are pretty good," he says.

"And you're pretty damn average," I say.

He rolls off and lies there beside me for a long time, the two of us not quite touching but almost, happy there together, looking up into the sky.

It's kind of like a date. It's definitely the best date with a guy I've had in three years, that goes without saying, but it's more than that. I mean, my dates with the ferals always ended up with me stringing their corpses up and disemboweling them. And even back with boys like Jared, back before everything went wrong with the world, I didn't feel like this. Like I wish we could just stay together in this ruined stadium forever and never leave.

We do stay a long time, playing, joking. We're still there as the light starts to fade. We're up at the top of the stadium now, in the uppermost row of the bleachers, because I've promised to show him how to do the wave. Hard to imagine doing the wave with just two people, but if you use your imagination you can make it happen.

I feel like I'm a totally different person, living in a totally different world. I feel like the world is just me and Sam and that that's all that matters, and I feel happy and relaxed. I try not to think of Kim. Every time I do, I feel guilty.

"Like this," I tell him, standing up and sitting down, standing up and sitting down. "Remember, no slouching."

And he's not bored. He's not just going along with it to make me happy. He is enjoying himself just as much as I am. I can tell from his broad smile, from the way his eyes smile, too, when he looks at me.

"You clearly practice this," he claims. Then he pretends like he's reading from a day planner. "Today's schedule: 7:00 a.m., wake up; 7:05 a.m., brush teeth; 7:10 to noon, practice the wave."

"Very funny," I say. "If you're going to do the wave, you've got to do it properly. Come on, do it with me."

I pull him up, forcing him to do the wave in the stadium. Up and down, up and down, up and down, until we're both laughing hysterically. Then, winded, we sit again. Our laughter slows, stops.

We sit in a comfortable silence for a while until I say, the old Allie coming back, "The world is coming to an end and we're practicing the perfect wave."

I look at him and he looks at me, and the two of us just sit there looking at one another. I don't want to leave. He doesn't want to leave, either. We want to be together. We belong together.

Wait a minute—am I insane? I've got my sister to think about.

Still, it's kind of nice just to look at him, and have him looking at me.

"Doc's working on a vaccine," I say. "I mean, she's always been working on a vaccine, but this time it seems like it's working."

"Yeah?" he says.

"Yeah," I say. "Maybe you won't have to leave after all."

Sam looks away. He doesn't believe it, I can tell, doesn't want to accept false hope. "It's getting late," he says, and I know this is the start of a good-bye. We might not see each other again, not ever. That's a corny thing to think. *Snap out of it, Allie!* But I don't want to snap out of it.

"I've been camping at the library in the town where we met," he says. "Food, supplies inside." And then he stops and turns back toward me, his expression at once hopeful and anxious. "You could . . . hole up there, too. . . ."

*Yes*, that part of me I'm trying to silence is thinking, *yes!* I feign anger, contempt. "With you?" I say. "Who do you think I am?"

His look drops fast and hard into embarrassment and shame. When he starts speaking, he's stuttering.

"I'm s-sorry—I—"

And then I laugh, punching him playfully on the shoulder.

"Relax. I'm just bustin' on ya," I say.

He loosens up and grins, his expression extremely relieved.

I'm relieved, too. Relieved that he's not too hurt, relieved that our time together doesn't have to end. Sure, it's a little cheesy of me to think that, but, well, that's how it goes.

## Chapter Thirty-six

# Allie

We walk down the sidewalk, past ruined, ransacked shops, past the bits of bone and hair and cloth I hardly even notice anymore, keeping to the shadows, being very, very quiet. We have both been doing this for a long time, and know almost by reflex how to travel carefully and safely. It's a good thing we do, because we've got other things on our minds now—we would probably be fucking up if this weren't second nature to us.

We've got our guns dangling at our sides, in ready reach. Sam's is between him and me. Eventually, he unslings it and slings it over the other shoulder, trying to be discreet about it, casual, just so there won't be anything between us. I almost tease him about it, but I know enough to stop myself—I want to see what happens next.

At first, nothing happens next. We just keep walking. And then I notice that he is letting his hand dangle next to mine, that every once in a while the back of it brushes against the back of mine. A little coy, I have to say. And so I decide to help him along. I reach out and take his hand in my own.

For a moment, he just lets his hand stay there, motionless and stiff, and then, suddenly, his hand comes alive and holds on to mine.

We don't speak. We just walk, getting closer and closer to the library. I glance over at him and he glances over at me, and we smile and glance, glance and smile, each of us intensely aware of the other person.

It's going well, moving along nicely—not exactly storybook romance, given the post-apocalyptic setting, but still. Then, suddenly, Sam's face falls, and he stops dead. After listening for an instant, he grabs me, pulls me behind a car.

"Did you hear—" I start to say.

"Not sure," he responds, but it's clear from his face he thinks he must have. "Let's move. Quick."

We are jogging now, padding along as quickly as possible while staying quiet, no more hand holding, back in alert mode, back to real life. How could I have let myself go like that? It's not smart. It's how people end up dead.

This time, I'm the one who stops abruptly. Sam slows and doubles back, but by then I'm moving again.

"You're right," I tell him as we both continue to jog. "They're tracking us. Tracking me." Because I know it must be me. They don't even smell Sam, don't think of him as anything but one of them when they think of him at all. I'm the one who smells different. "They're not far," I say.

Then, almost as if on cue, we hear the unearthly wail of a feral, howling in the night.

"Damn it," I say. "We know better than this." I reach around for my pack, but the pack is not there. How could I not have noticed until now? I think back, rewind the day, until I arrive at the moment where I see myself putting it down in the bell tower of the church and never picking it up again. I curse under my breath. I've just signed my death warrant.

"Shit, Sam," I say. "I left my bag with the extra blood back in the tower."

He looks at me. His brow furrows and his eyes dart around as he looks for a solution, some way out. The bell tower is far behind us now—we'd never make it. And the library is too far away. Then he looks at me.

"Your clothes, Allie," he says. "Take them off. Leave them here. Now."

I get it. Abandon my clothes and leave a smell source. It'll buy us at least a little time. I start undressing right there in the middle of the street.

"This is one hell of a way to get me naked, Sam," I say.

He smiles back, fleetingly. He's worried. I am, too. We hear another moan, closer now. Sam's face is pale and tense, and I'd guess mine looks at least that bad, maybe a lot worse.

My gun's on the ground, and I've managed to get my shirt off and my sports bra, too. I'm conscious that he's there, watching me, conscious of how weird a way this is to see someone you like naked. My face can't decide whether to blush from embarrassment or blanch with fear. I kick off my shoes and quickly pull off my pants, and then, in my underpants, I can't keep myself from looking over at Sam.

But he's not even looking at me. He's kicking through the rubble with his boots until he finds something and picks it up. When he turns back to me, I see it's a long shard of glass. I just have time to take this in when he draws it across his forearm, opening a long gash. I almost cry out, but manage to stifle it, and then think, *We're not just leaving a smell source, we're saving my life.*

He lets the shard fall and comes toward me, his face tight with pain. He's cupped his hand under the wound and is gathering the blood there. As soon as he's in range, he begins smearing it on me. I'm running my fingers along his wound, gathering blood as well, and smearing it. He massages his arm, milks the wound. We keep smearing and rubbing, and then he picks the shard back up and with a grimace opens the wound deeper to get a little more blood. It's at once terrifying and sensual, his hands and warm blood almost more than I can bear.

The ferals are wailing. They're getting closer—a pack for sure, and not that far away. I smear blood under my armpits and then bend down and pick up my shirt. I tear a strip off it and tourniquet his arm, and then we're running again, as more howls rise. We're hand in hand again, a strange pair: me, nearly nude and smeared in Sam's blood, and Sam, tourniquet already soaking through and blood dripping down his arm, as we run through the streets of just your everyday, ordinary, devastated, skeleton-ridden, post-apocalyptic American town.

We run faster, hearing the cries of frustration behind us. They've no doubt found my clothing by now, but don't know where to go from there. They've lost the scent. Fingers crossed that Sam's blood is enough to keep them from picking it up again.

Sam tugs on my hand, and we're in the street now, heading toward a large brick building that must be the library. We enter in a burst, and Sam darts to a supply pack right next to the front door, removing several bottles of feral blood. Hurriedly, he shakes them and douses the ground just outside the library, and then he slams the door shut.

He turns, his back pressed against the door, and looks at me like he can't believe we're safe. I can hardly believe it, either. And then he smiles, and I can't help smiling back. And then he takes a step and nearly faints. Immediately I'm beside him, supporting him, hardly aware of my nakedness.

"Come on," I say. "Let's take care of your arm. Where's your med kit?"

He takes hold of my arm and leads me to the nearby stairs. He's okay now, seems to be, but I'm there just in case he gets faint again. How much blood has he lost? More than is healthy, that's for damn sure.

He leads me to the second floor. We pass aisles of old, musty books and dusty corridors until we reach an open area between aisles, what must once have been a reading area. Sam gestures. He's pale now. His stuff is here, a rolled-out sleeping bag, a neatly folded towel, an extra gun, a first-aid kit, several bottles of water.

In the first-aid kit I find a tube of Krazy glue, some gauze pads. I open a bottle of water and irrigate the wound and then pat it dry with the towel, hoping it's relatively clean. Then I open the Krazy glue and squeeze it into the wound, pulling the lips of it shut as Sam winces. I hold them firmly as I count to twenty and then let go and examine my handiwork. Not exactly perfectly lined up—it'll leave a hell of a scar—but at least it isn't bleeding anymore.

"There," I say, "good as new."

I look up and find that he's staring at me. I stare back, suddenly conscious of my nakedness again, blushing a little. Then he reaches out and takes the towel out of my hand. He sloshes water onto a corner of it and begins to wipe the blood away from my body.

After a moment, I close my eyes. The damp towel makes my skin tingle as he daubs my face, my neck, my shoulders. And then he stops for a moment, and then, very gently, daubs clean the upper swell of my breasts.

I open my eyes and see he's watching me, his eyes smoldering. For a moment, time stops, and then I lean forward and kiss him. At first it's a gentle kiss, just a way of reaching out, exploring what might be there, but as he responds and as I respond back it becomes quickly more and more passionate, and both of us are very quickly swept away.

We fall slowly to the floor, still kissing. I can hardly breathe, my heart beating hard in my throat, my body feeling like it's on fire. My fingers are fumbling with Sam's clothing, bluntly nudging the buttons, tearing his shirt off, unbuckling his pants, and his hands are on my hips, easing my panties slowly off. For a moment, my hands get fumbly and can't do anything right, and then we're both naked and I'm on top of him. He pulls me close for another long kiss and my hands are all over him and his are all over me and I find him and slide around him, and then, for a very long while, I forget who I am.

## Chapter Thirty-seven

Harsh early sunlight poured through the windows, making motes of dust whirl in the air. Below, on the floor, on a sleeping bag that had been unzipped and opened like a bed, Allie and Sam slept.

Allie awakened first. Her eyes flicked around as she tried to understand where she was, finally coming to rest on Sam's arm wrapped around her. She lifted her head from his bare chest, looked at his face. For a long moment she just stared, considering him, and then she stretched forward and kissed him.

"Morning," said Allie, softly.

"Morning to you," said Sam.

They looked at one another for a long moment. "I should go," Allie finally managed.

Sam pulled her close and hugged her, and then, when she turned her face up, he kissed her, a deep, long, passionate kiss. He was the one to start it, but he was also the one to break off and pull away.

"Get the hell out of here right now or I'm locking you in this library with me," he said.

They shared a smile, laughter, another kiss, at the end of which Allie pulled her face away from his and just stared, her expression slowly sagging. *This is doomed*, she was thinking. He was leaving, he had to leave. She had just found someone, and now she was going to lose him.

"Come with me," he said. "You and your sister. The three of us could make it. Head down to the southern territories together."

She considered it. Maybe the two of them could make it, but the two of them plus Kim was a less likely proposition, and he knew it. She shook her head. "Traveling with us would be too dangerous for you," she said.

"There has to be a way," he said.

"I can't leave them, Sam," said Allie. "Not just Kim. The others as well. I just can't. Not now. I can't just desert them. You know that."

"But isn't it better to save at least a few of you? Why would you want to die with them?"

"All of us or none, Sam."

For a long moment Sam held her gaze, and then he sighed. He nodded. He knew. He shrugged. "Can't blame a guy for trying," he said.

She reached out and took his hand, squeezed it.

"Maybe you won't have to leave," she said. "Doc's made some progress with her vaccine. Maybe the vaccine will work and everything will be okay again."

Did she believe it? No, not exactly—she was still a skeptic. But she wanted to believe now, desperately.


Forty minutes later, she'd looted a Target for clothing and was back on her bike and cutting a swath down a forest path. They had agreed Sam would wait a day to see what happened with the vaccine, and she suspected he'd wait two at least—if the vaccine changed things, then there was no need for him to have to stay hidden. She went to the bell tower to get back her pack, did a little looting to justify the trip, and now she was heading back to West Staten. The whole way, she had peered around for ferals, but she had seen none, not even from a distance, which was a little unusual. Maybe, she thought, they had just moved on through and were continuing to head farther north.

*Yeah, right,* another part of her thought, *fat fucking chance.*

She slowed as she approached the farmhouse. She raised her radio, keyed it, spoke.

"Coming in," she said. "No visitors."

She slowed further, expecting the gate to open, but it remained closed. She glanced in her handlebar mirror, and that was when she saw it.

A feral. Close, maybe twenty yards behind her.

She slowed to a stop, keeping the bike in neutral, observing the feral in the mirror. It was *him*. She knew it. Scarface. He stood there, unmoving, waiting, watching her.

And then, from behind him in the brush, twenty more ferals emerged. A small army, stopping a few yards shy of their leader. *Oh shit*, thought Allie, suddenly feeling very afraid. She watched as the lips of two of them curled into a grimace and they started forward. They moved toward her, snarling—behavior she was more used to from ferals than Scarface's reaction—but she was surprised to find that the others stayed where they were. She flashed out her gun, ready to kill at least those two before the others tore her apart.

She was just preparing to shoot when she saw Scarface raise his arm high. Just as suddenly as they had begun running toward her, the two ferals stopped cold.

She watched Scarface, knowing that her life likely depended on what he did next. If she killed just him, what would happen? Would all the others suddenly go back to their usual feral behavior and rush at her? "How's the leg, motherfucker?" she called to him, not a yell exactly but louder than her normal voice. He gazed steadily at her, his expression unreadable, and then, suddenly, he turned, and disappeared into the brush. A moment later, the other twenty followed, filing silently away. Soon, it was as if none of them had been there at all.

*Did that really just happen?* she wondered—one feral directing the movements of a number of others, a kind of miniature army? That was very bad news. It meant at least one feral was smart and crafty and able to hold back his rage long enough to develop a plan, a strategy. The women were in real trouble. Maybe even more trouble than she'd already suspected.

Her thoughts were interrupted by the sound of the gate opening. She stared into the scrub for just a moment more, then resheathed her gun and settled back onto the bike's seat. Kicking it into gear she went through.

She drove through the camp, carefully navigating the safe path through the minefield. There was, she saw, something new up ahead, near the farmhouse—probably the reason it had taken so long to open the gates. It caught the sun, something large and glimmering. It had almost cost her her life—it would have, if Scarface hadn't held the others back. Why had he?

As she came closer, she saw clearly what it was: a huge retrofitted armored truck, ominous and impressive. She rolled up near it and parked, and then went in on foot for a closer look. It was fortified with two-inch steel bulwarks—not just the body, but every door, every window, every tire.

She stared at it for a long moment and then turned and strode away, entering the house.

The women were gathered inside the common room, and even before she reached them she could hear the rumble of worry and concern. She turned the corner and found them all seated and looking at Jacky, who stood in the front of the room, Doc beside her. Near them, also standing and a little to the side, were two women she didn't recognize, one of them tall and earthy, the other short-haired and wearing soldier gear, her body rock-hard and ripped.

Jacky made shushing movements with her hands, trying to stop the murmurs of the crowd.

"Everyone settle the fuck down," she said. "I know you have a million questions. Let's start with names. This here is Leslie," and at this the tall one nodded, "and Dallas," at which the soldier raised her fist. "They're from Hubbard. Some of you may know of it. It's about three hundred miles west of us. Their camp was hit by an army of ferals, months ago. Fifty-two women lived there. Dallas and Leslie are all that are left, and they're probably only alive because they were out on patrol when the attack hit. That's fifty dead." The rumbles started again, and Jacky folded her arms, waited for them to calm down. When they finally did, she said, "In their travels since, they have come upon a number of northern camps that have also been attacked. Including our neighboring camp, Huguenot." More murmurs. "Yes, Naomi's camp," she said, turning her head, picking up on whispers to her left. "They're gone. All of them. Wiped out."

The murmurs, when they came this time, were quieter, more subdued, tempered by fear and shock and grief.

"I know," Jacky said. "It's fucked, big-time. Dallas and Leslie are confirming something that has recently come to our attention," and her eyes floated to Allie in the back of the room. "The migration of thousands of ferals from the south into our region."

The murmurs were louder now, fear beginning to overcome the shock and grief. Allie watched their reaction, the terror in their eyes, the jerkiness of their movements. *These women*, thought Allie, *had no idea. They thought they could just keep on living here forever. I should have broken it to them slowly, over time. I shouldn't have kept it from them. I should have let everybody know the moment that I began seeing more ferals, not just Jacky.*

She caught Jacky's eye, saw the grim set of her jaw. *However it should have been done*, Jacky's expression seemed to say, *this is the way we're doing it. No matter how much of a shock it is, we have to tell them all of it now.*

"West Staten is dead. We need to leave. Not in months or weeks. We have days, maybe just hours," said Jacky, voice raised over the continuing murmurs. "We move south before winter hits. We don't have any choice."

The rumbling increased in volume, the confusion increasing as well. An older woman named Sabra stood, shouting to be heard over the others. "How?" she asked. "Just have forty-eight of us drive in a caravan a thousand miles south? We'll attract hundreds of ferals, maybe even thousands. We won't make it a mile."

The murmurs grew louder. A few women looked confused and kept glancing to Jacky for guidance. Other women were nodding, agreeing with Sabra. Others were whispering to one another, panic in their faces.

*Don't you get it?* thought Allie. *Leaving's the only way. If you stay here, you're dead.*

But of course they didn't get it. They hadn't seen the camp she had seen, hadn't seen how Scarface was out there right now, sizing up their walls, considering their security defenses. Jacky's telling them wasn't enough.

Jacky raised her voice. "We don't have the answers," she said. "I wish to God we did, but we don't. But we have to figure something out. We need to make a move before this area ends up being overrun."

"And how are we going to do that?" asked Sabra.

Jacky shrugged. "We're looking into every option," she said.

"Translation: we don't have any idea," said Sabra.

Jacky shrugged.

"We could take a boat," said Holly, her voice quavering. "I can pilot it."

"Where are we going to get a boat big enough?" asked Jacky.

"There are plenty of boats in the harbor," said Holly.

Jacky laughed and made a dismissive gesture with her hand. "What, you going to crew it with a gang of ferals? No fucking way we're getting near those boats." She looked around the room. "Anybody else got any better ideas?"

And with that the murmurs dried up. It was as if people were afraid even to talk, to do anything but just sit there, exchanging looks of dread. Scanning the crowd, Allie found Kim, who looked stunned. Allie started moving through the crowd and toward her.

And then Jacky stepped back and nodded to Doc, and Doc stepped forward to take her place. But it was a different Doc from the one Allie knew. Her playfulness and hippie poet swagger had crumpled. She was deadly serious for a change, and very focused.

"There's more," she said, and all eyes were turned toward her now—looking, as they always looked to Doc, for support and consolation.

Doc nodded to Dallas and Leslie. They glanced at one another, and then, taking a deep breath, Dallas stepped forward.

She was strong, Allie saw—that was immediately obvious from her corded arms, the power and confidence of her bearing as she walked a few feet to take center stage, the way no movement or gesture was wasted. But what was less obvious initially was how beautiful the woman was. She had chosen strength and survival over displaying that beauty, but once she began to speak it started to seep through again, and Allie found herself hoping that, in fifteen years, this was the kind of woman she would become.

Dallas let her glance travel slowly around the room. Silence fell. "Actually, three people survived the massacre," she said. "Two of us were female. One was a male." She waited a moment, but Allie knew what she was going to add before she actually said it. "An uninfected male. Nonferal."

Judging from the long, shocked silence, Allie was the only one who had seen what was coming. The other women were speechless and stunned, seemingly not even able to move. And then, suddenly, there was a tidal wave of noise, all the women talking at once, shouting questions, blabbering, crying.

*Oh shit*, thought Allie. *They're looking for Sam. They've come here looking for Sam. These are the women that kept him in a cage. That tried to breed him.*

What was she to do? These were the women who had drugged him, had treated him like a laboratory animal. On an abstract level, Allie could understand that—he was, after all, their one hope for salvation, and just a few days ago she'd captured him herself. But she'd listened to him, and she'd let him out. And now that she'd gotten to know Sam, now that she'd become friends with him, now that she'd slept with him, now that she'd fallen in love with him, she couldn't think of him that way. She was not going to rat him out.

"What's his name, Doc?" asked Allie as the noise died down.

"What?" Doc said.

"Even the ferals we assign names to," said Allie, trying to keep the anger out of her voice. "Why not just call him by his name instead of 'the uninfected male'? Doesn't he deserve that?"

At this, the room erupted again, women talking over one another.

"Please," said Doc, "stay calm. Time is no longer on our side."

She gestured to Dallas, who nodded. "This *male*," she said, emphasizing the word, deliberately not giving Sam a name, "escaped during the attack. We've been tracking him ever since, following him across the country. He moves often and swiftly. He doesn't know we're on his trail. We found some of his gear a few miles from here." *Oh no*, Allie was thinking, *oh no*, her mind racing. "He's twenty-one years old. We believe he is immune, but we didn't have time to run enough tests to be fully sure. We don't know if a child born from him will become sick, because the inseminated women in our camp were all killed in the attack."

*Inseminated women?* Allie thought, and thought of her night with Sam, and then of another woman in her place, then another, and another, and another, a whole line of them, and then, arising from some dead corner of her memory, there was that video recording, the one that had been sent to her phone on the last day when the world was still normal, but instead of her friend Brit and Brit's boyfriend, Damon, it was Sam and a series of women she didn't know. Her head was reeling. *No,* a part of her mind was telling her, *it wasn't like that, it couldn't have been. He was in a cage. They drugged him and extracted his semen.* But another part of her couldn't get the images to stop.

She shook her head to clear it. Kim, she realized, was peering back at her, concerned, wondering what was up with her. She tried to smile, to make herself look like she was okay, but, judging from the look Kim gave her back, she was sure she hadn't succeeded.

"Leslie and I will continue west," Dallas was saying, "in case he is still moving, see if we can pick up his trail. But you gals need to search this area. If we're all looking for him, he won't be able to hide forever. And we've found evidence that for some reason he's stayed here longer than anywhere else."

"What sort of evidence?" asked Allie.

"A gear stash, and evidence that he'd traveled back and forth from it," said Leslie. "A well-worn trail. Not his main camp, but a kind of backup. We left it as it was, not wanting him to know we were on to him." She turned to Jacky. "I'll show you on the map where it was."

For a moment more, Dallas stood before them, and then she nodded once, curtly, and stepped back. Doc took over again. She was smiling, but still serious, a kind of zealous fire in her eyes.

"I don't have to stress to you the importance of this find," Doc said. "He is the key to the future of our species, to the survival of our world. We need to find him as soon as possible. We absolutely cannot leave without him."

Allie looked like she'd seen a ghost, but nobody had seen it except Kim. All the others were too obsessed with the news to pay attention to the girl who always stood in the back and to notice she was white as a sheet, stunned. And then she realized that someone had said her name, that Dallas and Leslie were both staring at her.

". . . our best tracker," Jacky was saying. "She can tell you about the area after the meeting. Can't you, Allie?"

Allie, numb, just nodded. As the meeting began to break up around her, some women leaving, others gathering in smaller clusters to talk through the ramifications of the news, she just stood there, motionless, as if no longer aware of what was happening. She didn't snap out of it until she realized that Doc and Jacky were walking her way. But by the time her muddled senses realized this, it was too late for her to turn and escape.

Doc took Allie's arm and said to Jacky, "We'll put together various scouting parties, some to look for him, some to look for ways to get us all the hell out of here." She turned to Allie. "You're our best hunter," she said. "Go find him, Allie."

For a moment, Allie stayed stunned, unresponsive, as a thousand things flashed through her mind. Then she nodded. *Sure*, she thought. *I'll find him. Find him and warn him.*

"What about the vaccine, Doc?" Allie asked. "Wouldn't that change everything? Maybe, with that, we wouldn't have to leave. Maybe, with that, this uninfected male isn't as important as we think."

Doc looked confused for a moment, and then her face suddenly looked very old, very tired. "You haven't heard the news. Jacob Roman began bleeding out just after midnight," she said. Her voice broke as she spoke, her composure showing fissures, cracks. "He died early this morning. I'm out of ideas and resources. The uninfected male is our last hope, Allie."

Allie, in a fog of confusion and despair, somehow managed another nod. She turned away and moved off, her mind racing. *Last night it was like I had won the lottery*, she thought. *Today word is out and everyone wants my winnings.* She shook her head, laughed bitterly. No, it was so much more than that.

And there was Kim, right beside her, keeping pace with her.

"Are you going to look for him now?" Kim asked. There was fear in her voice, but excitement, too. Allie ignored her, kept walking.

"Let me come with you, Allie," said Kim. "I want to help."

Allie stopped and whirled on her. "You're not leaving this camp. It's too dangerous. You're not ready, Kim," she said.

"So—what—you've been back in town about ten minutes and you're heading out again?" Kim said, an edge to her voice that Allie hadn't heard before. "Too proud to accept help?"

For a moment, Allie stood there, unsure of what to say. Then she turned on her heel and headed for the door, and Kim, dejected and pissed off, could do nothing more than watch her go.

## Chapter Thirty-eight

## Allie

The last thing I want is having to worry about keeping Kim safe as I try to make it back to Sam faster than is humanly possible to let him know the cat's out of the bag and basically every woman in America has joined the manhunt for him. "Manhunt" is an unfortunate choice of words. But, then again, in another way, it's exactly right.

And so here I am, showing everyone how I'm so committed to finding this uninfected male that I'm leaving just five minutes after the meeting is over, having sidestepped Dallas and Leslie, even though I was out all night last night and just got back maybe an hour ago. But I'm zealous—fuck, yes, I'm eager to help the group—and if they don't believe that, maybe they'll at least believe that I've got enough competitiveness that I want to be the one who catches him. Whatever it takes to get me out of here before the others pour out as well and stumble onto Sam.

If they capture him, he'll likely die with the rest of us when the attack occurs. Even if they capture him and flee immediately south, we'll probably all be butchered and him along with us, particularly if they keep him caged up—which they for sure will, especially if Dallas and Leslie are involved. Or they'll kill all of us on the road, and then he'll be stuck in his cage in the middle of nowhere, slowly starving to death. But on his own he's more or less invisible to the ferals. He has to survive, and that's not just selfishness talking. Sam's the future. Not just of the camp but maybe of all of humanity. He has to go south—alone.

That's all I've got so far. Oh, and do not get killed by a feral in the process. But I'm hoping that more ideas will come to me as I go, that they'll just flow like water into my head when I need them, so that by the end of this Sam will be free and safe, we will both be alive, and the women of my camp will be less concerned with the lone uninfected male and more with just getting the hell out of Dodge before the ferals steamroll us all.

I'm out on my bike, and it's near dusk. It's foolish to be out this late, but at least this time I didn't forget my blood. I need to stay sharp, stay careful.

I stash the dirt bike in some bushes and then circle back and around and watch for a little while, to make sure nobody from the camp is following me. Wouldn't put it past Leslie and Dallas, those two bitches that kept Sam prisoner. When are they heading west to continue their search?

Nobody comes. No women; no ferals, either. So I thread my way into the trees, moving slantwise toward the library.

By the time I am out of the trees and on the edge of the town, night has fallen. I am careful on the streets this time, keeping to the shadows, waiting always a little longer than I feel I need to before deciding something is safe. But in the end I get there, and there I am, standing in front of the door of the town library.

Which, as it turns out, is locked.

"Sam," I whisper. "Sam." I scratch softly on the door, but of course nobody answers. I think about breaking the door down, but making a ton of noise doesn't seem like such a good idea with ferals roaming around. Plus, I remember now, it's bolted, so I'd probably have more luck digging my way through the wall next to the door than actually breaking the thing down. I think about just standing there for an hour and softly scratching and hoping he eventually hears me, but that doesn't seem like such a good idea, either.

Oh, what the hell, sometimes Allie's just gotta be Allie. I pound on the door hard—wham, wham, wham. "Sam!" I'm shouting, "Sam! It's me, Allie!" I can't do that for very long without rousting out the ferals, but I've got a few seconds at least. I hope.

And all of those seconds are used up before the door suddenly unbolts and Sam pokes his head out. He looks a little sleepy, but mostly surprised.

"Allie?" he says. "What's going on? What's wrong?"

I have all these things ready in my head to say. On the way, I've imagined myself saying something to get him mobilized and out of there. Instead, I say nothing at all. I just stand there until he pulls me inside and closes the door.


And then things start moving too quickly. We're kissing and then more than kissing and he's got my clothes half off and I'm into it, but, no, no, we don't have the time, every second counts, we have to stop, we have to, and so I'm pushing him away and shaking my head, and he's looking at me, confused.

I can hardly catch my breath. "They're here," I say.

"I told you they were going to swarm. We need to leave—now. Get as many women out as we can. Come on." He starts toward the window to take a look, but I've grabbed hold of his arm, have stopped him.

"No," I say, "Not the ferals. The women are here."

He just looks confused.

"Dallas," I say. "You know?"

"The . . . city?" he says. "Allie," he says, "I don't know what you're talking about."

I take a deep breath and I try to tell him, but it keeps coming out jumbled, or in bits and pieces, and for a while he just looks puzzled and confused, until, suddenly, the penny drops and he gets it.

"Ah," he says. "Oh shit. Her. From Hubbard. They're looking for me?"

"Not just them," I say, "my people, too. I'm supposed to be looking for you right now. That's what they think I'm doing."

He just stands there with his arms crossed, motionless. It makes me crazy that he is taking it this way. I've got to get him out of here, right away, and so I find his canvas bag and I start throwing his gear in. He'll thank me later, even if he doesn't seem to be too happy about it right now.

"I can buy time and send them on a couple of wild-goose chases,"

I tell him. "But you have to go now or they'll find you and lock you up—just like you said—and then you'll be killed with the rest of us when they attack—"

"Allie," he says. He takes hold of my arm. I try to shake him off, get back to packing, but he's got a good grip. "Allie, stop," he says, more firmly this time, and so I do. I turn and give him my *This better be good, you have ten seconds to tell me*, look and then wait.

"Allie, I'm not going anywhere," he says.

Hearing this, I freak the hell out. I push him, and then push him again, but he just stands there and takes it. I start hitting him in the face, trying to get him to wake the fuck up, but he grabs my wrists, immobilizes them. "Are you crazy?" I yell, trying to twist free. "Go, save yourself. You're too important—you're safer away from us. You and I both know we can't move all these women. We'll just die trying! And it's my fault you stayed too long. No more games, Sam, you have to go, and go now!"

He pulls me close, shakes his head. He's intense now, looking straight into my soul.

"This is not your fault, Allie," he says, his voice shockingly calm. "Listen to me. Ever since this all started, I've seen nothing but violence and death and fear. Then I met you and realized this world could be something else."

My heart's breaking. His words ripping through me like feral claws. I'm a basket case and I realize all the clichéd lovesick bullshit is real. I've become a blubbering, distraught, corny girl caught in an emotional tornado at the end of all things. I try to stay focused but it's so hard. I guess this is what happens when you fall in love.

"Sam," I say, "you have to leave. You have to."

"Look, I know the right thing for me to do is leave and go south to another camp. But if I go, I'll never see you again." He grabs me by my shoulders and puts his face so close it's almost touching mine. "Losing you after it took so long to find you—I couldn't stand that."

I can't believe that anyone would give up that much for me. Or maybe I can believe it, since I've done the same for Kim, but for me, someone giving it up for me? Am I worth it? I'm confused, because, if he is going to throw everything away for me, doesn't that make it my fault? And, finally, I'm conflicted because I love him, too, I want him to be safe, but I also want to be with him, don't want to lose him, not ever again.

But, no, I can't let him do it. I can't let him be selfish. He stays up here and he gets captured, and then he's dead. He has to go south. On his own. He has to.

I wrap my arms around him, trying not to cry. "What are we doing, Sam?" I finally manage. "What the hell are we doing?"

"I have no idea," Sam says. "Not the faintest clue."

"We need a plan," I say. I tighten my embrace on him. I've got to figure out how to get him to go south, even if I don't want to.


I don't know how long the hug goes on. Awhile, but it never feels like it's gone on too long, or even long enough. We hear a crash from outside.

I've already got my gun out, and a moment later, Sam has scooped his off the floor. I'm at the window and peering out.

"Ferals?" he asks.

A half-dozen silhouettes moving in the dark, flitting in and out of shadows. I stay still and watch them, feeling Sam's presence right behind me as he looks out and over my head.

I begin to nod yes, but then I get a better glimpse of one and realize that, no, they're not ferals: they're women. I grab my night-vision goggles and take a closer look. Jacky's there, Emma is, too, as well as other security from camp. Luckily, no Leslie or Dallas. They're armed, spattered in feral blood. As I watch, they move quickly, surrounding the building.

"They must have seen the candlelight," I say.

Sam grunts his assent. "How did they find me this quickly?" he asks.

I shake my head. "I don't know," I say. "Probably just the light. And dumb luck. I didn't think they'd get this far tonight."

I turn and look at him, and he looks at me. We've reached a point of no return, we know. Sam chose to stick around, and I wasn't able to coax him onto the road before Jacky and her crew showed up. Now we're both going to have to do some fast thinking or face the consequences of those decisions. If he stays, well, the future of humanity is at risk. If he goes, it'll break my heart.

"What do we do?" I whisper.

"I thought you had a plan," he whispers back.

I frown. "I'm thinking," I say.

"Think faster," he says, "they're here."

# Chapter Thirty-nine

They converged slowly, guns at the ready, still in stealth mode. Jacky motioned them forward one by one, slowly drawing the net tighter, closing in around the building that had a light flickering in an upper window. It wasn't a feral, they knew that: ferals had no use for fire, and no ability to make one. Which left only one possibility.

*Take it easy and slow*, Jacky thought. *We need this guy.* She moved the team in carefully, surrounding the building, someone in position to see every exit. Slowly, they sealed the target in.

But did they really need him? Jacky thought about it. She herself had no interest in men—Emma, neither. That didn't mean she couldn't see there was a practical purpose for them, if only to milk them for their sperm so you could have the species go on. Yes, the idea of life going on, of things not ending with this generation, even if things only lasted one more generation, sure, that was appealing.

Still, she wouldn't take it as far as Dallas. I mean, shit, give the man a name, let him have at least that small scrap of dignity even if you were going to milk his sperm. She'd been surprised that there hadn't been more of an outcry about that after what Allie said, but it got lost in the shuffle, she guessed—too much going on all at once. If she was thinking about it now, though, that probably meant some of the others were, too.

But as for men themselves, well, she'd just say it wasn't likely anyone would find her interested in anybody on that side of the gender fence. Emma, too, she was pretty sure was a lifer. The other women? Some of them were into women, sure, but more as a holding pattern to let them get their freak on until men showed up again. Nothing against them—you made do however you could—but, yeah, if a man showed up, there were going to be a few broken hearts.

They were almost to the door when they heard muffled sounds from inside, soft but insistent. What they were exactly, she couldn't say.

"Hold positions," whispered Jacky into her headpiece. The other five stopped, tense and at the ready. Jacky balanced her stance, leveled her rifle at the front door.

"We know you're in there," she called. "Come on out with your hands up!"

"Jacky," said a voice. "It's me. Allie. I'm coming out."

The other women groaned, let their guns fall. She'd have to work with them on that—they needed to remain at the ready until they were allowed their ease. That was what came from working with women with no military training. *Even if it is Allie, who's to say she isn't being held hostage?* she thought. No, she realized, Allie wasn't the kind of girl ever likely to be taken hostage.

The front door opened and Allie came out, hands above her head. *At least one of them follows protocol*, Jacky thought, and came forward to meet her.

"Christ," Jacky said. "We thought we'd found him."

"I was checking the buildings around here for any sign of him," said Allie.

"Anything?" asked Jacky.

Allie hesitated a moment, then shook her head. "Nothing," she said.

"What about the light we saw?"

Allie lifted the flashlight in her hand. "I was up there, looking around," she said. "Must have seen me."

Jacky nodded. *Not our lucky day*, she thought. "Personally, I think he's long gone by now," she said.

"You're probably right," said Allie.

"Sure, I am," said Jacky. "Hell, aren't I always?" She smiled in the dim light, then grew serious again. "That's why you should stop looking for him and come with us. I'm focusing on how to get us all out of here before the shit hits the fan. I have one crazy idea. We were headed to check it out when we saw the light there." She punched Allie in the shoulder. "Fuck, you got to be more careful, girl," she said. "Anyway, it's a long shot, but still. What do you say? Coming along?"

Allie nodded.

Jacky gestured, and the team gathered quickly around them. They moved away down the ruined street, just as silently as they had arrived. Nobody saw Allie, in the back, cast a glance over her shoulder at the library, her expression filled with sorrow and desire. There, in the window, in the moonlight, she thought she caught the quick blur of Sam's shadow and then the ghost of a pale hand against the glass. And then the window was empty again.

Or maybe that was just what she wanted to see. Maybe she hadn't seen anything at all.

They left the town and entered the woods, staying just within the tree line. Slowly, they moved along the forest's edge, skirting the road. Jacky led them forward without hesitation, still careful. And then, suddenly, she stopped.

"Suit up," she growled.

Immediately the other women began digging through their backpacks, taking out vials and jars of feral blood, smearing a new layer over their bodies and faces before proceeding. A few minutes later, she gestured at them again to stop; they stood there, silent and motionless, until a lone feral loped by and was gone.

Jacky led them down and around until they reached the defaced sign reading HARBOR AHEAD.

"This is your long shot?" Allie asked.

Jacky nodded. "I been thinking. That chick Holly might have been on to something. The whole place is full of boats. All we need is one. All we have to do is figure a way to get everybody on board and haul ass south."

"It's the beehive, Jacky. There are dozens of ferals there, maybe hundreds."

"Maybe we can come in by water," said Jacky. "Have someone swim over and go up an anchor chain, get a ship loose, just let it drift. We pick it up somewhere downstream."

Allie shook her head. "I asked Holly about that," she said. "Currents aren't right. Too sheltered. Probably the boat would just knock around for a bit and not go anywhere."

"Holly's sure?"

Allie shrugged. "Her dad ran the ferry. She probably knows."

Jacky nodded.

"So, okay," she said. "A little more fucking difficult. Get someone to swim out, or maybe two people, one to protect the other. Unmoor a boat and then start the engine, just take off."

"Ferals would be all over them."

"They carry jars of blood; put them on the second they're out of the water and on the boat. Motherfuckers won't smell them right away."

"They're too wet. It won't stay on. One of the ferals will smell them, and as soon as one does, they'll be swarmed."

"Fuck, all they need's a few minutes," said Jacky. "Just enough time to get the boat unmoored and the engine started. Run the engine maybe fifteen seconds and the boat will be far enough out that the current'll catch it, and the ferals won't be able to follow. The rest of us are downstream and get picked up after."

Allie shook her head. "They're not going to get anywhere. It's a suicide mission," she said.

Jacky shrugged. "Maybe it is, maybe it isn't. Let's take a look."

She took them a little farther, until they lay on their bellies in the vegetation crowning the crest of a little hill just beyond the edge of the forest. In front of them was the dirt road, bleached in the pale moonlight. Not far away, they could hear the disturbing howls and wails of ferals—not just one or two this time but many, many ferals, a cacophony of voices, an orchestra of protracted squeals. The women were tense; some even seemed terrified.

"Maybe some kind of diversion," Jacky said. "A fireworks show here, a few grenades, then a half-dozen women to coax them all out."

"Those women will die," said Allie.

"Sure," said Jacky, "but if it saves the rest of us, maybe it's worth it."

Allie shook her head. "It's not going to draw enough of them out," she said. "Still a suicide mission."

For a moment, Jacky was silent. "Fuck me," she finally said. "There's got to be a way. Say we just douse someone from head to toe in feral blood, maybe skin one of the motherfuckers and make a feral suit to wear. Go full *Silence of the Lambs* on them. They won't be able to . . ."

She trailed off. Allie didn't answer. She continued to stare down at the harbor, below them and about five hundred yards away. A calm inlet of water, it shimmered under the night sky. Boats of all sizes lined the docks, from fifteen-footers to yachts to midsize cargo vessels. Some seem in good repair; others were half sunk or capsized or simply dilapidated. Yes, there were boats there, if they could only get to them. That wasn't the problem. The problem was what stood between them and the boats.

The harbor had always been bad, but it was much worse than she'd ever seen it. Hundreds upon hundreds of black shapes constellated around the docks, moving and crossing back and forth. Ferals. Not only more than Allie had ever seen in one place: almost more than the total Allie had ever seen in her lifetime up to that point. The harbor was a whole city of ferals. From this distance it was hard for her to make out any details clearly, but it was clear there was an unnerving infestation of the entire area. They could not get through.

Jacky was shaking her head, shocked, disappointed, and scared.

"I was here five months ago," Jacky said. "There are five times as many of the motherfuckers now, maybe ten. You're right, this is suicide."

She turned to Allie, her face stricken with panic. She was whispering more softly now, her mouth close to Allie's ear, so that Allie would be the only one to hear. "I have no fucking idea how we are going to get all of our women south, Allie. It's just a matter of time before this army of ferals hits our camp. What the hell are we going to do?"

# Chapter Forty

## Allie

I'm running on almost no sleep, and it feels like I've been endlessly traveling back and forth between the camp and the world outside over the last two days—to see Sam, to see the shit storm that is the harbor, to patrol. Now Jacky and her crew are back inside, and I'm back, too, slipping off and fading away from the crowd as usual. Trying to avoid the sendoff for Dallas and Leslie, who are heading west in a few minutes to continue their hunt for Sam. If I don't go, I won't say anything stupid to them, won't let my anger flare in a way that makes them suspicious enough to stay and continue the hunt here. I can't have them around while Sam's still here. Shit, if they'd been along at the library yesterday, they would have seen through my story and stormed the place. And then Sam would be in a cage.

I'm just stripping off my gear when my baby sister starts in.

"You're back," she says.

I nod. "Nice of you to have noticed," I claim. I'm not trying to be an asshole; it just comes out that way.

She simply stays there, arms crossed, while I get ready to wash off. I frown, but she doesn't take the hint. Finally, I say, "What?"

"I want to go with the next search party," she says.

"No," I say.

"It's just like before we came into the camp," she says. "You insisted on showing me how to use a rifle, how to aim and shoot, but you never let me fire an actual shot. I'm ready, Allie."

"You're not," I say. I can tell she's getting upset, and it surprises me a little. Can't she see I'm trying to keep her safe? It was the same when she found out I'd been watching West Staten for a while before bringing her in. "How long?" she asked, and when I said a few months, she was pissed. Knowing that she would have wanted to go there immediately, I had to make sure it was safe first. I was protecting her, but she saw it as me keeping something from her.

"You don't get to decide what I do," she says.

"If that's the case, then why are you even asking me?"

That draws her up a little. I know why she's asking me: she wants my approval. No fucking way am I going to give her my blessing to go out and risk her life.

She opens her mouth again, but I've already gone to wash off.

"Hey!" she calls after me, getting angry. "Come back here!"

But I ignore her. I go into the bathroom and lock the door behind me. It is an actual bathroom, or used to be, back before the collapse. There's an actual showerhead, but it runs off a rainwater catchment system on the roof. Open the valve, and lukewarm water dribbles in. The water's not much cleaner than I am. A moment later, the door is rattling in its frame as Kim tries to get in.

"Go away, Kim," I say. I finish undressing, turn on the water, close the drain to catch it, and flick the lever over to shower, but I don't step inside. Instead, I wait, watching the water dribble into the tub, listening to the sound of Kim's knocking, hoping she'll go away.

"They need more people searching for him," she says. "They need more people searching for a way out of here. I can do it. You know I can."

*Yeah*, I think, *but you're not going to. I'm here so you don't have to do shit like this.* This is my baby sister, the one my father almost killed, the one who has more knowledge about how to act on a stage than about how to shoot a gun. She's not stupid—maybe she'd be fine out there—but I don't want to take the risk.

And then I catch sight of my face in the mirror and it hits me, all at once. I may not see Sam again. The ferals could come over the wall at any moment and slaughter us. I can't protect myself and I can't protect my sister. I want to be with Sam, right now, but I can't, I can't—I owe these women something, too. And it's because of me that he hasn't headed south, because of me that he is going to be captured and then killed. All I want is to have a life, but that is exactly what I am never going to be allowed to have. In this new world, nobody gets a life, and I have to take care of Kim. I want to take care of her, sure, she's family, but isn't there some way to do that and still have a life of my own? We may be alive, we may be uninfected, but we're still not really living, no matter how many crappy dinner theater–style plays Doc convinces us to throw, no matter how hard we try to pretend that everything is all right.

So I can't have a life. I don't get one. You broke your own rules, Allie. You let down your guard and allowed yourself to feel something in this godforsaken place. And now you're a god-awful mess.

The tub's got half a foot of tepid water in it now. I shouldn't take any more—there won't be enough left for someone else. I missed my chance for a shower. I step into the water and then crouch and splash it up and around me, cleaning the blood off, the grime. I soap up carefully and do it all over again, then sit down in the water, ignoring how chilly it is, and how dirty. Outside, Kim is still pounding, pounding, going on endlessly. She's angry, and getting angrier.

"I can handle myself, Allie!" she says. "You know that. You have to let me help!"

And then, a little later: "The camp is in trouble. We all need to be doing our part. I need to be doing my part." A pause. "Answer me!"

"Leave me alone, Kim!" I manage, my voice a little strangled.

She knocks again, and again, and again. It's just insane—she keeps knocking and knocking and knocking—and it starts to make me angry. I tolerate it as long as I can and then I splash my way out of the bath and rush over and yank the door open, and yell in my sister's face. "I am your mother! I am the only thing like a mother you have! I have to take care of you! I have to be the one who says, *You're not ready!* And sometimes I don't want to. Now leave me the hell alone!"

My words hang there harshly. Kim stands motionless, stung by this outburst. I'm half hidden behind the door, and she's standing there, and there's a moment when regret starts to well up in me and I'm about to say I'm sorry, but I fight it off. Instead, I go back into the bathroom and lock the door behind me and climb back into my cold bath.

## Chapter Forty-one

# Kim

The thing about Allie at the time was that she just held everything in, didn't share anything, just kept her grief and everything else all to herself. That was what she called "protecting me"—at least, that was part of it. She thought, I guess, because I was young, that I'd just be able to enjoy the life she was giving me, the safety she was giving me. Sure, I was young, but that just meant that instead of seeing right off what Allie was doing—the way she was keeping her grief to herself, the way she refused to ever relax—I just came to see it gradually. Or, rather, *feel* it. I wasn't stupid. I watched her, saw it all. I tried to make her happy, but it didn't seem to matter what I did. If I got deep into drama, like Doc wanted me to, Allie would tell me that I needed to do more target practice, that that was what really mattered. And if I said, Okay, I *have* practiced, I'm ready to start learning in the field, I'm ready to leave the camp—she would go ballistic. She wanted me to be independent but at the same time didn't want that at all. There were two halves of her, tugging me in different directions. No matter what I did, for Allie I was doing it wrong. She thought she was protecting me, and, sure, she was, but she was also holding me back, trying to keep me the same girl I had been when I was nine. Nobody wants to stay nine forever.

That evening, I'd waited up to talk to her, but she never came in. More and more she'd been like that, staying out all night, and with Holly no longer staying in the room now, it was just Beth and me, just two young girls. At night, that could get to me after a while. I'd start to hear every little noise, every breath, and before long I couldn't sleep at all. If Allie had been there, she'd have let me climb in with her. But she wasn't there.

So—a terrible night, wondering again where she was this time, wondering if I'd see her again. Just like it'd been back in the days before we came to the camp, where every time she left I'd wonder if this would be the last time I saw her. When she arrived late the next day, dead tired and dragged out, I was angry. When I was saying I wanted to go out and help search, what I was really saying was *I don't want you to leave me alone again*, and also *I want to be useful*, and *I want to be with you*, and *I want to be* like *you*. But when she said no, and said it again, and again—not even wanting to have a conversation with me about it, just withdrawing like she always did, just shutting me out—something shifted in me. And then saying I wanted to go out and help search became more than just words, became something that, stubbornly, I really wanted to do.

She shut the bathroom door hard for the last time, and I stepped back and back again until something caught behind my knees. I sat on the nearest bed, which was Allie's. In sitting down, I'd tipped her bag off the bed—clumsy Kim. She'd left the flap unbelted, which meant things inside clattered out and spilled onto the floor at my feet. When I leaned down to retrieve them, something grabbed my attention. Among the containers of blood and the knives and the first-aid kit and the night-vision goggles and all that other soldier stuff was a soiled piece of thick paper.

I picked it up and glanced over it. It was a map, drawn in thick pen strokes. I scanned it, frowning, and then turned the paper over. There was something on the back, too, words written in block letters. I stared at it, unsure what it meant. Who would Allie be in touch with that she'd have to meet outside the camp rather than inside? Was she seeing a girl from another camp? Was that why she'd turned away Holly? (I'd been awake for that, too: I'd seen a lot more of that courtship than Allie had probably wanted me to.)

I looked at it, puzzled, then made a decision. I decided to find out more.

Pulling the backpack up onto the bed, I went through it, pulling everything out. There, in the very bottom, carefully folded, was another note, same handwriting.

*YOU OK?*

I just stared at it. Allie had hidden this from me, the person who she said she was closest to in the world. I'd thought she was off keeping us safe, but instead it looked like she was seeing someone out there, hanging out with them, when she wouldn't hardly give me the time of day.

I crumpled the notes and threw them on the floor. And then, after a while, I got back up and smoothed them out again.

I'd made a decision. I knew just what to do.

## Chapter Forty-two

After a while, she was shivering. She stood shaking her head, gaining control, preparing herself to go out and face Kim. How much time had gone by? She'd really spaced out. It was dark outside the bathroom window, so it had been a while, but how long she couldn't say for certain.

She toweled off, examined herself in the mirror. She looked tired, a little pale, but that was all. Yes, she'd pass—nobody would know she'd been crying unless they looked at her very closely. She got dressed. Then she looked at the locked bathroom door and felt her guilt rising.

"Kim," she said. "I'm sorry."

She waited but there was no response. She took one last deep breath, opened the door, and stepped out into the bedroom.

"Kim—" she started.

But Kim was nowhere to be seen. The room was empty.

Suddenly the whole one-sided conversation rushed back to her. She began to get very worried about where Kim had gone.

She crossed quickly to the bedroom door and opened it to go out into the hall. Or would have: it was locked. She paused, confused, not quite able to believe it, and then tried the door again, rattling the knob. No: jammed, locked, not opening. Baffled, she jiggled it further and finally began trying to force it.

There was the sound of movement on the other side.

"Kim?" she called. "Come on, let me out. This isn't funny!"

There was no answer. She pounded on the door and shouted.

"Kim—is that you? What the hell is going on? Open the damn door!"

More noise from outside, and then she heard someone manipulating the doorknob. The door slowly swung open to reveal not Kim but Emma. Her face was cold and expressionless. She was holding her firearm, not directed exactly at Allie, but not deliberately directed away from her, either.

"What are you doing here?" asked Allie. "Why was my door locked?"

"You selfish cunt." When Emma spoke her voice was as hard and sharp as steel, and her eyes were cold.

Startled, Allie recoiled, and then began to move forward again, only to have Emma slam the door in her face. Fuming with anger, confused, humiliated, Allie had taken a few steps back to charge the door when she saw her canvas bag.

It was on the floor, the contents spilled out of it. *Oh fuck*, she thought, and dropped to her knees. She pawed through the items on the floor, running a quick inventory. Guns gone, knives gone, but her other gear was all there. Only the guns and knives were missing, she thought at first, and then realized, in a burst: Sam's notes. Like a schoolgirl, she'd kept them, and now they were gone, too.

*Oh fuck*, she thought again, her mind racing. She began pacing back and forth, then tried the door once more—still locked—and looked in the bottom of her canvas bag, where she had unstitched the lining and slid a flick knife in, a backup, just in case. The knife was still there.

She took it out, slid it into her boot. Maybe they hadn't been as thorough as she'd initially feared.

Dropping to her back, she inched under her bed. There, hidden in the back corner, in the dark, taped behind the frame's leg, was her backup weapon: her father's police-issue Glock.

She grabbed it and worked her way back out from under the bed. Quietly, she moved toward the door, then kicked it as hard as she could.

The lock buckled under the blow and the door swung open, surprising and jostling Emma. By the time she had recovered herself, she was staring down the barrel of Allie's Glock.

"Give me your weapon, Emma," Allie said.

"Like hell," said Emma, but made no effort to point her gun at Allie, either. There was fear in her eyes.

"Don't be stupid," said Allie. "We both know you have a lot to live for."

"You wouldn't," said Emma.

"I don't have to," said Allie. "Your safety is on."

And when Emma's eyes flicked down briefly, Allie rapped her hand hard with the butt of her pistol. Emma's gun clattered onto the floor.

"Actually, your safety was off," said Allie. "But you should have known that without looking. Amateur. Come on," she said. "Up and into the bathroom." And when Emma turned and headed toward the bathroom door, she struck her hard on the back of her head.

*Who knows?* wondered Allie. *Do they all know? Can I walk out of here, or do I have to sneak? What will I do if they try to stop me? Am I capable of killing another woman?*

She moved carefully down the hall, the gun hanging loose at her side, not all that noticeable unless you were looking for it. She tried to look calm, relaxed, but also walked quickly.

She went past a room with its door closed. She passed another door, this one open. A light shone from within, but the only woman that she caught sight of was sitting cross-legged on her bed and didn't look up.

Allie was just reaching the stairs when she heard a shout behind her. She broke into a sprint, clattering her way down three or four stairs at a time, and really accelerated once she hit bottom. She ran as quickly as she could, trying not to think about who was behind her, and then barreled around a corner right into Holly and two other women.

She recoiled and so did they. For a moment they all stared at one another, startled, and then Allie raised her pistol and pointed it at Holly's head, hoping she looked serious and deadly. The other two women started reaching for weapons, but Allie said, "Don't," and they froze, slowly lifted their hands.

"What did you do, Allie?" asked Holly, hurt and disgust painted on her face.

"Get out of my way, Holly," said Allie.

"What are you going to do, shoot me? It's too late, Allie! Jacky knows where you're hiding him. She has your little map. She's on her way!"

Allie elbowed her way past, pushing Holly into her two friends, and flashed out the front door. Breathlessly, she ran across the yard and leaped onto her dirt bike. She kicked the starter, revved the engine furiously, and roared off, paying no attention to the figure of Holly in her rearview mirror, shouting, waving.

## Chapter Forty-three

Six figures converged on the library, blocking all exits, moving sound-lessly, weapons raised. A candle burned on the second floor of the library. The streets around it were quiet and deserted—not a sound.


Allie rode hell for leather, outracing her own headlights, not slow-ing down for anything, the bike skidding and sliding. She had to get to Sam before they did, had to warn him, convince him to go south before it was too late. She had only her Glock, and she was riding at night without being smeared with feral blood, moving through prime feral territory because it was the quickest way. She was so busy keep-ing the bike on the road that she didn't see the two ferals emerge from the shadows, keeping pace with her, tracking her, just ten yards to her right.


The women moved into cover formation, surrounding the build-ing. Jacky holstered her pistol and moved to the front door. Wearing night-vision goggles, she quietly worked the door's lock, forcing in pick after pick until the lock clicked and the door eased open.

She drew her pistol and moved in, muzzle up. The ground floor of a library. It was quiet on this floor, and dark, the shelves still mostly intact, but with books scattered everywhere. She moved cautiously forward, listening for the slightest sound, careful not to dislodge any of the debris on the floor.

Halfway back, she found the stairs and ascended them, crouched, gun ready, silent. She stopped shy of the second-floor landing and just waited. No noise, no sign of movement, but there, farther along, a little flicker of light.

*Bingo*, she thought.

She counted to thirty in her head and then stepped up and moved forward, using the library shelves as cover, crouching low, ducking in and out of aisles. She moved toward the light, alert, gun at the ready.

Finally, she was sure it was there, just around the corner. She spun and planted her stance, ready to shoot.

But there was nothing to shoot at. There was one lit candle, and that was all. The man who had been there was gone.


She skidded and fishtailed, almost spun out, and then managed at the last minute to come out of it. She was driving too fast, not clearly seeing the road ahead. *Careful, Allie*, she told herself. *It won't do Sam any good if you end up dead.*

She slowed just a little, but not much. She'd be there soon.

She never understood later how she'd known they were there. They were behind her, out of sight, and, for once, silent. She must have caught the briefest flash of one in her rearview mirror, or the hint of one in her peripheral vision, but by the time she was aware of them, they were already making their move, leaping after her, trying desperately to catch her bike. In an instant she had the Glock out and was looking back over her shoulder, awkwardly firing. She hit one in the shoulder; he howled and went down in a heap, but he was up almost immediately, rushing like a tank after her. The other managed to bound in closer, ramming not into her but into the back tire of the bike, throwing it awry. She felt the tire slide and catch and the bike threaten to flip. To save it, she turned hard off the road to follow the slide. She crashed through the brush, trying to brake, but with the gun in her hand and her balance off she couldn't manage, and the back wheel, too, stayed squirrelly and unmanageable, out of skew or tire popped or both. The whole bike shook until she struck a little projection of rock and was flung over the handlebars. It felt like she floated in the air forever, and then she came down, hard.

She screamed at the impact, her shoulder searing with intense pain. Groping around as she winced, she realized that her machete had sliced through it, had bitten into her shoulder's flesh.

She managed to get to her knees. She was bleeding so heavily, she wouldn't stay conscious long if she didn't do something about that. She looked around to get her bearings, and there were the two ferals, advancing toward her menacingly, slowly moving in, predators anticipating a kill.

She reached into her belt for her pistol, but it wasn't there. She'd been holding it. She cast her gaze around and there it was—or something glinting, anyway—a dozen yards away. Too far. She would never make it before they got her.

There was really only one move she could make, and if she didn't make it now, it'd be too late. She reached for the machete, wrapping her hands tight around the handle, and tore it from where it was tangled in her flesh and clothing. The pain was excruciating, and she almost passed out, the whole of her vision going dim, but then she was more or less conscious again, shot through with adrenaline, blood soaking her arm and chest, the machete up and raised. She was even up on her feet now, stumbling but upright.

The ferals were keening, their faces upraised, breathing in the smell of her blood. And then, all at once, they were upon her, the unharmed one getting there just a little quicker. She dodged out of his way and brought the machete around quick and hard, slashing the throat of the wounded one. He dropped, his throat spewing a warm mist of air and blood. She spun around to chop at the other, but he was no longer there. And then, suddenly, he *was* there again, looming out of the darkness, not where she'd thought he'd be. She tried to bring the machete back around and into his side, but before she could, he drove his fist hard into her face and knocked her to the ground.

She lay there, dazed. Something took hold of her legs, and then she was moving, being dragged over the ground, her head jostling. She listened to the sound of the rocks scrape against the back of her head, felt the arms of the bushes pluck at her, watched a hazy procession of darkness and leaves go by above her.

But now she was focused again. There was her gun—the idiot was dragging her right past her own gun—it was only a few feet away. She dragged herself out of her torpor and twisted in the feral's grasp. Letting out a bellowing scream, she reached with her good arm as far as it would go, blood spurting out of the wound in the other shoulder.

A moment later, the Glock was in her hand. She thumbed the safety off and fired two shots in quick succession, and the back of the feral's head came apart.

He dropped her legs, took a stuttered step, and then pitched backward, ending up right beside her, looking at her, his face just a few inches from hers. For a fleeting moment, his monstrous visage softened and revealed beneath it something human. He stared at her with a hint of what she read as sorrow in his eyes, and then that faded and the eyes glazed over and he was dead.

She lay still for a long moment. If she hadn't had a feral next to her, the dead eyes staring at her, she might not have managed to find the energy to stand. As it was, it took all her strength to get up, and once up she just stood there, swaying, unsure if she'd be able to walk.

She leaned against a rock. She was covered in feral blood from the one who had died beside her—though how much good it would do with her own wound still active, she didn't know. She thought about binding her shoulder, but she didn't have the strength to tear off a strip of fabric or tie it off. She pressed her hand against it and tried to keep pressure on it, to slow the bleeding at least.

She paused, swaying, to think. She couldn't ride the bike—there was no way. No way she could get there in time.

Her mind was filled with mud. She just stood there, keeping the pressure on her wound. Then, breathing raggedly, wan and frail, she took a step, and another, and another, struggling into the forest.


How long had she been walking? It seemed like forever. Several times she almost fell, tripping on roots or thrown off by the unevenness of the ground. But each time she caught herself, making the wound in her shoulder well up with blood again. *How much blood do I have left?* she wondered, and tried not to worry about the way it was dribbling out of her.

Was she on the right path? She wasn't sure, but she thought so.

She'd been close when the ferals had taken her down, and she could see the woodpath below now, even in the darkness. She followed it.

Walking got harder and harder. She knew if she stopped she wouldn't be able to get going again. She continued carefully, stumblingly, forward. Just tried to keep moving.

When she saw the clearing and realized that, yes, she had been on the right path after all, she was so relieved she almost collapsed. There it was, the tree. Where she had almost died before, where she and Sam had exchanged notes. She was there, she had arrived.

She stumbled to it, falling in a heap at its base, still clutched her shoulder, trying somehow to staunch the blood. *I should have figured out a way to bandage it*, she thought. *Now it's too late.* But she tried to keep it elevated, tried to keep pressing on it.

Around her, the trees began to fade away, blurring into nothingness. She feebly shook her head, and for a moment the forest snapped back into focus. Then, slowly, slowly, it darkened again, and finally disappeared.


She was awoken by sounds—birds, she thought at first, but, no, as time went on they became clearer. *Words*, she realized finally somewhere deep inside her, and that was enough to rouse her.

"Allie," the voice was saying, "Allie, wake up. . . ."

Who was it? Was she late for school? No, it wasn't the voice of one of her parents. Why was the voice familiar? Jared? What was he doing in her room? No, not his voice, either . . . And then she realized, *Sam*, and it all came back to her.

She managed to make her eyelids flutter—like a bird, she thought— but couldn't go further than that. Then the birds were back—no, the words were back—and one of the birds or the words was fluttering against her face, against her cheeks, its wings slapping her skin lightly. This time, her eyes managed to open.

There was Sam, brow furrowed, eyes concerned. He had a flick knife out and was cutting away her camo jacket to get at her shoulder wound. He seemed frantic, anxious.

"Christ," he muttered, "you're bleeding so much. What the hell happened, Allie?"

Allie opened her mouth. Her teeth were chattering, her face bone white. "They didn't find you," she managed to say. "Thank God."

He shushed her, touched his finger to his lips. "Stop talking," Sam said.

She could feel him doing something to the shoulder, binding it up. She knew it should have hurt, but it didn't—the shoulder felt so distant and far away, like it wasn't part of her anymore, like it wasn't even part of the world. And then, suddenly, she was moving, and she thought for a moment that the feral had her legs again, that she'd never managed to get free from him after all—the pistol and shooting him had all been a dream. She kept expecting to feel her head jouncing along the ground, the sound of scraping deep within her skull, but it never came. No, she realized, the feral wasn't dragging her after all, he was carrying her. Why would a feral carry her? Why wasn't he trying to kill her?

They came a little ways out of the bushes, and the feral turned its head, and she realized it wasn't a feral at all but a man. Sam, she remembered.

"I got you now," he said. "You'll be okay."

She closed her eyes. Something began to nag at her. Where was Kim? Was she okay? Wasn't she supposed to be watching her? Protecting her? Who was going to look out for her when she died? She tried to speak, but nothing came out.

"Shh," said Sam. "It's okay. I have you."

Sam had her. She would be okay. She let herself be rolled by the gentle motion of his walk.

"Listen to my voice," said Sam. "Don't give up, Allie."

But she couldn't hear him. She was already unconscious.

## Chapter Forty-four

Emma was on the roof, in the highest crow's nest, still licking her injured pride. She rubbed the bump on the top of her head and winced. *Allie shouldn't have been able to surprise me like that,* she told herself angrily—*I should have been ready.* Jacky had told her so as well, had scolded her, laid into her. "What the fuck, your safety?" she had said. "That's the oldest trick in the book, straight out of the movies. What are you, a fucking amateur?" And then, with concern, Jacky had examined the lump on the top of her skull, before sighing and banishing her to the crow's nest. "Stay up there on watch until I tell you to come down," she said. "Any way you slice it, you fucked up." Jacky hadn't spoken to her since. She was giving her the silent treatment.

*I could have done something,* Emma thought. *Where did Allie even come up with a gun? We searched the room. I should have searched it better. I could have just locked her in the bathroom. I could have brought one of the other girls with me and then the two of us could have subdued her. I could have . . .*

But what did it matter what she could have done? She hadn't done it. What mattered was what had happened. She guessed she'd been put on watch both to punish her and to get her out of the way so that she couldn't see the others whispering and talking about how she'd fucked up. "It reflects badly on me," Jacky had told her, "having a girlfriend who can't even keep someone confined to quarters." That had stung the most.

She scanned the perimeter with her naked eye. Nothing there. No ferals tonight, for some reason—must be elsewhere. She'd just turned away and was preparing to beat herself up some more, when—

"Help! We need help! Now!"

Out of the darkness, couldn't see anything. There was something wrong with the woman's voice, too low somehow, like maybe throat cancer or something. And that, the quality of the voice rather than what the voice said, kept nagging at her, worrying her, until suddenly a dusty switch buried somewhere deep in her head clicked.

It was a man's voice.

No, she couldn't believe it. Dallas and Leslie had sworn there was a normal man out there and everybody believed it, but Emma couldn't get her head around it. She could hardly even remember a time when men had been anything other than ferals—even in her memories of her brothers, her father, they seemed to be grunting and shrieking rather than speaking. That whole time, from before, seemed like a dream, and it was hard for her to remember that males hadn't always been ferals.

No, the voice couldn't be male. Males no longer spoke, they just howled or shrieked or screeched before trying to tear your head off. And the only male they knew about who wasn't like that was on the run and wasn't likely to come here, if they could credit what Dallas had said about him. She was hearing things. Now she was both a fuckup and crazy.

She scanned the perimeter, trying to catch sight of whoever it was. For a moment she saw nothing, and then, out of the darkness, a dim figure approached the fence, walking along it toward the gate.

She squinted. Not a feral. A man. She could tell by the way he walked. Or maybe that was a trick—Allie had said the ferals were evolving, getting smarter. Maybe this was part of it, too. Her heart began to beat very fast, and she felt dizzy.

"Open the gate!" he cried. "She needs help!"

She raised her rifle to her shoulder and looked through the night scope and saw him suddenly more clearly. A young, possibly hand-some face contorted by an expression of distress. Could it possibly be a man? She lowered the rifle slightly and saw that he was hold-ing something, or, rather, someone—Allie. The girl was covered with blood, and he was, too. Her head was joggling loosely to the side with each step. Had he hurt her? Was he a feral after all? Emma couldn't tell if Allie was alive or dead. She let her finger tighten on the trigger.

At the gate, he stopped.

"I have Allie!" shouted the man. "She's hurt! Open the goddamn gate now!"

Emma hesitated. He could talk, but did that really mean he wasn't the same as the other men, the ferals? Who was to say that it wasn't him who had mauled Allie, that this wasn't part of some elaborate trick, and that as soon as the gates were open a whole bunch of other ferals would rush in? She hesitated, unsure of what to do. WWJD? What would Jacky do?

"Please!" he cried out. "She's dying!"

She waited, her finger still on the trigger, let her finger tighten. She held it there, aim steady, but she couldn't quite pull the trigger. What if she was wrong? What if it wasn't a trick? She waited, watching for the creature to give itself away, to show it wasn't human after all, but when nothing happened she shuddered. What would Jacky do? She lowered her rifle and slung it. A moment later, she had the trapdoor up and was sliding down the ladder as quickly as she could, shouting for help.

## Chapter Forty-five

He waited outside the gate for what seemed like forever, standing there, holding her. From time to time he shook her softly, just to get a reaction, just to make sure she was still breathing. *Hurry*, Sam kept thinking, *hurry*.

"Hang in there, Allie," he told her. "You're almost home."

Her eyelids moved a little without quite opening. Blood bubbled a little on her lips, so he knew she was still breathing. At least, for the moment.

How much time had gone by? One minute? Two? He couldn't tell, but finally there was a whirring sound and the gate swung open. He slid his way in, walking forward with Allie. Emma was there waiting, and Doc and Jacky, all recognizable from Allie's descriptions of them.

As soon as they saw him, they gasped. Their faces looked stunned, as if they couldn't believe what they were seeing. Then the largest of the three, Jacky, said to him, "Stop right there."

Sam stopped.

"She needs help!" yelled Sam. "What are you waiting for? She's lost a ton of blood! Help her now! Now!"

"Don't fucking move," said Jacky.

A number of women started rushing around, some running back into the house, others pulling a stretcher out from where it lay beside the porch.

Sam gave a cry of frustration. He took a step forward.

"Freeze!" said Jacky and lifted her gun to point it at his head. "Do not take another fucking step!"

"She's going to die!" said Sam.

"So are you if you're not careful, asshole," said Jacky. "You're in a minefield. Your left foot is about six inches away from one."

He looked down and saw it, the dull pressure pad rising just a few centimeters above the dirt.

"Oh shit," said Sam.

"'Oh shit' is right," said Jacky. "Now, if you can bring yourself to listen to directions from a woman, take two steps to the left."

Carefully, he did.

"Two short steps forward," she said, but in the middle of his second step she said "Stop!"

He put his foot down so suddenly he nearly fell.

"I said short steps," she said.

"Those were short steps," he said.

"Not short enough," she said. "Shuffle left again, slowly. I'll tell you when to stop."

He did. She moved as well, squinting, observing the path between them, and then nodded.

"Now walk straight toward me," she said. "You'll be okay."

He nodded and moved slowly and evenly forward. When he was still a few feet away, the women kicked into action. Doc rushed forward along with a few others and pulled Allie away from him, laid her flat on the stretcher, and began to minister to her wound.

For a moment Sam watched, feeling helpless, and then Jacky and four other women rushed him. He dodged the first almost by reflex, not turning his eyes away from Allie, but another had her hands on him by that time, and he hadn't shaken her off when yet another was there. He stopped resisting, let them grab his arms and zip-tie them behind his back, keeping his eyes fixed on Allie as long as he could as they rushed her away.


She lay asleep on the same surgical table in Doc's lab that was used for autopsies of the dead ferals. She had been cleaned up, the blood sponged off her face, the wound on her shoulder cleaned and rebandaged now. A small bag of blood hung from an IV stand beside her, and an intravenous line had been fed into her arm. The color was coming back into Allie's cheeks.

She felt a pressure on her arm, a tightness, and heard a pumping sound, like someone was inflating a bicycle tire. When she opened her eyes, she saw the blood pressure cuff that encircled her arm. Dana, the blonde whom she'd seen Holly hanging with earlier, stood beside her, holding a stethoscope under the cuff and looking at her wristwatch, silently counting her heartbeats, her mouth moving. Allie groaned.

Dana removed the stethoscope. She scribbled something onto a clipboard, then turned toward Allie, smiling.

"Allie," she said, her voice open and kind, "how do you feel?"

Allie peered around, confused, still not quite sure of herself, nor quite sure where she was.

"Do you know who I am?" Dana asked.

"You're Dana," Allie said.

"That's right," said Dana. "I'm glad that you remember."

"How long have I been out?" Allie asked.

"A few days," she said. "Nothing to worry about."

*Nothing to worry about?* thought Allie. *When the ferals are getting ready to swarm?*

"Where's Doc?" she asked. "I have to talk to her."

"She's been with you this whole time, helping you through. I've been helping her out. Kim's been here, too." She pointed to the bag of blood hanging from the IV. "That's from her," she said, "and not the first pint she gave. I made her go lie down."

Allie lifted her hand, but winced when she felt the pain in her shoulder. Where had that come from? She let the hand fall. "What happened to me?" she asked.

"You lost a lot of blood," said Dana. "A few more moments and you wouldn't have come back. He saved your life by bringing you here."

Her look changed, becoming suddenly more focused. "Sam. Where is he?" she asked.

"He's with Jacky and Doc," said Dana.

"Where?"

"Look," said Dana, "it's nothing to be worried about. You need to—"

"Did they put him in a cage?" asked Allie. "Was he in a cage here in the lab, like an animal?"

"Allie . . ." started Dana, but from the way she looked away, Allie knew he had been.

Allie cursed under her breath. She sat up in the bed and swung her legs out. When she felt the IV drip pulling at her arm she tore it out; blood began to spill slowly onto the floor.

"Allie, no!" said Dana, moving to the bed. "You need to rest."

Allie ignored her. She got her feet on the floor, almost slipped in the blood, but, jaw clenched, struggled to maintain her balance. When Dana reached for her to try to coax her back into the bed, Allie snapped at her. "Get the hell out of the way or I'll punch you in the face, Dana."

For a moment, Dana stayed where she was, and then, seeing how great Allie's need was, how impossible it would be to stop her, she stepped out of the way.

"You're making a mistake," Dana said. "We're just trying to help you." But Allie had already stumbled across the floor and was on her way out the door.

She stumbled down the hall, memories of struggling through the woods flashing through her. She had limped about halfway down the hall when she began to be conscious of voices, and then realized almost as quickly that she'd been hearing them for a long while. The sound grew louder as she moved forward. By the time she was exhausted and needed to stop and get some rest anyway, she realized it was coming from a half-open door just ahead: Jacky's security HQ. She stopped to lean against the wall as she caught her breath and peered in.

Inside were two dozen women or so, around half of the camp. Most of them were leaning back against the walls or standing with their arms crossed, focused intently on the middle of the room. In the center, Jacky and Doc were on their feet, pacing around one another, arguing. Jacky looked angry enough to hit someone, and Doc, for once, did, too. They were debating something, back and forth, but Allie was focusing on just staying upright. She hadn't been able to concentrate on what they were saying. Now, leaning against the door frame, a little steadier, she could begin to make it out.

"*I'm* being shortsighted?!?" Jacky said, throwing up her arms.

"Yes, you are," said Doc. "In other words, business as usual! Stick to what you know, Jacky, and leave the rest to those of us who really know something."

The crowd had realized Allie was there, and a ripple ran through them. The women closest to her looked at her and drew away, perhaps shocked by her appearance, the bloodstained gauze on her shoulder, the blood spattered on her legs, the fact that she was dressed only in a hospital gown. Or maybe still shocked by what she had done, hiding a male. Even Jacky and Doc paused their heated debate for a few seconds, glancing at her as the ripple passed beyond them. And then the women on the far side of the room moved a little, too, and, for just an instant, through the gap, she saw Sam.

He was in the rear of the room, leaning awkwardly against the wall, a guard to either side of him holding him firmly by the elbow. He was muzzled, and his wrists were bound. He didn't seem upset or anxious. More than anything, he just seemed resigned to whatever fate awaited him. It was as if all the fight had gone out of him.

But not Allie. Rage grew within her, bubbling to the surface. She exploded into the room, moving as quickly as her injured body would allow, rushing toward Sam.

"Jesus Christ!" she yelled, but her voice was weaker than she expected when it came out. "He is not *feral*!"

All heads had turned her direction, and all eyes were on her now as she barreled toward Sam.

"How can you treat him like this?" she asked the faces around her as she pushed her way closer. "This is exactly what he said you would do!"

She reached him. Their eyes locked, and he shook his head a little, trying to get her to stop, but she ignored the gesture. Her hands were up and on his face, touching and caressing it, trying to yank the muzzle off.

Suddenly someone folded her arms around Allie and pulled her away. Jacky. Allie struggled against her grip, gasping in pain as she moved her shoulder, trying and failing to break free.

"Enough!" cried Jacky. Allie had caught Sam's eye again, was watching him as she was pulled farther and farther away. He was shaking his head, his eyes telling her to relax, calm down. "After the shit you've done," Jacky said, "you need to keep your mouth shut." She firmly placed Allie next to a guard and gestured toward the door. "Get her the fuck out of here!" she ordered.

But Doc was there, too, just to the other side of her, and had one hand on the guard's shoulder. "She stays," said Doc, a strange intense authority in her voice that was altogether different from the way she normally talked.

"Like hell," said Jacky.

"It's a purely practical consideration," Doc claimed. "She might have something to add that can help." She turned to Allie. "But keep quiet, Allie," she said, "or we will have you restrained and gagged, like him."

For a moment, Allie kept her gaze on Sam, the latter pleading with his eyes for her not to pick a fight. Finally, she sagged, looked down, and nodded. "I'll be quiet," she said. She made her way to her habitual spot, lurking in the background, near the door, quickly realizing as she did that all the women and girls were eyeing her coldly, some with real venom. She looked away from them, ignoring them, staring only at Sam as the debate continued.

"We begin testing *now*," said Doc. "For all we know, he has the virus and it's just lying dormant. He could be a carrier. We need to find out why he's the way he is."

Allie grimaced. She had to bite her tongue to keep from speaking. But there was Sam, still looking at her, calm, calming her, not breaking her gaze, his eyes telling her not to do anything foolish.

*Or at least they are if I'm understanding them correctly*, thought Allie. What if he was saying something completely different? Something like: *Watch me. Stay focused. When the time comes, we'll make a break for it.*

"You smoking too much, Doc?" Jacky said. "This area is infested.

It's time to leave—now." She pointed at Sam. "And that one will help get us out."

"The risk is too great," said Doc.

Jacky shook her head. "It isn't," she said. "Justified risk. He claims that the ferals leave him alone. It'll work."

"Jacky, it's been three years. Surely, the batteries are dead by now. This is a pipe dream."

Jacky folded her arms over her chest. "We've got batteries of all sizes here, at the camp, fully charged. Can't be that fucking difficult to swap them out."

"What about fuel? Fuel doesn't last that long."

"If it's gasoline, sure, there's no chance. But the big boats run on fuel oil. A full tank of that might still work, even after all this time, as long as we have enough battery power to heat it. He goes to the harbor, gets a boat, clears it of ferals, and brings the boat to—"

"And just how do we get on this boat?" Doc interrupted. "The shorelines and beachheads are crawling with the things."

"Let me finish," said Jacky. "The bridge. We board from the Bayview Bridge."

Doc opened her mouth to speak and then shut it again. Her look was one of thoughtful consideration. Jacky had her attention. She had the attention of every woman in the room.

Jacky walked slowly to the chalkboard on the far wall. She began to sketch on it—neat, swift chalk diagrams, circling bits of them here and there.

"We wouldn't have to go near shore," she said. "We make our way onto the bridge, which is clear of ferals unless they're using it to cross to somewhere and which can be defended." She pointed at Sam. "He pulls the boat up beneath it. Then we harness down from the bridge and get the hell out of here. We can't travel by land—we go by sea." Her eyes searched around the room until she found whom she was looking for. "Holly grew up on boats—her father ran the ferry. So did Ellie and Jenna—they had fishermen for fathers. Any of the three of them could pilot us down to the southern states, easily."

A few of the women in the room were nodding, Allie saw, already buying into the plan. Others were muttering, shaking their heads. Doc remained somewhere in the middle, not sold but not rejecting it, either, more thoughtful, still contemplating.

After a moment, Holly spoke up. "Why wouldn't he just run for it when we send him on this mission? Why would he come back with a boat?"

The other women turned to Jacky, eager for her answer. But she didn't have one. She remained silent, darting looks at Sam, trying to judge if he was to be trusted, unsure of how she felt. Could a man ever be trusted, even if he wasn't feral?

The women were beginning to get antsy when Doc spoke. Her voice was quiet and measured. She looked straight at Allie. "He wouldn't leave her behind," she said.

Allie narrowed her eyes. She hated that Doc was using their relationship as a kind of leash for Sam, and hated, too, that Doc, even though she'd only just met Sam, had already read him—and her, Allie—like they were open books.

"Is Doc right, Allie?" asked Jacky.

Allie thought. Yes, Doc was right, she knew it, but did she want to put Sam at such risk? The ferals left him alone when there were one or two of them—or at least didn't seem to know what to make of him for long enough so that Sam could bring them down with a machete. They didn't immediately identify him as a threat. But what would happen when he was in the middle of hundreds of them? And would it work with someone like Scarface, with the evolved ferals? Saying yes might be sending him into a death trap.

"You can see from her face that I'm right," said Doc. "Look, it's not a terrible plan, but it's too risky. We keep him here, radio Dallas and Leslie, bring them back, find out if they can get us the records of the tests that were already done at Hubbard. That will give us an edge. His blood could help us develop a vaccine—a child born from him, a male child, could be immune. He's too valuable. He can't be out of our sight ever again. We have to come up with something else."

Jacky threw her hands into the air. "Jesus Christ, it's the same shit, over and over again! We have nothing else!"

From there the discussion became a yelling match, shouted accusations back and forth between Jacky and Doc, with the women around them starting to murmur as well and beginning to chime in, until the whole crowd was roiling, fighting with one another, the confusion growing stronger and stronger. Allie stood there in the midst of it, dizzy, swaying. She pressed her hands to her temples, tried to clear her head, tried to remain calm, to think, but finally just lost it.

"Shut up!" she shouted as loud as she could manage. "Shut the fuck up!"

The noise lessened, everyone a little stunned by her barked yell. Women began to turn to face her.

"We have to let him go!" she said. "He's in too much danger with us! Let him go south alone! He'll find another camp! Don't you see—"

Jacky folded her arms across her chest and gestured to Emma. "Get her the fuck out of here!" she said.

The closest guard rushed Allie, several other security officers following quickly in her wake. They grabbed her as she struggled, tried to get away. Sam started forward, yelling something through the muzzle, but the guards to either side of him caught his arms and, when he continued to struggle, tripped him, immobilized him on the floor. Emma and her crew dragged Allie toward the door as she resisted, feeling her injured shoulder quickly going numb.

"Get off of me!" she cried.

And then something inside her cracked and broke, and she was scratching and clawing—biting, even—doing everything she could to stay inside the room, near Sam. She didn't want to be separated from him again, ever again. Kim, too, was yelling, crying out Allie's name, and hitting and kicking one of the guards, trying to get her to let go of her sister. The guard turned around and backhanded the girl, knocked her off her feet like she was swatting a fly, and Allie had flashes of her father knocking her mother across the room. "Stop it," Doc was yelling. "Stop it!" But nobody was paying attention. Meanwhile, though Allie struggled as if possessed, she was being drawn, slowly and inexorably, out of the room.

An earsplitting noise, sudden and intense, a protracted blaring siren, echoed through the entire farmhouse. The chaos and fighting stopped on a dime, the guards dropping Allie abruptly to the floor and looking for Jacky. It was the warning alarm. Trouble. Sam was shouting into his muzzle, something desperate but too muffled to hear.

"Get to your posts," shouted Jacky. "Now!"

The women hurried out, a mass exodus. Allie managed to get to her feet. Pushing against the flow of women, her shoulder dressing now sodden with blood, she tried to make it to Sam, but was intercepted by Doc.

"You're bleeding again," shouted Doc over the sirens. "You never should have gotten up in the first place." She grabbed her uninjured arm. "Let's go."

For a moment, Allie resisted, staring past Doc at Sam, who had managed to roll over onto his back and sit up. Whatever she saw there, whatever she read in Sam's eyes, relaxed her. She let herself be guided out of the room, never taking her eyes off Sam as she went, as the sirens continued to blare.

## Chapter Forty-six

Jacky pushed her way through the crowds and to the ladder, scrambling up as quickly as she could. The trapdoor at the top was already open, and she had started speaking even before she was all the way up and into the highest crow's nest.

"What the hell's going on?"

"There!" said Brandi, the security officer on duty, and gestured. Her hand was shaking.

Jacky pulled herself all the way onto the platform of the crow's nest and came to the edge. She squinted, peered out at the forest.

"Oh my God," she said. "They're here."

Whatever she'd expected, this was much worse. An army of ferals surrounded the camp, gathered just outside the ten-foot wall topped with barbed wire that edged the outer perimeter. There were dozens upon dozens of them, a roiling, restless mass. They shuttled back and forth, pacing, but never touched the fence, never crossed an invisible line. It was as if they were waiting for something, as if something was holding them back. There were far more of them, Jacky realized, than the women and their defenses would ever be able to handle. The camp would be quickly overrun.

"What are they doing?" Brandi was asking. Jacky heard the question through a kind of fog. For a long moment, she didn't respond at all. Then she just shook her head. "I don't know," she said. "I don't know why the motherfuckers haven't attacked already."

"What are we going to do?" Brandi asked.

Jacky grabbed Brandi's rifle, quickly raised it, and squeezed off two shots. Two ferals fell, their heads blurred with blood. She thrust the rifle back at Brandi, hard, then reached for another rifle off the rack. "That's what we do," she said. "Fucking keep killing them until they kill us."

## Chapter Forty-seven

## Allie

I'm in Doc's lab, letting her patch me up. I wanted to stay with Sam, wanted to hold, to touch him, one more time, just once more, wanted to take that ghastly muzzle off him and free his hands, let him stand up and be a human being again, but when I met his eyes he was telling me to go, go, get myself taken care of, now wasn't the time. And so I went, letting Doc lead me away, but I kept my eyes on him the whole time, and if those eyes had started telling me something, anything else, trust me, I wouldn't be here now.

Doc has out dental floss, which she's using for sutures, and a long, thin, nearly circular needle—the kind of thing that used to be used, she told me once when she was a little stoned and I was watching her sew up the foot of a girl who had stepped on broken glass, to mend the fabric wings of airplanes. "But that was years ago," she'd said, "and if someone hadn't figured out how good these were for sewing up flesh in a pinch, well, they probably wouldn't exist anymore."

That's what I'm trying to think of this as: that I'm watching someone sew fabric, something inanimate that has nothing to do with me. I'm trying not to feel the pinch and hot sear of the needle plunging through my flesh where I tore out my stitches. The siren is still blaring, which doesn't help any—it makes me more conscious of the pain—and Doc, between sutures, as she draws the thread tight and prepares to insert the needle again, keeps looking at me over the top of her glasses, considering me, assessing me, judging me. I'm hoping to hell that this isn't what I think it is, that the ferals aren't going to come pouring in, that we'll have another day or two to get away.

"I got to get up," I say. "Have to help take care of the ferals."

"There's plenty of people out there," she says.

"No," I say, "this could be the big one."

"If it is," she says, "which I doubt, then you'll be able to fight them from right here."

When I try to sit up, she pushes me gently but firmly back down on the table.

"You're not going to do anybody any good unless I get these stitches in," she says. She's right: if we're about to be overrun, it's time to get sutured up and as battle-ready as possible. I grudgingly give in.

I'm in enough pain that it's hard for me to keep any kind of mask up. I'm worried that she's seeing me. All of me.

"Don't look at me that way, Doc," I finally say.

"What way?" she says. "How am I looking at you?"

"No," I say, "don't pretend you don't know what I mean as a way of distracting me. Don't say anything," I say. "I don't want to hear it."

"I don't know what to say," says Doc. "For once, you've rendered me speechless."

"Well, that's an accomplishment," I say.

She doesn't say anything for a stitch and a half, but then she can't help herself. "I should be saying, 'You stupid, selfish girl—what were you thinking?'"

"Didn't you just say that?"

She shakes her head, deliberately. "No," she says slowly. "I don't blame you, Allie. I don't blame you at all."

And then she looks at me full in the face, and I see that, yes, her eyes are interested but they're not full of blame. They're brimming with understanding, and empathy.

She goes back to the stitching. Almost done. Then I can get up and go find a rifle and start killing ferals. "One day, you can tell me his story," Doc says.

I nod, and then, realizing she's looking down, focused on the suturing, say, "Okay."

"Right now, though, you'll tell me his one thing."

And that, for just a moment, draws me in, makes me ignore the alarm blaring down the hall, makes me stop imagining picking off ferals as they swarm over the wall. For that moment, I don't say a word, wondering if I should tell her anything at all. I want, in so many ways, to keep Sam all to myself. I don't want to betray him, don't want to share him with anyone, not even with the people I love. But another part of me remembers why we did this with the ferals we'd captured: it was a way to make them human, make them individual, make us remember there were people hiding inside. Doc is saying she wants to know Sam as a *person*, that she wants to *think* of him as a person, and it is hard for me to think of that as anything but a good thing. If she and the others start thinking of Sam as a person, maybe they'll take his muzzle off.

"He . . . talks to himself," I admit. "Out loud. And he doesn't know he's doing it." And I think of how amazing that was, just hearing his voice, even when it wasn't speaking to me. Hearing a man's voice not squeal or howl or bark but actually talk for the first time in three years.

Doc nods, watching my face the whole time. Something about what I say or the way that I say it gets to her. I see her eyes glisten.

Outside, the sirens continue blaring. They've never gone on so long before. Which makes me think that I was right, that this is it.

Doc turns and looks at the window. "What the hell is going on out there?" she wonders aloud.

"You know what's going on, Doc, even if you don't want to admit it," I say tiredly. "Now, make yourself useful and find me a gun."

## Chapter Forty-eight

The security room was empty of women; they had all fled to their positions. The only one remaining was Sam, bound and gagged, still sitting on the floor, forgotten for the moment as the alarm sirens roared. He stayed there, and waited, and listened. How much time did they have? he wondered. Had the ferals already started over the walls? Would he manage to get out of this one as he had the last attack, or would he be left here on the floor, hands tied behind his back?

*At least I'm not in a cage*, he thought. He could get to his feet and take off, eventually find something he could cut the zip-ties off with. It wouldn't be easy, but it wasn't impossible, either.

His gloomy meditations were interrupted by movement in the hall. What was it? A moment later, a group of young faces poked around the doorway. They stood there in the frame, watching him. Four, maybe five young girls, silent, tense and poised for danger, stealing quick glances at him like he was some kind of circus freak.

He watched them for a moment, and watched them watching him. After a while, he could no longer resist. He contorted his face as much as he could, wearing the muzzle, and growled, loud, then roared, rocking his torso forward.

The girls uttered high-pitched screams and fled madly away. All except one, who remained behind, unaffected, staring at him from the doorway. About twelve years old. After a moment, she cautiously entered and slowly approached him.

He watched her come, moving closer and closer. She looked familiar to him, which was strange. And then, after a moment, he realized why: she looked a little like Allie. Suddenly he knew who she was. He wondered what she was up to, but he let her come, remaining still. She came right up to him, stopped just in front of him, and slowly reached out to touch the muzzle. And then she reached around to the side of it, unbuckled the straps, and tentatively removed it, letting it drop to the floor.

It felt good to have the muzzle off, to have his mouth and cheeks exposed to the air again. He licked his lips, swallowed. When he spoke, his voice was cracked, rusty.

"Thanks," he said. And then, when she didn't say anything but just stayed there, looking at him, "You're Kim, aren't you?"

"How did you know that?" she asked, surprised.

"Your sister's been telling me about you," he said. "You don't happen to have a knife, do you? Something I can cut myself free with?"

She shook her head.

He sighed, nodded. "We'll worry about that later. Look, for now you need to douse yourself in feral blood. Do you know where they keep the stash?"

Kim thought, nodded. "I know where a few jars are," she said.

"Slather it on, and on those other girls, too. Get a gun or two if you can. And then hide. In a minute, they're going to come swarming over the walls. Don't let them find you."

Kim nodded and started for the door. But before she got there she turned back around, looked at him.

"Can I ask you a question?" she asked.

"Sure," said Sam. "Shoot."

He was expecting something to do with the imminent invasion. Instead, it was, "Do you . . . do you love her?"

Sam didn't even have to think. "Very much," he said immediately. He waited to see how she took the news; she didn't react one way or the other. "But I would never take her away from you," he said.

Kim just stared. *What's going on inside your head?* Sam wondered.

Slowly, Kim backed out—just like her sister, not willing to take her eyes away from Sam until the very last moment, until the moment she was gone. The alarm droned on.

## Chapter Forty-nine

Jacky had dropped two more and they fell, but the others didn't go anywhere. They just moved restlessly back and forth, without leaving and without coming closer. Something was holding them back. She hesitated, wondering if she should keep firing. How many shots could she fire before they rushed in? Four seemed to be okay, but what if the next one brought the whole pack rushing forward? The more shots the women fired, the more likely the ferals were to swarm—Jacky was sure of it. And there were so many; what good did picking a few off do?

Maybe they'd just leave, she told herself. Just turn around and fade into the bushes, giving the camp a chance to pack up and clear out. There was no real reason this would be the case—it didn't fit with how ferals acted—but there was also no real reason for them to congregate like they were doing. They would chase someone, but if there wasn't anybody in sight, they would fade off into the bushes and go looking for other prey. Like Allie had said, they weren't acting the way ferals normally acted. Which meant that anything could happen.

So—Allie had been right. They were fucked. They should have left already. And now maybe it was too late.

Brandi grabbed her arm hard. A line of ferals gave their howl and rushed forward, clambering up the fence surrounding the property.

"I don't fucking get it," said Jacky. "The motherfuckers have never done anything like this before. They're not chasing anyone. This is straight suicide."

Jacky fired, then fired again, picking off a feral here and there, and a moment later Brandi was following her lead. Though a few ferals remained heaped at the bottom of the wall, the rest started to climb it. Another few fell or got stuck on the barbed wire, but the majority crested the fence; they tore skin, left bits of themselves hanging, but, undaunted, they kept coming.

They leaped down, inside the perimeter now, and began to run madly toward the main building. After only a few footsteps, they struck the mines and exploded, going up in a shower of dirt and flesh and blood, the explosions ringing loud.

*That's it*, thought Jacky, *they'll retreat now.*

But a moment later she heard another series of howls. As she watched, a new wave of ferals threw themselves at the fence. They clambered up to the top and fell over, started running just as the others had done, and a moment later were blown to pieces. But this group got a little farther.

A third wave was gathering. Everyone was firing now, all the women in all the lookouts on the roof, all the women on the porch of the farmhouse, trying to kill them, but as each one fell, another took its place.

"If they keep coming like this," said Brandi, "all our mines will soon be gone."

Jacky reloaded and raised her rifle again, readying herself to shoot a few more before they got to the mines. The ferals were still gathering. She peered through the night-vision scope, letting her focus wander. There was something behind the army. Or, rather, someone. Thirty yards back, half hidden in the brush, watching his fellow ferals climb into the enclave and die violently, was the one Allie had called Scarface. Jacky observed him, wishing she was a trained sniper. She was preparing to squeeze off a shot when he abruptly turned and stalked off, limping as he went. She followed him a little farther back, until he reached another group of ferals, maybe twenty, maybe thirty—hard to say, given the vegetation between her and them. They were waiting, strange and hideous and unmoving among the trees. Just waiting.

She squeezed off a shot, and in a flash Scarface was gone, hidden somewhere.

Jacky lowered the gun. "Oh my God," she said. "They're waiting."

"For what?" asked Brandi.

"For what you said," said Jacky. "The mines to be gone. This is some kind of plan. These motherfuckers are getting rid of the mines, throwing themselves on them like kamikazes, so that Scarface and the rest can make it all the way to the farmhouse." She shook her head. *Shit,* she thought, *I didn't get far enough, didn't even get around to mixing the napalm.* "Without the mines, we don't have enough firepower to stop them. We're doomed."

## Chapter Fifty

There had been an explosion, which they expected—usually, if a feral got it in his head to climb the walls, that was how it ended. But that had been followed almost immediately by several more.

"More than one made it over this time," said Doc, wrinkling her brow.

They stayed still, listening. A moment later, there were more explosions, then still more.

"That's not just one or two of them climbing over the fence," said Allie. "They're coming in."

There were a few more rounds of explosions, the noise shaking the house.

"How many mines are out there?" asked Doc.

"Not many more than that," said Allie.

One more explosion, and then silence. Suddenly gunfire started up, more than just the stray shots they'd heard earlier. Now it was relentless, coming from everywhere all at once, a dozen or more weapons, the howling of the ferals drawing nearer.

Allie was on her feet and getting dressed. Doc had moved to a weapons cabinet and was grabbing guns. She tossed several to Allie, took one for herself. They heard a scream not far away, terrified and long, and cut off abruptly, and then more screams, more wails, a kind of unearthly symphony arising in the house around them.

"They're inside," said Doc.

A figure flashed by the door of their room, running down the hallway. A feral. Allie rushed to the door, leaned out of it, and shot the feral in the back of the head. Hissing, it collapsed into the wall and died.

"Lock the door after me, Doc," she said. "Don't open it for anyone. Hide behind a table or something. Shoot the bastards if they come after you."

"Where are you going?" Doc asked.

"To find Kim," she said. "And Sam."

She left. Doc locked the door and took up a position behind the lab table, her gun aimed at the door. She waited.

## Chapter Fifty-one

He could move a little, and at least now his mouth wasn't muzzled, but his hands were zip-tied behind him, impossible to get at. When Kim had left him, he'd tested his bonds to see if he could get free, but to no avail. A few scattered shots, and then there'd been the explosions, just a couple at first, then explosion after explosion, and at that point he knew all too well what was going on. He struggled his way to his feet. He'd get out, find Allie, get someone, anyone, to cut him out of these zip-ties, and then do what he could to help. He saw himself again back at the old camp, looking over the carnage of the mutilated bodies, slowly digging holes to bury the five youngest. Maybe that was what he would be doing here. In his mind he saw a flash of Kim, dead.

He started forward at a half-run—and a second later was thrown off his feet, wrenching his arms. What the hell? He turned around and looked behind him, saw the line running from his wrist ties to the ring in the wall. His hands weren't only tied: when the guards had thrown him down they had tethered him to the wall.

He tugged at the tether; it seemed secure. He looked around for something to cut it, but there was nothing. Even if there was, how could he have held it? He cursed in frustration. He was stuck.

A moment later, the gunfire began again, volley after volley. The sounds rose feverishly, drawing nearer and nearer until he was certain they were coming either from just outside the farmhouse or from down the hall.

And then there was that unearthly feral moan and the high shriek of a woman. Now they were inside. He saw a dark shape flash by and hurtle down the hall. Feral. Not all that interested in him—he didn't smell right—clearly in pursuit of someone, a woman.

Outside, sounds of war rose. He remained helpless, tethered, unable to flee or help. He stamped his feet, so frustrated he was going out of his mind, helpless. He gave a roar of frustration and only realized once it came out how close it sounded to a feral's cry.

There was a click; the lights went out, and he was thrust into darkness.

"Allie!" he cried. She was out there, maybe dying or even dead, and there was nothing he could do.

His voice was lost among the screams and the wails and the machine-gun fire, the general cacophony like the sound track for hell.

It felt like hours but was probably only a few minutes before the gunfire decreased. Slowly, the human sounds were whittled down to faint screams. There were a few final bursts, a few baying feral cries, and then a silence fell, eerie and profound. As if all that was left in the world was Sam, sitting in the dark, listening to the sound of his own breathing.

He wasn't in a cage, but he might as well have been. He was just as stuck as he had been in the last camp when the ferals had swarmed. Even worse: this time, nobody was going to come let him out.

He pulled hard on the tether. No, it was strong and well attached, not likely to break. He walked in the dark, stumbling, sweeping one foot over the ground in front of him, listening for the sounds of things moving, trying to imagine from the sounds a likely object that would save him—a sharp piece of metal, a shard of glass, a knife. When he found nothing, he sat down again, his back against the wall. So this was how it would end. He and Allie had been right all along. Coming to the camp was a death sentence.

A dragging sound, not too distant. Sam's eyes had adjusted enough now so he found he could make out the doorway, a patch of lesser dark in the general dark. He kept his eyes on it, waiting.

He caught the flicker of a flashlight beam in the hallway and only then knew for certain it wasn't a feral. It was getting brighter, coming closer to him.

"Hey," he whispered. Not so loud that he'd draw the attention of the ferals, if any of them were left in the camp, but, he hoped, loud enough so the person would hear. When there was no response, he repeated it a little louder.

"I'm here," he said, when he saw something cross into the door frame. The beam of the flashlight skewered the darkness and blinded him momentarily. Then it was lowered and he saw only afterimages, which slowly faded to reveal a woman, emerging from the darkness, walking toward him.

"Allie?" he said.

It was Doc. She was out of breath—anxious, maybe.

"Hello, Sam," she said, her voice surprisingly calm.

"Thank God you're here," he said.

She began to cut through the zip-ties, sawing back and forth weakly on them for a good minute with a knife, the light of the flashlight shivering like water the whole time. Why was it taking her so long? He could hardly stand to wait, could hardly keep still. But then they fell off, and the tether along with them, and he was finally free.

He stood up, chafing his hands.

"Thank you," he said.

Doc nodded, her motion barely visible in the darkness.

"Let's go," said Sam. "Where's Allie? Wasn't she with you? Have you seen her? For God's sake, let's go find her!"

He was already halfway out the door when he realized Doc wasn't following. He turned around and retraced his steps.

She was sitting on a chair, perched oddly, like a bird. He went to her.

"What are you doing?" he asked, exasperated. "Come on!"

Doc looked up at him. Her face was serene, and when she spoke she still had that same unnerving calm.

"I'm going to sit down now," she told him. She repositioned herself slightly on the chair. "Okay. I'm going to rest here."

"What?" asked Sam, baffled. "What are you—"

The flashlight clattered from her hand. Sam quickly picked it up and shone it back on her, and that was when he saw the blood, a lot of it, leaking from Doc's lacerated abdomen and chest: a deep, fatal wound. Seeing how bad it was, he was surprised she had managed to free him.

"Oh God," said Sam.

"It's okay, Sam," she said. "I don't mind dying. Come close. I want you to listen to me now."

He brought his head down close to hers. Though she was fading, she struggled to raise her hands and managed to get them high enough to rest them lightly on either side of his face. She drew him closer, until their faces were almost touching, and then she spoke, using every ounce of strength she had left.

"Get out of here," she said. "Get out and stay alive. You are everything. Everything. Go. Don't look back."

They stayed there like that, Doc's hands warm and dry against his face, as she waited for him to pull away and he waited for her to release him.

"Is she alive, Doc?" he asked.

Something about that question seemed to break Doc's heart. He watched a shudder tear through her, felt it as well in the trembling of her hands. And then she released a juddering cry from deep within. She fought against the emotion, trying to push it down, grabbing on to Sam's face even tighter.

"The scientist in me tells me I should tell you the woman you love is dead," she said. "But I can't do that. I don't trust the scientist anymore."

For a moment, Doc didn't say anything. Anxious, he waited for her to go on.

"They took her, Sam," she said. "Alive."

Doc's hands fell from his face, and Sam reached down, squeezed them. "Thank you," he said.

She nodded silently. "When you see Allie," she said, her voice hardly more than a whisper now, "tell her my one thing . . . tell her my one thing was . . ."

She trailed off. She was still breathing, blood pumping feebly from her stomach. And then her breathing stopped, and she was dead.

## Chapter Fifty-two

The whole house was a bloodbath, scattered with heaps of dead ferals and the corpses of women. He moved through it rapidly, checking for pulses and plucking guns when he failed to find any, taking up a clip from where it lay on the floor a little farther on. He was barreling for the door, running all out, when he heard something: a whimper, the whimper of a young girl. He pulled up short and stopped, listening.

It was coming from behind a closed door, just back down the hall. The crack at the bottom of the door had been doused with feral blood. He went to the door and started to open it, then thought better of it.

"Are you okay in there?" he asked. "It's me, Sam. I'm coming in."

When there was no reply, he slowly opened the door.

On the floor just inside was a dead feral. He'd been gutted, torn open. His viscera were everywhere. When Sam opened the door wider, he saw, in the far corner of the room, Kim.

She was smeared head to toe with feral blood. Crouched behind her were two women as well as several very young girls, all of them smeared as well, the smell of blood very strong in the air.

Kim stood alert, a pistol in her hand. As Sam came forward, slowly, toward the shell-shocked women, Kim kept positioning herself to stand between them and him, protecting them. *Must run in the family*, thought Sam, impressed.

"Are you okay?" Sam asked.

Kim immediately nodded. The others hesitated a little longer, but in the end nodded as well.

"They took your sister, Kim," said Sam.

Kim nodded. "They took a lot of us," she responded. "Holly, Jacky, pretty much everybody they could."

Sam gave a sharp nod. "We're all getting out of here. I know where the ferals have taken them—the harbor. I just don't know why."

One of the younger girls started crying.

"Where do you keep your weapons?" Sam asked. "Let's go get them back."

# Chapter Fifty-three

He left his quad there, on the side of the road, just a little shy of the defaced HARBOR AHEAD sign. "*Stay Back!*" the graffiti read. "*Hell Ahead!*" He ignored the warnings and continued on, dragging the heavy canvas sack along on the ground behind him.

He worked his way, panting, to the top of the small hill just shy of the harbor and stopped at the hill's crown to rest and reconnoiter. From somewhere, the distant wails of ferals rose out of the darkness like a demonic choir. A few hundred yards ahead, he could see the dim shadows of boats—some large, some small. The harbor was teeming with movement, dark wraithlike figures passing back and forth in a kind of elaborate and at times almost geometrical dance. Ferals in their hive, Sam thought.

Would it work here? he wondered. When there were one or two in the wild, they didn't know what to make of him, and usually left him alone unless they were provoked. But that was lone ferals, out in the middle of nowhere. Here, in their hive, it might be a different story. They might be all over him simply because they didn't recognize him, no matter how he smelled to them.

He hauled the strap of the bag back up onto his shoulder and started down the hill.


He dragged the bag along, slowly. At some point he crossed into the hive, but it was hard to say where that was exactly. First there were just a feral or two, and then there were dozens. They milled near the roadway, lithe and muscular and inhuman. They were quickly near him, looming up suddenly in the darkness, sniffing him, moving all around him, scrutinizing him. He kept still and kept his eyes lowered, trying to appear less of a threat, and holding his breath, trying to hide his fear. After a moment, they snorted and seemed to lose interest in him, and slowly wandered away.

The smell was terrible. Most ferals were in the later stages of the infection, lean and attractive, perfect and deadly creatures driven by rage. But some still had blood and pus coming from their eyes, mouth, and nose, as if the illness was asserting itself again, the veins on their faces and chests and arms unnaturally swollen, writhing like worms. Others seemed to be having muscular spasms, their limbs tightening and flexing in a way that seemed unnatural, almost enough to snap their own bones.

They kept coming up to him. It took a few such encounters for him to realize that he didn't have to stop as they sniffed him, that he could just keep walking. But even then he kept expecting to be torn apart.

As he moved farther into the hive, the cacophony of feral wails crescendoed into a ghastly, earsplitting noise. It seemed to come and go like a wave, a near silence followed by an intense and reverberant roar of deafening sound. He could see a little better here, with the moon above twinned by its reflection in the bay, everything caught in a gray and grainy light.

It was an earthly version of hell. Some of the boats were half sunk, others spattered with filth and blood. The docks and boats were crammed with the teeming masses of the ferals. The boards of the docks had collapsed and rotted in places. The ferals stalked about, some staring skyward and howling, others feeding on carcasses, still others lying on the dock's edge and convulsing feverishly. There were also groups that had clustered in strange, unmoving throngs, their eyes dull, as if they were machines that had been deactivated and were just waiting to be turned on again.

He continued stubbornly onward, dragging his sack behind him. They were leaving him completely alone now, not as interested in him as the ferals on the edge of the hive had been, perhaps assuming in advance that he was one of them.

The boards that composed the docks were littered with parts and piece of bodies, gobbets of rotting flesh—half-eaten deer, dog, and horse carcasses, bones, and smears of brain. The ground was sticky from blood and gore, and stank badly. Even in the near-darkness, he could see squirming white maggots everywhere, and sometimes heard them pop beneath his feet.

A feral loomed up suddenly, just beside him. Sam jolted to a stop, and stiffened with fear as it came close and closer still, sniffing Sam's neck. It stayed there for a long moment, smelling him, exhaling its hot, rancid breath on his skin. And then, just as suddenly as it had appeared, it was gone.

Sam breathed a raspy sigh of relief. The wails around him kept ebbing and flowing, from thunderous to almost silent. He stood in the heart of the maelstrom, wondering where to go.

He started in one direction, but a moment later he second-guessed himself and started heading in another. Where was he to find the women of West Staten? Was he already too late? Had the ferals already torn them apart?

And then, in the trough between wails, he heard something that could have been a scream, a woman's scream. But was that really what it was? He wasn't sure, not exactly; he stayed still and waited, ears pricked, hoping he'd hear it again.

It took him three more cycles of wailing to pick it up again between roars. There it was, muffled but definitely a scream. His head whipped toward the sound and waited. Another round of wailing, and he found the source: a nearby cargo ship.

Dragging the sack behind him, he headed for it.

## Chapter Fifty-four

The deck of the cargo ship was packed with ferals, and there was something different about them. Whereas the others seemed to be wailing at random, wandering, only partially aware of one another, these ferals seemed fully aware. They wailed and bellowed at one another, the threat of violence heavy in the air. Ferals out on the hunt didn't fight each other, unless it was over who'd have first choice of the meat of a kill, but these seemed tense and ready to spring at one another. Itching for a fight. Eager to dominate. Alphas vying for power.

He hesitated at the top of the gangway, wondering if it was safe to board. They were bellowing back and forth at one another, faces sweaty and filled with aggression. He began to hear different tones in the sound, as if they were expressing a kind of primitive language.

He was still waiting, wondering what to do, when the wails became frantic on one part of the deck. The ferals turned, as if a single body, to focus their attention in that direction. There two ferals circled one another, shrieking. The ferals closest to them had backed away, forming a barricade around them, a circle. The crowd surrounding them wailed, and it felt to Sam like a kind of boisterous jeering, an incitement to fight.

The two ferals feinted toward one another and away, snarling, their claws raking at empty air. At first it seemed like a sort of elaborate dance, a display of dominance, but all at once, for reasons that Sam couldn't understand, the tone of the circling changed. Their stances became more fixed and aggressive, their teeth were now exposed in a permanent snarl, and their eyes had focused on one another in a way that suggested they couldn't see anything else.

They leaped forward and attacked one another, moving so swiftly that they were little more than a blur of fists and nails and teeth rolling about. And then they were apart, bleeding and torn, circling again. The crowd of creatures around them began to wail venomously, absorbed in watching one of their own tear another of their own to bits. The pair closed again, another terrible frenzied blur, and when they separated this time, both were panting heavily. One was missing an ear, but it had bitten off the index finger of the other and was chewing on it now, furiously masticating. It spat out a gobbet of bone and flesh. The ferals on the edge of the circle fought for the scrap. Again the pair circled, waiting for the next opportunity to close, as the maddened ferals around them screamed with rage, egging them on.

Sam moved from the gangway up onto the deck, staying near the edge of the crowd, moving slowly around, always looking down, never meeting a feral's eye. He was carrying the heavy bag now, the muscles in his arm bulging, and trying to make as little noise as possible, trying not to draw attention to himself.

He had made it about halfway around the deck when he saw a feral turned away from the action, observing him. He stopped, held still, made himself small.

The feral continued staring, unblinking, just watching him. It shifted a little, turning its body toward him. And then there was a cry from the circle and a long arc of blood shot up into the night sky, spattering onto the deck between Sam and the feral. The ferals roared, and the one that had been watching Sam turned away for a moment, distracted. As soon as he did, Sam moved as unobtrusively as he could to the hatch leading belowdecks.

As he started down, he expected at any moment the attentive feral to come after him, but nobody came.

It was very dark, no lights at all. He reached into his bag and extracted the pair of night-vision goggles that Kim had found for him among Allie's things, carefully affixed them over his eyes.

The companionway was a tight circular staircase, and he had to lift and edge the bag through it to make it go. At the bottom was a long passage, fluted slightly at each edge; the ceiling down here was hung with ductwork and pipes. It smelled rank here, foul, of rotted flesh and oil and stagnant water.

The passageway came to an abrupt end, opening into a warren of other smaller passageways and compartments, catacombs of storage and mechanical spaces. It was hot down here, almost unbearably so, and through the goggles the air vibrated with heat distortion. The cacophony of female screams was audible again, the volume of the sounds increasing with each step he took.

He hesitated at the end of the passage and then chose a new one, the one the screams seemed to be coming from. He was moving faster now, driven on by the urgency of the women's cries.

The passageway twisted around in an odd knot and then straightened again. He could see, up ahead, an open doorway, with two ferals standing under the lintel. They could see him—he could tell by the shift in their attention when he turned the corner—but they didn't move, didn't hiss or menace him. They just sniffed the air, and then one snorted a little, dismissing him as unworthy of any sustained interest.

The shrieks were coming from behind them, in the compartment beyond. Slowly, he moved forward. The ferals just stayed as they were, paying him no heed. He set the bag down with a clank, and that interested them for a moment, but then they turned away again.

Painstakingly, Sam opened the bag and removed a machete, interposing his body between it and the ferals. He approached them, machete held at his side, tight against his upper thigh.

They watched him come. They wailed once as he came close and then opened their mouths in snarls, not sure what to make of him, keeping him at a distance. Focusing his eyes down and making his body small, he got a little closer—then rapidly slashed the machete up and through the throat of the first and into the temple of the other. Warm blood sprayed all over his chest and arms as the first feral pitched over. The second stumbled, struck the wall, and shook his head, blood pouring out from beneath the flap of skin the machete had raised. He turned toward Sam and leaped, just in time to have his throat skewered by Sam's blade.

As the feral fell, it tore the machete out of Sam's hand. The creature lay thrashing on the floor, air hissing out of its throat, until Sam stomped on its head and cracked its skull apart. He wrenched the machete free and began to put it back in the bag, then thought better of this and slid it into his belt. *Two down*, he thought to himself, *ten thousand to go.* He stepped through the doorway and into the room beyond.

For a moment, he was unable to take it in, unable to understand.

It was a mechanical room. Three large, upright cylindrical objects covered with dials and gauges occupied a good portion of one-half of the space. The rest was full of large rusted pipes with wheels to open and close them, vents and cables snaking everywhere.

On the cold steel flooring, between the pieces of mechanical equipment, a dozen women were lying on the floor. They were not dead. Not all of them. Some were nude, some were bloodied, all were cowering in fear, trembling, traumatized to the point of utter helplessness. They were lying in filth, rotting bits of animal carcasses flung here and there among them. Only one of the women wasn't trembling. She sat with her back against a large boiler pipe, unmoving. When Sam came closer, he realized that she was unconscious, breathing shallowly.

"Oh my God," Sam whispered.

He forced himself to look at each woman carefully, one after another. None were women he recognized from Allie's camp. Many of the others had clearly been here a long time—weeks at least, maybe months. Impossible to say.

That they were alive struck Sam as strange—ferals usually tore women to shreds. Bile started to burn his throat.

It also meant that there was a chance that Allie was still alive as well.

He stood there, uncertain what to do. After a time, he moved over to a woman trembling in the corner, curled up tight on herself in fetal contortion, eyes closed in terror. As he drew near and she heard his footsteps, she began to whimper.

"Just kill me," she whimpered. "Please . . ."

He bent down beside her. "It's okay," he said. "I'm here to help you."

Her eyes sprang open, staring blindly into the darkness. She uncurled and rose to a kneeling position, clutching herself, her face riddled with shock, as if she was certain she must have imagined what she'd thought she heard, as if certain that she had finally gone mad.

"Hello?" she said. "Hello? Is someone there?"

"It's okay," said Sam again.

"Who are you?" she said. "Why is your voice so deep? Are you a . . . man? Are you real? Oh my God, can the monsters speak now?"

"I *am* a man," he said, "and, yes, I'm real, and uninfected."

She began shaking her head. "No," she said. "I'm imagining it. I've gone crazy. You can't be real."

"Cover your eyes," Sam said.

He reached into the bag and pulled out a flare. When he had lit it, he left it sizzling on the deck and removed his goggles, allowing the woman to see his face.

At first she kept her eyes covered with her hands, blinded by the glow, but gradually she moved them away, blinking. She stared at Sam's face for a long moment, astonished, and then, slowly, reached out to touch it. He let her, staying there unmoving as she caressed his jaw softly, making sure he was real.

"I don't understand," she said. "Why aren't you one of them?"

"What is this place?" Sam asked. "What are they doing to you?"

At the question, the woman tightened on herself further, her face contorting. And then she relaxed, her face filling with sadness. Lightly, she touched her bare stomach.

"I have one of them inside me," she said. She gestured to the women around her. "We all do," she said. "Every last one of us." She gave Sam a look of anguish. "Please kill me. Please kill us all," she said.

It took a moment for what the woman was saying to sink in. *A breeding ground*, Sam realized. *This is a breeding ground for the ferals.* He turned his head, peered at the other women around him. They were all looking at him now, attentive—some of them still shaking, some of them rubbing their arms, but all listening. Women had been brought here alive, then raped and impregnated. The monsters had figured out a way to perpetuate their own species. They weren't killing women, they were using them to breed. The methods were different, but it still brought back bad memories for him.

"Kill us," the woman said again.

Sam shook his head. "I am not here to kill you," he said. "I am here to kill the ferals that did this to you." He reached into the bag, withdrew a pistol, and handed it to her. "Come on, you can help. Follow me," he said.

She took the gun, regarding it with a kind of mute wonder. Sam stood and walked across the room. He was just bending down near another woman when he was startled by the sound of a gunshot, resounding over and over in the enclosed space. He turned just in time to see the woman's body collapse, the back of her head spread now across the wall behind her, as the gun clattered onto the floor. The nearest woman was looking at the gun hungrily; before Sam could react, she had scuttled crablike across the floor and scooped it up, smiling madly, and was holding it against her temple.

"No!" cried Sam, but it was already too late. The shot resounded, throwing her head hard to one side. She slumped to the floor.

Before another woman could grab hold of the gun, he crushed the flare out with the heel of his boot, leaving them all in darkness. Quickly he brought the night-vision goggles down again, in time to see several of the women on their hands and knees, feeling around, faces hungry, searching for the weapon. *They can't imagine that there's an escape*, Sam realized. *They know they're going to give birth to a monster. This is the only sure way out.* He quickly located the gun himself and stuck it back in the bag.

He stood there paralyzed, watching them.

"Please," he pleaded, "I'm trying to help you. I can get you out of here!"

When they realized they weren't going to find the gun, they began to wail in frustration and confusion. "No," one of them said over and over again, "no, no, no!" Another turned in circles, round and round. "Just kill me!" another groaned. "Kill me before they come back."

Sam stared. What could he do for these women? What could anyone do for them? If he got them out into the light, back among other women, who would love and care for them, perhaps in time they would recover, perhaps they would be happy eventually that they hadn't died here, in filth, belowdecks on a ship. But none of them could see far enough into the future to get even a glimpse of that. No, none of them could see into the future at all. They had been living minute to minute for months now, unable to see, their lives reduced to nothing. They didn't believe in the future. Considering what they'd gone through, how could he blame them?

"Who wants to live?" he finally asked. "Who wants to make the ferals pay for what they've done?" Most of the women didn't respond, just kept moving around on their hands and knees, searching hopelessly for the gun, for the only sure way out. But one stopped moving. Very slowly, she raised her hand.

Sam went to her. "What's your name?" he asked.

"Mar-Marjorie," she said, searching for his face in the dark but not finding it.

"Marjorie," he said. "Good. I'm Sam."

He pushed a flare into her hand, folded her fingers around it. "This is a flare," he said. "Do you know how to use it?"

She took it, her brow furrowing. "I . . . I think so," she managed.

"Do you think you can lead these other women out of here?"

"I . . . don't know," she said.

"Can you try, Marjorie?"

"Yes," she said. "I can try."

"Good," he said. "Light the flare in a few minutes, and see what you can do with them. I'll scout around and then come back and take whoever wants to go. Do you want a gun? Just in case the ferals come back?"

"N-no," she said.

"You're still alive, and you know your name. Now try to make these other women remember their names as well. There are more women here—we're going to find them and get out together. And then we kill all these motherfuckers. If you're going to die, take one of them down with you."

She'd opened her mouth to respond, but he wasn't listening anymore. He'd heard more screams, some feral, some female, and sounds of commotion, not far away. He darted out of the room and hurried toward the sound, pulling the bag along with him.

As he came closer, he heard grunts and cries, a struggle of some kind. He moved as fast as he could with the bag, glancing into the rooms as he passed them. More women, nude, bruised, but alive. All the rooms were full of them. Dozens upon dozens of them. They shook, cowered in filthy corners, lay curled in balls. Through the night-vision goggles, their expressions were dead and they looked like ghosts. All those camps . . . He realized that the children he'd buried were the lucky ones.

Sam continued frantically, searching for Allie. The passageway forked in two, and he took the larger passageway, the one the noise was coming from. When he reached the end of that, he saw, through an open doorway, a throng of ferals, maybe a dozen of them, in the middle of a large compartment. They were facing away from him, occupied by something inside the room—wailing, screeching, pacing rapidly. Rabid, feverish, they were unable to take their gaze away from whatever was before them.

Machete out now, Sam moved farther into the chamber and drew closer to the frenzied ferals, until he finally began to catch sight, around heads, through gaps in the crowd, of what they were facing.

It was the women from Allie's camp. They were backed against the wall, bloody, their clothing torn, but they were protecting one another, fists raised, continuing to fight back, even though it was useless. In front of them, thrown to the floor, was Jacky. Scarface stood over her menacingly. He circled her slowly, as Jacky tried to keep her hands up to protect herself, tried to spin to keep him in front of her, guessing where he was in the darkness by the wails he was making and by the shuffling of his feet.

There was a commotion within the group of women, and Sam's heart leaped as he caught a glimpse of Allie. She was in the middle of the crowd, trying to break free so she could help Jacky, despite not being able to see her in the darkness. But the other women were holding her back, trying to keep her from getting killed.

Sam slid the machete back into his belt, reached back into the bag, and rummaged around.

Now Scarface struck, two quick jabs past Jacky's hands that hit her hard in the face and left her dazed. When he went in again, it wasn't to hit her, but to tear her clothing apart with his talonlike nails.

Stunned, she tried to stop him, tried to fight back, and he hit her again and again, until she was nearly unconscious. A moment later, he had jumped atop her and was straddling her. He started to force her legs open, scrabbling to tear apart her jeans. She began shouting, and the shouts quickly became screams. All the women were screaming now, horrified by what their imaginations suggested Scarface was about to do to her.

Sam's hand closed around the grip of the weapon he'd been looking for. He drew an Uzi out of the bag. He checked the clip, popped off the safety, and pointed it at the backs of the ferals.

"Get down!" he screamed.

He could see that Allie immediately recognized his voice. Almost instantly she was yelling, "Down! Down! Down! Now!"

All the women hit the floor, covering their heads, cowering low. The ferals, hearing him, began to turn his way, mouths opening in snarls, but Sam was already pulling the trigger, releasing a nasty barrage of gunfire. He drew the weapon along the line of them, keeping the barrel level as it threatened to pop up, cutting the ferals in two.

It was over very quickly. The ferals were all down, most dead, some wounded and well on the way to being dead, except for one: Scarface. He'd been low enough, straddling Jacky as he was, not to be hit. Now he was scrambling to his feet, eyes locked on Sam. Fuckers could see in the dark.

Sam took aim and pulled the trigger, but the clip was out. He reached behind him to grab another clip or another gun from the bag. Scarface was wailing, about to leap, while Sam fumbled with the bag and backed into the passageway, when there was a sharp cry and something erupted through the feral's chest. Scarface reached down, astonished, and his hands closed around the jagged end of a rusted piece of pipe. His eyes rolled back in his head and he fell, revealing Jacky behind him, her lip curled in disgust and rage.

"You fucking wail and I can tell where you are, even in the dark, motherfucker," she said, and kicked him to make sure he was dead.

Sam lit a flare. The women rose, eyes squinting. They looked at the massacred ferals and embraced one another, weeping. When they saw

Sam, they looked shocked. Allie was one of the first on her feet. She ran to him, hugged him. She grabbed his head in her hands and drew him close, gave him a kiss fueled by relief and terror.

Then she pulled away, looking at him as if trying to memorize his face, and, after a moment, said, "We have to find Kim."

"One step ahead of you. She's safe. We're going to go get her and the rest of your camp now."

Allie's eyes filled with tears, but before she could say anything, feral wails arose nearby. Sam gently pushed her away, kicking into gear. He rapidly stripped his shirt off and threw it to Jacky, who put it on, muttering thanks. Then he opened his bag and began extracting flashlights and guns, lots of guns, handing them to Allie to distribute to the others.

"Which one of you knows how to handle this ship?" asked Sam.

"Holly does," said Jacky.

Holly stepped forward. "Here I am," she said. "Right here. Not this ship exactly, but I don't think the engine'll be all that different."

"Any chance it'll start after three years?"

Holly thought. "Like Jacky said back at camp, if it runs on fuel oil, it should," she said. "If the tank is full enough so there hasn't been too much condensation. The biggest problem is going to be the battery."

"Thought of that," said Sam. He slapped the bag. "Took a fully charged truck battery from what was left of West Staten. We can connect it up."

"That might work," Holly said. "If we're lucky."

"Looks like you're going to get your cruise after all," said Allie to Holly. "Only it's going to be a little different from what you thought, maybe not so romantic."

Holly snorted. "Anything that gets me out of here qualifies as romantic."

Sam nodded. "You and Allie are with me," he said. "The rest of you need to clear the boat of these motherfuckers."

"This one's okay," said Jacky to the woman next to her. "He's got the right attitude. Plus, he'll give you the shirt off his back." She turned to Sam. "Leave it to me," she said. "We'll wipe the fuckers out."

## Chapter Fifty-five

They moved rapidly through the ship, Jacky running the women in tight formation. As they passed other compartments, they shouted in, encouraging the other women either to join them or to barricade their doors and wait out the fight. Marjorie, holding the flare, had become more confident, and she had coaxed a few others of the abducted into action as well. Sam didn't know how they'd hold up in a firefight, but at least they could fight back. They were ready to die fighting. It had to be better than what the ferals had forced them to go through.

Two ferals darted out from a side room and were blown backward by shotgun blasts, their chests exploding. Sam and the others were moving fast now, hauling ass, guns up and blazing as they killed every feral they came in contact with.

The passageway split in two and the team split as well, Jacky sending half the women down the other way. "Follow your training," she said. "Anybody gets killed, God forbid, the next in rank takes over. Fight until nobody is standing."

The women nodded and left, rushing away. Jacky and her team set off again, with Sam and Allie and Holly following.

About halfway down the second passage they entered, Holly stopped and said, "There's a sign for a companionway. It'll take us in the right direction." She opened the door, but was bowled off her feet by a feral. It straddled her, slavering, and was lifting its fist to strike her when Allie lopped off its head with her machete.

"You're a beast," said Sam.

"Takes one to know one," claimed Allie.

They pulled Holly up. She was stunned, a little disoriented, but otherwise okay. Behind the door where the feral had been was a narrow tube with a ladder leading upward.

Sam turned to Jacky. "This is where we get off," he said.

"You don't want me to send a squad up ahead of you to clear the way first?" asked Jacky.

Sam shook his head. "You're going to need everyone you have just to hold them off long enough to get this tub in motion. Plus, we have a secret weapon."

"What's that?" Jacky and Allie asked at once.

"Me. I smell like them," said Sam. "They won't know I'm coming until it's too late."

Jacky nodded once, curtly. "I thought I smelled something," she said, and thumped his shoulder. "And thanks." Then she motioned, and she and the others took off, continuing their movement through the ship, intending to slaughter every feral that got in their way.


Allie and Sam and Holly looked at one another in the dim glow of the flashlights.

"I remember being taught 'ladies first,'" said Sam. "But, considering the circumstances and that something may be waiting up top that wants to kill you, maybe I'll go ahead."

"What?" said Allie, smiling, "You don't think I can handle them?"

He smiled back and handed her his gun. "Hold this," he said. Immediately she looked worried. "I need both hands free to climb," he explained. "And I've got this"—he slapped the machete dangling at his side. "If I have to start killing them, this will draw less attention."

Allie nodded. He could see that she hated being left behind, even if only for a few moments—hated, too, being separated from him. He felt the same way, but it had to be done.

He turned to Holly. "How far up is it?" he asked.

She shrugged. "How should I know? How large is the ship? The bridge will be at the top. There's maybe a deck above this one, maybe two. Take this all the way to the top if it goes that far. It'll either take you to the bridge or out on the top deck somewhere. Hope for the bridge."

He nodded. With Holly's help, he strapped the large industrial battery that had been in his sack to his back, like a backpack. He lowered his night-vision goggles into place and started up the ladder. The noise of his feet ringing on the rungs sounded exceptionally loud to him. He kept climbing as the darkness grew around him.

He reached a platform and saw the first doorway. The door was open, the passageway outside a bustling mass of ferals. One caught sight of him and watched him come up the ladder, leaning in through the doorway to get a closer look. It sniffed him, coming very close, and then turned away, quickly losing interest.

Sam climbed up until he could stand on the platform and then removed the machete and rammed it through the creature's back. The feral went down without a sound, slumping into the door frame, its blood dripping and puddling there. He waited until it had mostly bled out and then kicked the body out into the passageway, closing the door behind it, smearing all the cracks with the creature's blood.

He kept on climbing, and came at last to a hatch door; the wheel was just above his head. He reached up and turned it. Nothing happened. He tried again, putting as much force as he could into it. Still nothing moved. He thought for a moment, pulled the machete from his belt, and began to hammer on the wheel with the handle, his fingers jarring with each blow.

After a while, he could feel a kind of dust on his hand, which he figured for rust. When he sheathed his machete and tried again, it still resisted, but then there was a creaking sound, a high screech, and slowly the wheel began to turn.

The air in the room above smelled different from the rest of the air in the boat, and it took him a minute to realize why: it was clean. Or not clean, exactly—it was dusty and stale, sure, but what it didn't smell of was rotting flesh and excreta and filth. The bridge had remained sealed since before the virus, and except for a thin layer of dust, it looked just as it must have looked before—one of those odd rooms he had come across every once in a while where it seemed that people had gone out for a little while and might at any moment come back in and continue to lead their lives.

He clambered up and looked around. It was a large room, illuminated by moonlight through a wraparound window that looked out over the harbor. In the back was a door, its panel cracked but still intact. There was a steering column and a dashboard panel. A jacket had been left folded over the captain's chair. When he picked it up, it fell apart. Moths fluttered out of the scraps.

He moved closer to the window and looked out. Below, he could see the flitting shapes of ferals rushing back and forth across the deck in the moonlight. He returned to the ladder and rapped on it with the blade of the machete—three short taps, then a pause, then three more. After a moment, he heard the sounds of movement on the rungs below and knew they were on their way up.


First thing Holly did upon reaching the top of the ladder was rush to the control panel, leaning over and squinting to see it in the darkness. Allie came up after her. Sam helped her up, taking the gun she offered him.

"How does it look?" Allie asked.

"I've got to have a light," said Holly. "I've got to see what I'm doing."

Sam handed her his flashlight. He gestured to the window. "Point it at the floor and try to be quick," he said.

She turned the flashlight on and shone its beam at the panel. Together, she and Sam wired in the battery.

"Let's hope this thing starts up," she said.

"Just hurry," said Allie. "We're beginning to attract attention."

Sam looked out. It was true. Some of the figures on the deck had caught sight of the light flickering in the bridge and were standing motionless, watching. A few had begun to clamber their way toward it. On the docks, too, ferals were beginning to pour toward their boat.

He heard the sound of gunfire behind him, a single shot, and turned to see a feral corpse slide back down the shaft they'd just come up. Howls came from below as Allie dropped her gun and flipped the hatch back in place. Together, they spun the wheel on this side of it, locking it.

"I guess they smelled us after all," said Allie.

Holly was playing with the controls, hitting buttons, moving levers, working fast. The lights flickered on overhead and there was a wail outside: the ferals saw them clearly now. A second later, the lights had flickered off again, but the damage had been done.

"I don't know if this is going to work, guys," said Holly, half turning toward them. Suddenly the front window of the control room shattered in a hail of glass, and two feral males clambered in.

Sam fired at the one on the right, hitting it once in the side and spinning it round. When it came up again, snarling, he shot it in the face. Allie had taken the other one out with a single shot before it even set foot on the bridge floor.

"Enough complaining," said Allie to Holly. "Get this thing started before we run out of ammo."

Holly frantically hit buttons, turned keys. Now there was a roar and, beneath that, the fluttering thrum of the engine. For a moment they exchanged a look of triumph, but then the engine died.

"Keep trying!" yelled Allie. "Hurry up!"

More ferals were running onto the deck of the cargo ship from the docks. Down below, Jacky and her crew were firing, getting rid of the creatures as quickly as they came, but their ammunition wouldn't hold out for long, either.

"I'm try—" a frustrated Holly had begun to shout, when, with a roar, the engines fired up, revving to life. The lights flickered on above them and all through the ship. Down below, the ferals wailed, but they could still hear the cheers of the women, who were now, finally, beginning to believe that, yes, they might actually escape with their lives after all.

"Get us out of here now!" shouted Allie, and fired at another feral clambering through the shattered window, heedless of how he was getting cut. Holly pushed a lever and the boat started forward; the gangway slipped away and crashed onto the docks, and the boat started to move—until it was abruptly jerked to a stop.

"Fuck me, we're still moored," said Sam.

"Too busy right now!" yelled Allie. "You'll have to take a rain check."

And then they were side by side, guns aimed, firing, picking off ferals the instant they appeared in the shattered window.

Holly threw the boat in reverse and backed it up, the craft shuddering. It struck the dock behind them with a crunch and a jerk that knocked Sam off his feet. He scrambled up quickly. Holly had held on to the console, and was still up. Allie, too, had somehow maintained her footing.

"Hold on," Holly said. She grabbed a lever and yanked it down hard, as far as it would go.

The big boat lurched, its engine whining, and then slewed drunkenly, slowly gathering speed. Through the side window, Sam watched the rope grow taut and then catch, and they were jerked to a stop momentarily. Then there was a grinding sound and the whole railing on one side sheared off, taking the rope with it. They were away.

## Chapter Fifty-six

Dawn was just starting to break, a roiling fog filling the air. It was eerily quiet, and Bayview Bridge was entirely hidden in a white haze.

When the two armored trucks arrived, they did little to disrupt the silence. They were driven quietly, carefully, at little more than a few miles an hour. They crept out of the fog, slowly maneuvering their way through the husks of ruined cars, making their way soberly but persistently to the bridge.

They drove out onto the middle of the span and stopped. For a few minutes they just stayed there, engines ticking beneath the hoods, and then that sound faded, as if they were just two additional motionless and unoccupied vehicles.

The rear doors were flung open. Women poured out, a dozen of them, all armed. They moved slowly, scanning their surroundings; the majority of them immediately assumed guard positions, while the remainder moved to the edge of the bridge and peered down into the mist below, searching for the boat. All of them were survivors of the attack on West Staten—women and girls who had hidden or barricaded themselves in or managed to become so spattered with blood that the ferals didn't notice them.

"I don't see anything," said Dana.

"They'll be here," said Kim.

"How do you know he didn't just run off?" asked Dana. She was whispering so that the others wouldn't hear, only Kim. "He's a man—we can't trust him."

Kim shook her head. "Allie trusts him. That's all I need."

"If he went to the harbor, he's dead. They're all dead. We need to run. Now."

"They'll be here," Kim said again, the expression on her twelve-year-old face sober and assured.

———

A half hour later, the fog had rolled all the way in and thickened, engulfing the entire bridge and the water below. The women were beginning to grow restless. Kim had relieved one of the others and was on guard duty now, keeping an eye on the south end of the bridge, peering into the white haze. Nearby, Emma and a few others secured ropes to the electronic winches on the front of each truck. They tested the first one; it whirred to life, the coiled steel cable spinning onto the spool and pulling the attached harness and rope up.

"Think it'll work?" asked a girl.

"This was made to pull a truck," said Emma. "So lowering you won't be a problem."

Having tested the harness system, they had nothing to do but wait. The guards remained in their positions, weapons drawn. The girls and women around the winch stayed where they were, in a tight bunch, hugging their own arms. The women standing at the edge of the bridge stared down into the fog, hoping to catch a glimpse of the boat. They all remained silent, their sense of helplessness making the tension rise even further.

There was a wail, still at a distance but not as far away as they would have liked. They tensed further. The guards pointed their weapons at the fog. It was so thick now, it was hard to see more than a dozen feet. Another wail, perhaps from the same feral, perhaps from a different one. Was it getting closer? Too hard to tell. Better off assuming that it was and then, happily, be proved wrong.

And then the wailing started to become more and more regular. Louder and louder, definitely coming closer. One of the girls in the group standing beside the winch started stepping from one foot to the other and back again. Before long, she was pacing a tight little circle on the bridge.

"We have to leave," she said, talking to anyone who would listen.

"You're right," said another. "They're not coming."

The others were getting antsy, too, beginning to whisper to one another, to pace, anything to relieve the tension. Only Kim remained where she was, motionless, seemingly unfazed, weapon raised and pointing into the mist.

"They'll be here," said Kim, without turning her head. She seemed almost to be talking to herself.

"Come on," said a third, her voice beginning to rise, "let's get back in the trucks and drive out of here."

"Ferals are faster than the trucks," said the second woman.

"They're armored—we'll be okay."

"They'll just turn them over and wait until we come out."

"Be quiet," said Kim, her voice level. "Not so loud."

More wails rose, long and shrill, sounding very close now. Fear began to rise in the women as well, swelling to the bursting point.

"Christ," said one, "it sounds like an army."

"They're getting closer."

"My sister will be here," said Kim. "Sam will be here."

"We can't see, we can't see," said one of the girls, almost hysterical now. "How will we stop them?"

"Everyone just calm down," said Emma, though she looked anything but calm.

"We're sitting ducks here," said the girl.

"We have to leave!" said another, hardly any older.

"We can't leave!" said Emma. "We're committed now. It's us or them."

The screeching was loud now, nearly deafening, the sound of many, many feral voices, all of them full of rage. But something had changed, something in the air. Not quite a sound but almost, as if there was something you could nearly hear, just not quite. They stood, holding their breath and attentive, trying to catch some hint of what it was.

Emma was the one who first figured it out. It wasn't a sound at all, but a vibration, something they were feeling through their boots.

"They're on the bridge," she said. "Both ends."

Several of the women raised their guns, pointed them here and there, but there was nothing to aim at—in the fog, there was nothing to see.

The wails continued, growing louder, the vibrations stronger. Slowly, the women withdrew, moving back toward the trucks, their weapons raised, searching frantically for any sign of movement, anything they could shoot at. Not knowing what else to do, they began to clamber back in.

And then, suddenly, the blast of a foghorn. Kim broke ranks, ran to the edge of the bridge deck, and looked down. There it was, the dim shape of the ship's smokestack below, though most of the rest of the vessel was invisible in the fog.

She turned around, her face lit up. "They're here!" she said. "Come on, let's move!"


They traveled slowly along the deck, stepping carefully over the piles of the dead. Besides Sam and Allie and Holly, there were the women they'd rescued from West Staten and various other women from at least a half-dozen camps. Some of these latter were pregnant and clearly traumatized. Those women who could were moving from body to body, administering to the wounded, throwing the corpses of dead ferals overboard. Their own dead they kept nearby, in a neat row beside the base of the conning tower, hands crossed over their chests. Jacky was doing a final pass with another few women. Less for ferals this time—they'd gotten all of those—but just to make sure that they hadn't missed anyone, that there wasn't someone curled up under a piece of machinery, rocking back and forth, terrified, unaware that she had been liberated.

Ammo was mostly expended. Sam was moving among the dead, checking pockets, looking for a stray unused bullet here or there. A few of the women were giving him looks of thinly veiled hostility, as if he were violating the dead, but Allie understood what he was doing. She knew how necessary it was. A single clip, even a single bullet, might make the difference.

Allie was staring into the fog. "How can she see to navigate?" she asked.

"I don't know," said Sam. He bent over and picked up a shell, but cast it overboard upon discovering it was just a casing. "She probably can't. She's probably just trying to remember what the river looks like and hoping that we'll get lucky."

They began to hear wails again, up ahead, out of the darkness. After a moment, Allie realized they were coming not from the shore but from somewhere above them.

"Shit," she said, "They're on Bayview Bridge already. We need to hurry."

Above, on the bridge, everyone was moving now, not just Kim, clambering back out of the trucks, their faces tight and pale with fear. For a moment they all stood looking at one another, nobody quite willing to take the lead, and then young Kim stepped forward and took charge.

"Right," she said. "Set up two firing lines. One facing south. The other north. Everybody else on the ropes."

For a moment they just stood there, unmoving.

"Hurry," said Kim, "now!"

And then they were sprinting, as if by arrangement splitting into two groups. One hurried north, setting up to blockade the bridge there, taking cover behind the old and desiccated cars. The other went south, doing exactly the same. Rifles raised, they stared down the barrels of their weapons at the fog as the feral moans continued to get louder. They waited, hoping they could meet the onslaught when it arrived.

"I can't see anything," said Dana from the line.

Her hands were trembling. Kim watched her glance over at the woman in the line next to her, Tamara, and saw she was shaking as well. And then Kim took a long, deep breath, trying to steady her breathing; she could only hope that when the ferals came she'd be up to the task.

In between the two lines, several women were working the steel winches attached to the trucks, playing out a little cable. They were securing people to each respective winch harness, preparing to lower them to the deck of the boat below.

Suddenly the wails and gibbering of the ferals fell away into silence. The only thing that the women could hear was the sound of their own breathing and the clank and snap of the harnesses. They all froze, exchanged looks.

Seeing the pylon loom up near her, the side of the boat scraping gently along it, Allie realized they were there. But in the same instant she registered that the wails of the ferals on the bridge above had stopped. A very bad sign. They'd found their prey and begun to stalk it.

Allie cupped her hands around her mouth and looked up. "Let's go!" she yelled. "Now! Now! Now!"

Up above, they heard Allie's cries rising out of the mist. The two women who had been secured to cables climbed over the bridge's guardrail and began to lower themselves, as other women worked the electronic winch mechanisms on the trucks behind them, hitting the levers that caused the steel cables to release with a whirr and lower the women into the fog.

The evacuation had begun.

The women plunged down into the fog, past the ominous shape of the smokestack. They could see a little more of what was below as they descended further, the vague shape of the deck, figures looming from it and gradually taking on the form of humans, then of humans they knew: Allie, Jacky, Sam. They hit the deck hard, the cable still paying out for just a moment before the reel ran out and it stopped. The women already on deck rushed forward, caught them, and began to unharness them. Allie was saying something neither of them could make out at first—they were confused and still a little panicked, struggling their way out of the harnesses.

One of them said, "The ferals are coming," and Allie said, "I know. Is Kim there?"

The woman worked her leg free. "She's okay, she's there."

And then, before they could sort it out further, gunfire started above, punctuated by the howls of ferals. One woman was completely out of the harness now, and the other was nearly there, with Jacky and Sam helping her.

"Is Emma up there?" Jacky asked the second woman, who nodded. Jacky's face showed a strange mixture of happiness and dread. She and Emma hadn't had a chance to make up since Emma had been knocked out by Allie. Jacky had been giving her the silent treatment to teach her a lesson, and then, suddenly, the ferals came. Life was too short for such bullshit.

Sam helped the woman get her foot free and then tugged on the cable and shouted, "Take it up!" It went whirring back up into the mist. He turned to see how Allie was doing with the other new arrival, but she wasn't there. The harness was gone, too.

"Where is she?" he asked the woman standing there, even though he was sure he already knew the answer.

"Up," said the woman with kind of dazed wonder. "She went up."

Up above, Kim, Emma, Dana, Tamara, and the others were armed and ready, staring into the fog. For a moment it was quiet, eerily so, except for the whirring of the cable. A few seconds later, the cable ran out and even the whirring stopped. Kim watched the fog in front of her, trying not to blink. They would come, she knew. And when they came, she would have to be ready.

And then something strange began to happen to the fog in front of her, something that took no more than a second or two. A shift, a subtle change, and then the fog was swirling, undulating, something moving within it. And, as if synchronized, the ferals broke through en masse, from both sides at once.

Kim started firing. Dana and Tamara were firing, too, on either side of her, and those on the other side of the bridge were firing as well. The ferals fell, wailing, some still groaning and writhing, until the women put them out of their misery. Then it was quiet again, and Kim was quickly reloading.

She hadn't quite finished when another wave burst through, howling. She started firing from the hip, not even having the time to raise her weapon. How many clips did she have left? Another two, maybe a third. How many more waves would there be?

The ferals coming at them dropped near enough to spatter them with blood. Kim reloaded again, quickly this time, and had the gun up before the third wave came, aggressive and quick, trampling over the dead bodies of their fellow ferals. Kim had killed the ones coming at her when she saw out of the corner of her eye two coming at Tamara, who still had her weapon down, trying to reload. A moment later, the ferals had grabbed her and were heading back the other way, into the mist.

Kim took a few steps, giving chase and firing, but her shots missed—she was too worried about hitting Tamara to aim precisely. She had stopped moving and was just starting to take careful aim, hoping to get a shot off before they vanished into the fog, when three quick gunshots rang out behind her, and both ferals went down.

She turned and there was Allie, cresting the guardrail, firing even as she pulled herself over it and onto the bridge. She locked eyes with Kim and smiled, and Kim spun and fired almost at her, taking out the feral that had gotten through the other firing line and was there next to her, preparing to take her sister out.

"Nice shot," Allie acknowledged, wriggling her way free of the harness. "Now you need to go."

Kim shook her head. "Tamara's hurt," she said. "She goes."

For a moment, Allie hesitated; then she nodded once, curtly. She and Kim rushed forward and grabbed Tamara, dragging her back. They harnessed her in quickly and lowered her over the side.

As soon as Allie hit the lever and sent her down, she and Kim went to stand near the trucks, side by side, and, working as a team, kept firing wildly at the ferals that were streaming their way.


Sam grabbed the unconscious Tamara and lowered her to the deck. He unstrapped her quickly, stealing glances back up into the fog as he did so. The gunfire was still popping; this was the only indication that Allie was still alive.

## Chapter Fifty-seven

# Allie

We fire and fire, sometimes side to side, sometimes back to back, the ferals coming from everywhere, every direction. It's a real shit storm, but Kim's holding strong. She's quite a warrior—but this is it. We are both going to die. Another woman goes down by winch, Dana, and then two more. I trip the levers with my foot to lower and raise the winches while still firing at ferals, trying not to waste a single bullet. There are only a few of us left now: Kim and me on this side, Emma and two other women on the other. How long can we possibly hold out?

I'm firing, still carefully picking them off, when I hear the click-click-click of Kim's empty gun.

"Give me a clip," says Kim.

"Time for you to leave," I say.

"Not without you," says Kim.

"No choice," I tell her. "I'm older."

Still firing, I hook Kim into a harness. I can tell she wants to resist, and would if she still had any bullets left. Gradually, more and more ferals are emerging from the fog, nearly surrounding us now. Emma and the last two women are trying to keep them back, strafing them, but there are so many now, far too many.

I see one shoot forward, lightning fast, and grab one of the women, dragging her screaming off into the fog. Before long, that may well be me. The other ferals keep advancing. They fall one by one, but there are always more to step in and take their places.

"No," says Kim. "Stop it! You have to come with me!"

"Just go, go, go!" I shout.

I've started to push Kim toward the edge of the bridge, kicking and elbowing her and generally driving her forward, still firing here and there, the ferals getting close now, far too close, when, suddenly, something grabs me, wrapping itself around me. I struggle, expecting to be dragged off into the fog by a feral, hoping I can get one arm free and take a shot, at least take this one out with me. But this one doesn't move, just holds me there, in place. When I brace my feet and look down, I realize a rope is wrapped around my waist. That doesn't make any sense—ferals don't use ropes. And the arms that are holding me are normal, human arms. And one of them is lifting the end of the rope, on the end of which is a hook, and harnessing me to the same winch as my sister.

Confused, I turn, struggling against arms that restrain me. Out of the corner of my eye, I catch a glimpse of Jacky, just a few feet away, laying down covering fire. It doesn't make sense. Jacky is down below. Or was. Why did she come up here? And then I realize: *She just followed your example, Allie. She just hitched a ride.* I twist a little farther and see that the arms around me are Sam's. He is pushing both Kim and me toward the guardrail.

"Time to go," he says.

I try to break free. Like hell am I going, not without him. I'm the warrior, not him. He can't do this to me. He can't stay behind without me.

"I'll be right behind you," he claims. He pulls me close. "I love you," he says. His voice is calm and serene, and that as much as anything freaks me out, that, despite all the shit going on around us, he can zero in like that and say something in a way that makes it burn right into my soul. And say he'll be right there in a way that makes it sound like good-bye.

Without warning, he pushes Kim and me over the side. We're hanging there, swinging, and I'm knocking into my sister, getting twisted up with her. He's smart. If it was just me, I'd be able to pull myself up, grab on to the bridge, and get up there beside him in a flash. As it is, I can only hear footsteps as he runs across the deck of the bridge and flips the lever.

I've managed to grab one of the struts, but just with one hand, and when the lever goes it means that I've got all Kim's weight on me, too, and the cable's descending. If it were just me, or if it were someone other than Kim, I'd hold on and try to pull myself up and go back up for Sam. But as it is, I'm realizing I can't hold on forever, and if I hold on too long it'll mean Kim and I fall all the way to the deck without the support of the cable. And so, without my mind really deciding it exactly, I let go. I scream on the way down, scream Sam's name. I want him to remember me. I want him to know that he's making a mistake. And, most of all, I want him to figure out a way, somehow, to get back to me.

And then my sister and I are dangling in midair, swinging on the end of the cable hard enough to knock against the side of the smoke-stack on the way down. We're twirling around one another in mid-air, descending, trying to steady ourselves, until here comes the deck, toward us, and hands are on us now, holding us, steadying us, bring-ing us safely down. They're unhooking us, and I'm helping them unhook Kim, but as soon as she's out I'm trying to stay in the harness, trying to get them to haul me back up, back to Sam. "Let me go!" I'm shouting. But, no, they won't let me, they won't listen to me, they're dragging me away, they're dragging me away.

## Chapter Fifty-eight

Sam flinched when he heard the way Allie called his name—it almost folded him in two—but there was no time for that. The bridge was awash with death, and if you stopped paying attention even for a second, you'd be the next one to die.

Emma was down, her throat torn out by a feral who lay now in a pool of blood near her. Jacky had Emma's head pulled into her lap and was trying to staunch the wound, but, no, Emma was already dead, she had already bled out.

"Jacky," said Sam. "Jacky. It won't do any good."

When Jacky finally looked up, he saw her tear-stained face, the pain in her eyes. She already knew. "I missed my chance to say good-bye," she said.

He shot a feral coming up behind her, then another, who had come over the top of one of the trucks. Jacky slowly lowered Emma's body and settled it gently on the bridge; then she rose.

"Let me at those motherfuckers," she said.

"Be my guest," said Sam.

Besides them, two women remained on the bridge. "Harness up!" Sam shouted at them. "We'll cover you." And then he and Jacky held back the onslaught while the two women both managed to hook on to the remaining cable and make their way to the edge of the bridge.

"Ready?" cried out Sam between shots, and when they cried an affirmation, he kicked the lever and the cables spun down.

"Just you and me now," said Sam to Jacky.

"Oh, great," said Jacky. "Only one man left in the world, and it's my luck to have to spend the last moments of my life with him."

They stood side by side, then back to back, firing, always firing, turning back and forth in the middle of the bridge, protecting one another. They'd just gotten a good rhythm going, were really working as a team, when he heard the click-click of Jacky's gun and realized she was out of ammo. A few more shots and he was, too.

He unsheathed his machete, and saw that Jacky already had one of her own out. A moment later, they both had the same thought and made for the trucks, but they were cut off, a swarm of ferals on the roof now and coming around the sides. They turned and moved in the other direction, toward the guardrail, thinking to climb down the cables manually, but this way, too, was blocked, and, to make matters worse, some of the ferals were starting down the thin cables toward the boat below.

Sam and Jacky exchanged a look. Simultaneously, they raised their machete blades and brought them down hard on the cables, cutting a few of the strands and notching their blades. They raised the machetes again, brought them down again, and this time they cut through, so the ferals already on the cables fell rapidly downward until, with a crunch, they struck the deck below.

*That's it,* thought Sam. *No getting off the bridge now.* They'd exchanged their own escape for protection for the women below. It was, Sam couldn't help feeling, a good trade, the only thing to do.

"Kill as many as you can," said Jacky.

"Go down swinging," Sam answered.

All around them, the ferals closed in, coming closer, and closer, and closer. And then, as if one, in a snarling, terrible mass, howling, they leaped.

## Chapter Fifty-nine

# Allie

I'm still screaming, still trying to get them to let me go back up there. The gunfire stopped a few minutes ago, which isn't a good sign, but the fact that the ferals are still up there and still screaming means that one or both of our people are still alive. They've got to be alive. Sam has to be alive. I can't lose him.

And then there's a faint whistling sound, and the cables thump down onto the deck; a few ferals crash down with them. Two are killed by the fall, but the last one is still wailing. Even though his legs are broken, he keeps trying to get at us until Kim steps forward and, as if it's second nature, sends a bullet through his head.

And that's the end. There's no coming down for Sam now. The fall's too great; the ferals proved that when they smacked into the deck. Sam's not coming back.

"Sam!" I'm shouting. "Sam! No!" It's strange. It's almost like I'm watching someone else shout, hovering above myself and just observing, not being able to make her, make me, stop shouting. From above, I watch myself struggling and fighting, trying to leap into the water and swim to the edge and then climb up the bank, but they're holding me down, keeping me from going. It takes four of them.

"He's gone, Allie," Kim keeps saying over and over again, "he's gone."

And I can't stop myself. I'm still screaming when Holly suddenly opens the throttle, and the ship slews and is turning about, back in the direction we came, west at first and then, eventually, when the river curves, south. And now I'm snapped back into my body, and everything that I was watching from a distance is up close, almost too much to bear.

Prologue

# THE WORLD TO COME

And so, despite all expectations, despite all that could have gone wrong, we survived. My sister and I are still alive. We lost the two women who had led us: the doctor who was working hardest on developing a vaccine, the badass security chief. Lost, too, the only uninfected male that we knew of. Setbacks, yes, but we were still alive.

For a long time, Allie didn't want to be. For a long time, our roles were swapped, and even though I was just twelve I had to be the grown-up, had to be the one in charge, keeping her going, making her eat, forcing her to put one foot in front of the other. She thought she'd never get over Sam—she didn't want to get over Sam. Her heart was broken and she didn't want it ever to mend.

But hearts are funny that way. Over time they always mend, whether you want them to or not. You find reasons to go on, small reasons to keep on living, and the more days that go by, the more reasons you find.

We motored down the river, Holly proving to be an excellent pilot. From time to time, ferals caught our scent and trailed us, but we kept the boat to the middle of the river, and though they might follow us for a mile or two, they always left off in the end. And when they stayed longer than we wanted, we got out the rifles and our few remaining bullets and took care of them that way.

It was true, what Sam had told my sister: the ferals were moving north. The farther south we traveled, the fewer of them we saw. We went south until it started to feel safe, and then went even farther south, and finally stopped, where there was a dock, where we could board the boat again quickly and easily if we needed to. We began to make sorties out, *weaving through the trees, looking for a place to call home. After four or five trips inland, we found trees that were arranged in straight rows, an orchard that had run wild for several years, and, through it, this place.*

*When we first found it, it was just a deserted mansion. There was a body in the living room, a woman killed years before, her body a moldering mess now. Other than that, the place was unoccupied, and in good condition, big enough to house us all with a little jostling. Plus, there was a fence around the property—hardly enough to keep the ferals out, but a good start, something we could develop quickly and effectively.*

*We built up the fence and strung the top of it with barbed wire. On the roof of the mansion we built crow's nests, lookout points, just as we'd had back at the old place. We always manned them, taking turns baking in the hot sun, waiting, watching.*

## Chapter Sixty

# Kim

"Hey, sis," I say, "time to wake up."

We're in our new place, and Allie and I share a bedroom, just the two of us. It has nothing to do with me: Allie's the one being given special treatment. I'm just along for the ride.

I get up from my bed and stand near hers. She's asleep now, her face fuller than it's been in months, her hair long and lustrous. For a while, she stays sleeping, and then her eyelids flutter and slowly open.

"How do you feel?" I ask.

She nods. Then she reaches down and pushes the sheets aside and caresses her belly.

It's big now, though far from as big as it'll get before the end. She's four months along, maybe five—she won't tell me when she and Sam actually met and how long it was before they started—well, you know—so I can't figure it out. But I'll be an aunt soon, in just another four months. Or, maybe, five.

We get dressed and go down to the dining room. About thirty people are here now—all the rest of the women from the camp, but some new faces as well. Some of the women Sam found in the beehive, and then a few others that either wandered along or that we discovered ourselves when one of our scouts was out searching for food. We're not back to the numbers we used to have, nowhere near as big a camp as we were before, but we'll get there.

We sit and eat, laugh and chat with the others. Allie's no longer so standoffish; something has changed with the pregnancy. It's as if for three years she was holding her breath, waiting for something to go wrong, and, sure, lots of things went wrong, but a few went right, too. And now she's got something that she didn't have before: hope.

---

I've taken over the training of the up-and-comers. Allie in her third month was sick constantly, always vomiting, and there's nothing that takes the fun out of learning how to use a weapon like your teacher puking all over you. So I took over. Didn't ask permission—I just did it. It was supposed to be temporary, but even though she's past the puking phase now, Allie hasn't asked for the job back. It's hard for her to let go a little, relax a little, but now that she has and has seen that the world hasn't fallen apart as a result, I think she's glad she did.

We're at the shooting range, me and a bunch of young girls, none of them even in their teens yet—ten and under, all of them. I've got them lined up, pointed in the right direction, and am walking behind them, watching them as they shoot. I stop and scold one, my voice professional but harsh. It's not a voice that comes naturally to me, but if I remember my sister using that same voice on me, it comes out right. And I have to admit it works: these girls are a little scared of me even though they're almost my same age. But, more important, they're learning, making fewer and fewer mistakes.

I stop behind one girl. "You're letting the weapon handle you, Lisa," I say. "One day you'll be caught out there, with no blood, and you'll need to be able to handle a rifle."

I say it seriously and coldly, and I can tell by the way the others fidget that they're all impressed. They'll remember. And then I turn and smile at Allie, watching from just outside the range, and she gives me a conspiratorial wink. She knows what I'm doing. She knows who I'm pretending to be.

But we've also hit a balance. It's not all weapons all the time. Allie learned something from Doc after all: that life has different parts to it, and that even in hard times you can't give some of those up and still feel alive. If you're going to really live, you have to take on life in all its parts. Otherwise, you're just marking time.

We're down in the basement, all of us working together to build sets for the new play. Allie and I are working on a backdrop together, hammering in back supports. Later, we will paint it, or I will—since she's pregnant, I don't know that it's such a good idea for her. In the old days, we would have just Googled "okay to paint pregnant?" and in fifteen or twenty seconds, or maybe even less time, we would have figured out what the risks were. Now all that knowledge, all that opinion, is lost. All the things we used to be able to have at our fingertips, we can't get to anymore.

"Who's playing Rapunzel?" asks Allie.

I've been waiting for her to ask this. I steel myself. "Maybe Dani," I say.

"What?" she says. "Her audition sucked. She didn't have enough vulnerability."

"I can work with her and get her there," I say.

"But there are the others who were so much—"

I cut her off gently. "It's right for her," I say. "You'll see." And she accepts this.

Later, Holly comes and gets her, takes her down for an examination. "You want to come along?" Allie asks. I don't really—I've got a lot to do to get ready for the play—but I can tell by the way she's asking that she wants my company, and so I go.

We go to another basement room, this one with a generator and a number of pieces of medical equipment, including a portable ultrasound that Allie scavenged from a hospital once she knew she was pregnant but before she started to show. Holly's decided to be our doctor, at least until someone comes along who is more qualified. She's managed to find a number of medical textbooks at the library in the town nearby—funny how we don't care what the towns used to be called anymore—and she studies them night and day, trying to make sense of them. At first it seemed hopeless—like it does to Allie with Dani and the play—but now she's started to get the hang of it. Even so, both she and Allie are hoping the delivery will go easy and she won't need to attempt a cesarean.

The other women, the pregnant ones that we saved from the boat, two of them were having boys, and they got enough of a glimpse of their babies on the monitor to know they'd be bringing something feral into the world. They might not have kept the babies anyway, even if they were girls, considering the way they'd gotten them—too much of a reminder. But if they'd been healthy, maybe everyone would have forced them to keep the children. Glad that fight didn't take place. The third one is having a girl, and she wants to have it. She figures if it's a girl it's because the real father's the man the feral used to be rather than the feral himself. I couldn't go through with it, but she is. More power to her. She's a survivor. We all are.

So—Allie's on a cot, her stomach all covered with gel, and Holly is sliding the ultrasound wand over it. I'm there beside her, and after a while she forgets, more or less, that I'm there. She's just talking away, chatting with Holly about everything and anything. The reason I know she's forgotten about me is that she says, "I don't think Dani can handle the Rapunzel role. I think Kim may be asking too much of her."

"Kim's right there," said Holly.

Allie looks over. "Oh," she says. "Oh yeah. Sorry, Kim."

"No problem," I say. "I'm used to being forgotten."

Allie laughs a little at this, and I'm expecting Holly to laugh, too, but she's not laughing. She hasn't even heard: she's looking at the monitor, absorbed in it, staring at the image from the ultrasound. I've noticed, but Allie hasn't. She's still chatting away, and it's only when Holly's been silent for a good minute that she realizes.

"What is it?" Allie asks, and again there is some tension creeping into her voice, some fear. The old, hypervigilant Allie starting to come back. "Is something wrong?"

"No, nothing wrong," says Holly. She keeps staring, is slow to continue. "Your baby turned, Allie," she says. "I can finally see what sex it is."

My heart gives a little leap, like a fish. I'm watching Allie, watching the way emotion floods over her from this unexpected news. I reach out and take her hand.

"Should I get the others?" Holly asks.

Allie snorts. "Are you crazy? Tell *me* first!"

Holly opens her mouth to speak, but she can't say anything, and that's when I know what she's going to say. She takes a deep breath, starts over.

"It's a boy, Allie," she says.

And Allie squeezes my hand so hard that I'm afraid she's going to break the bones. It's big news, the biggest. It means that we might have a chance, that, since the father is immune, the baby might be, too—humanity might go on. Holly and Allie look at one another in utter disbelief and joy, absorbing the enormous implications of what they've just learned. They're smiling and weeping, and so am I, all of us embracing, crying. We can't believe it. A boy. A boy!

## Chapter Sixty-one

# Allie

I'm alone now; my sister and the other women are down in the common room, celebrating my news. It's a new beginning. Nothing's sure, nothing's certain, the world is still a hellish place, but we have at least a shot now of starting again, of having humanity stumble on and move forward. To build civilization up again and this time know when to leave well enough alone, what to mess with and what not to. We're on the verge of a new beginning, and it feels overwhelming and enormous.

I celebrated for a while with them. I've given in to that now, accepted that I'm a part of the group, and I'm surprised how much I've come to like it. But then, pleading pregnancy and exhaustion, I excused myself, said I was going off to bed to make an early night of it. Even though it wasn't even quite dark outside yet.

I meant it, too. When I said it, I think I meant it. Only, once I was on my own, I didn't want to go to bed. So, instead of going to bed, I came up here.

I'm up in one of the crow's nests, looking down at the camp, out past the fence, scanning the land all around, considering the world, my life, this child. The air is hot, with a slight breeze. I just stay there feeling it, looking out at this place of ours, my hand resting softly on the curve of my belly.

"What are you going to name him?" Holly asked me, back in the clinic, just after she'd discovered I was having a boy. At the time, I'd just shrugged. And later, too, at the party, I'd let the women suggest names, let them run through the gamut, with a little half-smile on my face. But I knew what I was going to call him—have known ever since I found out I would be having him. I'm happy it's a boy—if it is a boy. Those portable ultrasounds are hella grainy, and maybe Holly was seeing what she wanted to see. But, boy or girl, doesn't matter. The name I've got in mind works both ways.